I0736493

A strange man has come to save her…but is he friend or foe?

Anderson Merritt's been kidnapped, but when a stranger comes to rescue her, she isn't sure he is who he says he is. He claims to work her father's boss. But someone close to Andi set her up, and now she doesn't know who to trust. Every man she's ever known has seen her only as a tool to get to her father or his money, so why should this one be any different? As the sparks between them ignite, and the danger escalates, Andi has to choose—go off on her own or trust that some men really are what they seem.

He doesn't want to hurt her…but he may have to if she doesn't come willingly.

Ex-CIA black ops specialist Levi Komakov doesn't believe in hurting women, but when the place is set to blow and Andi won't cooperate, he has no choice to but toss her over his shoulder and carry her out of danger, determined to keep her safe in spite of herself. But the beautiful little spitfire doesn't make it easy for him. With her abductors seemingly always one step ahead of him, Levi suspects there's a rat in the woodpile, but who? Could it be someone close to Andi's father, someone in the FBI, or someone in the family Levi works for? When a new threat appears, and even the CIA can't help him keep Andi safe, Levi puts everything on the line—but will it be enough?

KUDOS FOR *DEAD MEN DON'T*

"I am really big on action thrillers and mysteries that feature detectives or spies, the CIA, etc. So a book featuring a former black-ops guy as the leading man? I'm sold. So, Andi gets kidnapped and Levi gets called in to rescue her. And to make things worse, it's an inside job. Andi doesn't even know if she can trust Levi, and this just complicates things more. I absolutely adored Andi and Levi, both apart and their chemistry with each other. This book was also well-written, it flowed very nicely. This is a part of a series, but can be read as a stand alone. I do plan to read the other books in the series." ~ *Shelf Life*

"*Dead Men Don't* is an action thriller that comes with everything that is indigenous to this genre. A plot that demands your curiosity, adrenaline, and full attention. A central character that excels in evading danger with a swift flick of his hands. In short the book has everything that usually goes into an action thriller but then there is also the romance quotient that overshadows the entire book which makes the book more of a romantic thriller than an action/spy thriller. The language and narration is flawless in terms that it runs smooth and flows without any obstructions. The build of the story is so good that it absorbs the readers pretty quickly into the book." ~ *Read, Think, and Watch*

"This thriller/romance/adventure story sizzles with action in diverse settings — a secluded, well-guarded estate, a remote mountain cabin, headquarters of a crime family, and a harem in a desert palace, all believably created. Pepper's characters ring true, and we learn a good bit of information about self-defense for women as well as how to prepare for a black-ops mission, planning, weapons, fight strategies, and explosives." ~ Linda Pirtle, *Venture Galleries*

"I did not know what to expect when I started reading this book. I was pleasantly surprised. It is not often that black ops tough guys actually have hearts of gold—or that spoiled little rich girls have backbones of steel! I really can't say any more without giving away the plot so I won't." ~ Miki of *Miki's Hope*

Books by Pepper O'Neal

Love Potion No. 2-14

Blood Fest Series

Blood Fest: Chasing Destiny

Blood Fest: Cursing Fate

Black Ops Chronicles Series

Black Ops Chronicles: Dead Run

Black Ops Chronicles: Dead Men Don't

Black Ops Chronicles:

DEAD MEN DON'T

Revised Edition

Pepper O'Neal

A Cibola Press Publication

To Levi's real-life counterpart.
Thanks. For everything!

And to my sister, Cynthia (1950 ~ 1968)
On whom Andi was based.
I still miss you!

Author's Note

When my Black Ops Chronicles series first came out in 2011, I had made my organized crime family a member of the Mormon Mafia, on which I had done a considerable amount of internet research. And I quite liked the conflict between religion and crime. However, since that time, I have discovered that many of the sites I used for my research on the Mormon Mafia contained deliberately inaccurate and inflammatory information put there by people with an axe to grind, thus making me wonder if there is actually a Mormon Mafia at all. As my purpose in writing fiction is to entertain my readers, and I have no wish to spread inaccurate and inflammatory information about an organization which may not even exist, I have decided to remove the Mormon Mafia from the book completely and to use the Greek Mafia instead. I can at least be sure that they do exist and the information on the internet about them comes from reliable sources and not from someone with malicious intent.

GLOSSARY

AED: Acronym for Automatic External Difibulator, a portable device to restart a person's heart.

AO: stands for area of operation and usually refers to where a battle or tactical event takes place—where the mission is carried out.

Black Ops: short for black operations—covert mission that are highly clandestine and often outside of standard military protocol, or even against the law. They are called black operations because they are carried out in great secrecy, usually with no official records of the mission being kept.

Blowback: the consequences of a mission or action.

Camo: short for camouflage.

Camo Paint: military makeup that come in shades of black, brown, gray, white, dark and light green which is painted on a soldier's face to help conceal him or her.

Collateral damage: damage to things that are incidental to the intended target. Frequently used as a military term to refer to the accidental or unintentional killing or wounding of non-combatants and/or destruction to non-combatant property during attacks on legitimate enemy targets.

Connected: Connected (with a capital C) means associated with organized crime as in belonging to or working for an organized crime family.

FUBAR: pronounced foo-bar, is an acronym for "F***ed Up Beyond All Recognition," often used by the military personnel to describe a blown mission or a catastrophe.

Ghillie Suit: a camouflage suit designed to resemble foliage and primarily used to hide snipers and Special Forces soldiers in combat situations.

Intel: short for intelligence, refers to information pertaining to the mission.

In Country: Short for in the country.

IVIS: An acronym for Integrated Vehicular Information System—an information-sharing system that allows what one person or vehicle knows to be known instantly by the rest of the team.

Mole: a spy, or an insider, who is giving information to the other side.

MOS: Acronym for Military Occupation Specialty, or in other words, a soldier's job or skill set.

Murphy's Law: the name military personnel commonly give the saying, "Whatever can go wrong, will go wrong."

Outfit: another name for the mafia in America

Point Man, Point Position, Taking Point: the man in front, scouting out the mission and relaying information back to the rest of the team. The point man is usually some distance from the rest of the team.

Seventh Floor Authorization: a term used by CIA officers to denote whether an operation is approved by the heads of the CIA, whose offices are located on the seventh floor of the CIA headquarters building in Langley, Virginia.

Sit Rep: Short for Situation Report—a statement of conditions in the field on an operation, mainly with regard to the location of the enemy.

Six or Your Six: Directly behind you. Also, meaning "your back" as in "I've got your six," or "Watch your six." Short for "six o'clock" from the military style of giving directions based on a clock—used especially by fighter pilots to alert their wing men to the location of enemy planes.

STAT: a code, mostly used in hospitals, meaning immediately or right now.

Stockholm Syndrome: also called "capture bonding" is a psychological phenomenon where hostages bond with their captures and take their side against rescuers.

The Company: what CIA officers and others in the know call the CIA.

The Farm: the CIA training facility near Williamsburg, Virginia.

Victimless Crimes: refers to crimes which are illegal but do not violate or threaten individual rights, such as gambling, prostitution, adult pornography, and smuggling of alcohol and tobacco. Also called crimes between consenting adults.

Wiseguy: a highly ranked individual in a crime family.

CHAPTER 1

Wednesday, March 27th, 5:21 p.m., the estate of Darren Merritt, near Springfield, Massachusetts:

No! This can't be happening!

The last thing Andi expected to encounter on the grounds of her father's estate was an ambush. Headed to the stables for her rendezvous with Donald, she'd had her mind on romance and her fingers toying with the beautiful opal pendant he'd given her last night. *Can I trust him?* she wondered. *Or is he just another gold digger after Father's money?* Lost in her thoughts, she paid little attention to the stranger approaching her.

Until he spoke.

"Excuse me, miss."

His rough voice grated on her ears. Nerves tingling, she backed away. He followed—big, muscular, and hulking. *Geeze, he looks like a thug.* Incongruous in his three-piece, navy-blue suit with its tiny white pinstripes, he made the hairs on the back of her neck stand up. She stuffed the opal necklace under the neck of her T-shirt and continued backing away. "Who are you?" Chills skittered up her spine. The man *oozed* violence and malicious intent. "You're t—trespassing," she stammered. "This is private property!"

Focused on the guy in front of her, she didn't notice the other two come up behind her until she felt a hand on her shoulder—and the prick of a needle in her arm. Vomit rose in her throat. Hot and bitter, it choked off her breath. She swallowed hard, forcing the vile mess back down so she could scream.

She fought them. Rage and panic poured strength into her muscles as she twisted, scratched, and kicked. But it did her no good. The men overpowered her and stuffed her into a cloth bag reeking of dirty socks and stale cigarettes. The thick, heavy material muffled her cries for help, echoing them back on her. Screams turned into sobs then into hysterical giggling as the drug took effect.

The world dimmed. Faded to gray. And went black.

8:10 p.m., the Sydarian Embassy, Washington, DC:

"Did you get the package?" The words, calm and quiet, displayed none of the seething tension Ambassador Jamar Farahani held inside. He hated working with scum like this—dirty, violent, uneducated. But that was the only kind of man who would undertake this type of job.

"Yeah, we got her," replied the rough voice on the other end of the line. "When are you coming to pick her up?"

"Tomorrow. Maybe. It depends on the weather. Right now, they will not let any planes take off from the airport. Not even private jets." Jamar's hand tightened on the phone as he watched the snowstorm outside his windows. "There is supposed to be a break tomorrow. So hopefully, I can get out then."

"If that's the best you can do, I'll just have to sit on her for a while. But get here as soon as you can. My guys are getting restless."

"Just make sure nothing happens to her, Johnson." Jamar's voice turned cold and hard. "If she is raped, beaten, or even scratched, you and your men will not get paid. Understand?"

"Yeah, yeah. I'll make sure nothing happens. But the sooner she's out of here, the better. She's such a looker, it's hard to control my men."

"If she was not 'such a looker,' she would not be worth as much money, and you would not be getting paid your over-inflated fee." Jamar turned away from the windows. And the storm. *Dammit!* The goal had been within his reach, then this happened. "Tell your men I will examine the package thoroughly when I get there. If there is a mark on her, they will not only lose the money, they will not live long enough to regret it." He paused to let that sink in. "I hope I have made myself clear."

"Yeah, I got it." Johnson's voice had risen nearly an octave. "N—Nobody'll t—touch her."

"See that they do not." Jamar disconnected, fighting the urge to throw the phone against the wall. If Johnson's men did what kidnappers of young women normally did, the buyer would not pay full price. A knock at the door jerked him out of his dark thoughts. "Come in."

Basaam brought in a tray of coffee and pastries. "Did they get the package, sir?"

Jamar scowled at his assistant. "Yes, they got her. But I do not know what kind of shape she will be in when I finally pick her up." Still frowning, he took the cup of coffee Bas handed him. "If Johnson cannot control his men, she may not be worth very much to the buyer."

"Surely, for what you are paying them, they should be able to control their…urges." Bas put a chocolate eclair on a small plate and handed it over. "Shall I call Ahasama and give him the good news?"

"Not yet. I do not want to report success until the

package is safe in our hands. Ahasama tends to deal harshly with disappointment. Very harshly."

Jamar looked at his watch then out the window at the storm. He hoped it did not last much longer. Both he and the package were running out of time.

Thursday, March 28th, 5:04 a.m., the apartment of Levi Komakov, Boston, Massachusetts:

"Bloody hell, what now?" Still more than half asleep, Levi fumbled for the ringing phone. "This had better be *good*."

"Levi?"

"Jonas?" Levi bolted up into a sitting position. His friend and employer, Jonas Demopulus, never called him at home unless there was trouble. "How bad?"

"Bad enough. Son, I need you here." Jonas sounded tired. "Will you come?"

"Of course, I'll come, old man. You should know that by now."

A weak chuckle came down the line. "Actually, I do. But it's still more polite to ask."

"Nothing's polite at five in the morning," Levi argued, glancing at the clock. "I'm on my way."

"How soon can you get here?"

"If you want me awake and functioning, it'll take me an hour. Otherwise, thirty minutes." Levi could hear Jonas conferring with someone else but couldn't tell who.

"An hour will do."

"I'll be there."

Levi hung up the phone. So it was urgent, but not life or death. Still, whatever it was, it was bad.

He reached across the bed for the hand that wasn't

there and groaned. His wife Leanne had been dead for over two years, but he still reached for her every morning, after dreaming of her each night. Murdered—when she was six months pregnant—by a drunk driving the wrong way on the freeway, her death had left a hole in Levi's soul that he couldn't seem to fill. A former sergeant in the British SAS, he was a man who would have killed, if necessary, to protect his wife and unborn child. But he couldn't even go after the bastard who'd murdered her. The bugger had died in the crash, along with Leanne.

Levi had always known that life wasn't fair—he'd just never realized how bloody *unfair* it could be.

He threw off the covers, rolled out of bed, and stretched. He'd have to forego his morning run, he realized, then he closed his eyes, disappointed at the flash of relief he felt. He was getting older, slowing down.

Losing his edge.

At thirty-four, he could still do most of the things he'd done at twenty-four, but running a six-minute mile now took seven and a half.

He went into the kitchen, flipped the switch on the coffee pot, and headed for the shower. Maybe the trouble waiting for him at Jonas's estate would be big enough to get his mind off his own problems.

Yeah, and maybe I should be careful what I wish for.

5:11 a.m., a cabin in the Cascade Mountains on the Yakima Indian Reservation in southern Washington:

Fear and rage. They seemed to be the only emotions Andi had left. The only ones she remembered, anyway. As if she had never known anything else, they filled and consumed her.

When she'd awakened from her drugged sleep, the sack she'd been shoved into was gone. Now she lay, bound and gagged, on a lumpy double bed. Her mouth tasted like muddy cotton. The ropes around her wrists and ankles bit into her skin. For hours she'd lain here, watching the sky outside the barred windows grow lighter—as day one of her abduction passed into day two. She'd stopped struggling, defeated by the emotional and physical pain. The ropes were too tight, freedom impossible.

What did they want with her? She shuddered as thoughts of what men usually wanted from women flashed through her mind. *No. Oh, please, no.* Panic flared up again, and she fought the ropes until she lay curled into a ball, sobbing and exhausted.

Would anyone come to help her? No one had seen her being abducted. Had Donald reported her missing when she hadn't shown up for their date? Or was he *in* on it? From what she'd overheard the men in the next room say, someone close to her had arranged her kidnapping. Her father? Donald? Could it really be true? But who else could have given the kidnappers her picture, her schedule, and the best time to ambush her? Not many people had known exactly where she'd be and when.

Jonas Demopulus, head of the crime family her father belonged to, might send someone to help. The rumors in the Family said he didn't allow innocent people to be hurt. Then again, he might not even know she'd been abducted. If her father had tipped off the kidnappers, he wouldn't have called Jonas for help.

Damn, if only she could get to a computer! She was an expert hacker and had broken into the FBI's database more than once for her father, checking for arrest warrants on his men. Only this time, she'd put out an abduction alert on herself. But she doubted the kidnappers would loan her a laptop, even if she asked.

Exhausted from the effects of the drug, her ordeal, and the questions she couldn't answer, Andi drifted off to sleep, praying that someone out there—somewhere—would come to her aid.

5:53 a.m., the estate of Jonas Demopulus, outside Boston, Massachusetts:

Levi walked into Jonas's study and found a surprise waiting for him. "Special Agent Wilson," he said warmly, shaking the FBI agent's hand. "What brings you here?"

"Mr. Komakov." Wilson looked relieved to see him. "We need your expertise," he said, picking up a manila file folder from a stack of papers on Jonas's desk and handing it over.

With a twinge of unease, Levi sat down, opened the folder, and scanned it. "Anderson Merritt," he read out loud. "Goes by Andi." But he saw nothing in the file that would explain why he'd been called in. There was a brief dossier and a color photo, showing an exquisite young woman—probably mid-twenties—with auburn hair to her mid-back; ivory skin; and striking, almond-shaped, honey-colored eyes. According to the file, she was five feet, eight inches tall, one-hundred-thirty pounds. Just about perfect. He whistled. "Nice. *Very* nice. She's a bloody beautiful girl. And if your information's correct, she's also intelligent, stubborn, very sheltered, and a bit of a handful." He looked from Wilson to Jonas. "But other than wondering who I'd have to kill to have her, I don't see what the problem is. Is the FBI after her for something?"

Jonas cleared his throat. "Andi is Darren Merritt's daughter, Levi. She's been kidnapped."

"Bloody hell! Sorry." Levi winced, appalled by his thoughtless comments. "By Darren Merritt, I assume you mean your guy in Springfield." He remembered meeting the underboss once but hadn't been impressed with him. "Did he ask for your help?"

"No. I knew nothing about this until Wilson called me early this morning."

Levi rubbed a hand over his face. "You've lost me, guys," he confessed, handing the file folder back. "You said you needed my expertise, which I assume means my particular brand of skills." Jonas and Wilson both nodded, so Levi continued. "The FBI has a whole *team* of professionals who handle this kind of stuff—all younger and in better shape than I am. If the young lady's been kidnapped and you guys are involved, what can *I* do?"

Wilson didn't answer directly. Instead, he said, "I've checked out your background, the part that's not classified, anyway. You're experienced in covert operations—or should I say 'black ops'—and you've had paramilitary training with the British SAS. After you immigrated to the US from England, you worked in some capacity with the CIA for a while, but nobody there will say what you did." When Levi said nothing, Wilson smiled. "Mr. Demopulus tells me you're a dangerous man to your enemies but a savior to your friends. He also says you could out-stalk a leopard."

"What does my background have to do with anything?"

"Are you willing to work in an *unofficial* capacity?"

Levi couldn't stop his snort. "You mean *more* unofficially than I usually do?" He looked from Wilson to Jonas and back again. "Look, just tell me what the situation is and what you want me to do. Then I'll tell you if I can do it. Fair enough?"

Wilson nodded. "The girl's being held in a cabin on

the Yakima Indian Reservation in southern Washington," he said. "We know exactly which cabin, even which room."

"*Exactly*? How the bloody hell did you manage that?"

"Technology," Wilson said with a tight smile. "The problem is there's a conflict between the tribal authorities and the FBI. We won't reveal the source of the information on the girl's whereabouts, so the tribal authorities won't accept that the girl's there. Unless we can show them some concrete proof that she is, other than claiming we have a confidential informant, the tribal authorities won't allow our hostage rescue team to come in and retrieve her. And we can't just go up and knock on the door to get the necessary proof, or the girl will likely become collateral damage."

He sighed and shook his head. "The bottom line is the bosses are all sitting around playing with their dicks while the victim suffers."

"So what you're telling me," Levi said, remembering why he'd left the CIA, "is that politics is interfering with the rescue of a kidnap victim?" He studied the man. "That doesn't sound like the Special Agent Wilson *I* know."

"That's why I'm here," Wilson admitted without apology. "The Powers That Be have decided to negotiate with the tribal authorities rather than take any direct action. So my hands are tied."

"And you remembered that I don't like innocents getting hurt any more than you do, right?"

"That's right. I also remembered how effective you were in rescuing Tess Horton in Mexico a few years ago. So when I got the word that the victim wasn't the Higher Ups' first priority, I—" When Levi raised his eyebrows, Wilson shrugged. "That's not what they *said*, but it's what they *meant*. Anyway, I thought of you, so I called Mr. Demopulus and—"

A knock on the door interrupted them. Jeff, one of Jonas's attorney advisors, came into the room, followed closely by Garry, his assistant, carrying a tray loaded with coffee cups and pastries. "We were passing, saw the light under the door, and heard voices, so we assumed there was a meeting going on." He gestured for Garry to set the tray on the coffee table in front of the couch. "We thought you could use an eye opener."

"Thank you, Jeff," Jonas said. "And you, too, Garry. That was very considerate of you."

Jeff looked at the three men, the file in Wilson's hand, and the stack of papers on the desk. "Is there anything I need to know, Jonas?"

"Not at the moment, Jeff," Jonas said dryly. "You normally don't need an attorney until *after* the crime's been committed."

"Right," Jeff said dryly. He eyed all three men again then beckoned to Garry and left, closing the door behind them.

Levi passed around the coffee before grabbing a cup for himself. "So let me see if I understand what you're saying. You can't do jack shit to get this girl out of there, so you want me to go onto federal property, by myself, armed and unauthorized, and *unofficially* rescue her. Correct?"

"Yes."

"That's what I thought."

"Can you do it?" Jonas asked. "I'll get you whatever gear you want and anything else you need."

"You're just a sucker for a pretty girl, aren't you, old man?"

"Absolutely."

But Levi knew it was more than that. Jonas hated to

see innocents suffer as much as Levi and Wilson did. The fact that Jonas focused on "victimless crimes" and didn't allow his organization to hurt civilians was the only reason Levi had agreed to work for him in the first place. "To answer your question, yes, I can probably do it," he confirmed. "I'll know more when I see the layout of where she's being held." He turned to Wilson. "My question is, *how* unofficial is this operation going to be?" When the man gave him a blank look, Levi clarified. "If I get in and get out with the girl, am I going to be in trouble with your troops for breaking the law?"

"If you get in and out without getting caught, then no—I don't know you and have no idea that you're even involved."

"Gee, that sounds just like what I used to hear from the SAS and the CIA. And if I get caught?"

"If you get caught, you were not acting with any official authorization, but I *will* do whatever I can for you," Wilson assured him. "I strongly recommend, however, that you *not* get caught."

"That sounds familiar, too." Levi thought for a moment, wondering how to broach his next question. *Hell, might as well be blunt.* "To do this as covertly as you seem to want, I'm going to have to kill any hostiles, whether they pose a direct threat or not." He paused, sipped his coffee. "I don't normally like to do that, but in my book, kidnappers rate right up there with terrorists and don't deserve any mercy. So I'm okay with it this time. But are you?"

"As far as I'm concerned, you can kill every one of the bastards."

"Good. That's settled." How could he *not* go? A woman or child in danger was a call to action no honorable man could ignore. And Wilson had known he'd go even before he asked. *So what hasn't he told me?* "I'll do it, but I have one more question," he told the FBI agent. "What don't you want to tell me?"

Wilson averted his eyes. "As of yet, there hasn't been any ransom demand."

"Bloody hell!"

8:23 a.m., the Sydarian Embassy:

Jamar stood at the window, cursing the snow. From the looks of it, there wouldn't be a break anytime soon. He'd thought about taking the train south, out of the storm, then chartering a plane once he'd left the bad weather behind, but that would leave witnesses as well as a paper trail.

Bas poked his head through the doorway. "Boston on line one for you, sir."

Jamar nodded then stomped over to the phone on his desk. "Why the hell did you not call me on my cell phone?"

"Because the feds can *eavesdrop* on cell phones, you idiot," said a familiar voice. "I've worked for a crime family long enough to know not to give out sensitive information on anything but a land line. As a matter of fact, I'm calling from a payphone in town, since I don't know if the phones on the estate are bugged."

"I see. So why did you call?"

"We have a problem. Demopulus may be sending someone to rescue the package."

"How do you know?"

"An FBI agent showed up at the estate early this morning. About an hour after he got there, Demopulus's trouble shooter, Levi Komakov, came in, almost three hours earlier than normal. They were still holed up in the study when I left to call you. What else could they be planning?"

"I have six guards on her, and it is in a very remote location," Jamar said. "Do you think we really need to worry?"

"If they send Komakov, we do. The guy's a freaking ghost. Trained by the British SAS *and* the CIA—if you believe even half of the rumors about him—he's no joke."

"How much do they know?"

"I won't know for sure until I check the tapes. But someone must have called the FBI. It wasn't her father, so we've probably got a mole, which means they must have some idea of where she is, or they wouldn't have called in Komakov."

"Great. That is just what we do not need." Jamar sighed. "I will call Johnson and warn him. I will also send him some more men. Though, depending on the roads, they probably won't get there before sometime tomorrow. Meanwhile, you try to find out how much they know and what they intend to do about it." Jamar considered the man at the other end of the line for a moment. "Is there any way *you* can take out this Komakov?"

"Not a chance." A dark chuckle traveled down the line from Boston. "Even with my training, he'd gut me like a fish. Unless I managed to shoot him in the back. But I'm not sure he doesn't have eyes in the back of his head. What do you think about moving the package?"

"I do not trust Johnson to do it safely and I am stuck here. I could not get my plane out of the airport last night as I had planned. I probably will not be able to leave until this evening from the look of things." Jamar scowled at the snowflakes whipping past his window. "I cannot drive. The snow has closed too many roads. So I was considering taking the train south out of the storm first thing in the morning and chartering a plane."

"Why can't you do it now?"

"I have a meeting this afternoon that I cannot afford to miss. If I could have gotten out last night, I would have been back in time for the meeting, but it is too late now. It will have to be tomorrow." Jamar massaged the back of his neck to ease the tension. "If I leave first thing in the morning, I could be there by tomorrow afternoon. But I do not like the idea of witnesses and an untrusted flight crew. Or a paper trail, for that matter."

"Dope the package and put her in a box, for Pete's sake. Then she's just cargo to any witness or flight crew. All any paperwork will say is whatever you write on it."

"Yes, good. An excellent idea." Jamar played the scenario in his head but saw no downside. "I will be on the first train south in the morning. You see what else you can come up with and let me know. If this Komakov is going to attempt a rescue, he will have to be good."

"He is. So just make sure Johnson's expecting him."

CHAPTER 2

8:42 a.m., the cabin on the Yakima Indian Reservation:

The men had taken off the ropes and gag around sunrise, given Andi a sandwich and a glass of water, and even let her use the bathroom—once. Then they'd taken her coat and shoes and shoved her back into the bedroom. They hadn't said one unnecessary word to her or answered a single question.

She lay on the bed and listened to them talk. They were calling her "the package" now. Apparently, they were waiting for someone to come for her so they could get paid, but whoever it was had been delayed by the weather Back East. And it seemed someone else was coming who shouldn't be. They sounded worried.

At least she hadn't been raped. Yet. For a while she'd entertained thoughts of escaping. But even if she could get through the bars on the bedroom window, she couldn't run through the woods without shoes. Or a coat. At least not as fast as she'd need to.

Her wrists and ankles were sore and bruised, she was cold, she had a headache, and she was totally exhausted. Obviously, her nap hadn't done her much good.

She fingered the opal pendant Donald had given her,

missing his smile and the warmth in his eyes. She'd been obsessed with him from the moment she'd met him three weeks ago, thinking about him almost every second she was awake. Was he really that different from all the others, or was it just an act? Impossible to tell at this point, but her instincts told her he was one of the good guys. And even if she couldn't trust him, the necklace offered a lot of comfort now in her fear and anguish. It was gorgeous and probably valuable, and she was surprised the men hadn't confiscated it along with her shoes and coat. Maybe they just hadn't seen it under her T-shirt. But then they hadn't taken her purse either. Just her freedom, self-respect, security, and any hopes she had for a future.

Tears welled up in her eyes. She tried to blink them back, but they fell in spite of her efforts, silent as the snow outside. What was going to happen to her? Just thinking about it made her shudder.

8:51 a.m., the estate of Jonas Demopulus:

Levi listened intently as Wilson explained where the girl was being held. When Levi ran out of questions, Wilson handed over a map, diagrams, and the picture of Andi then took his leave.

"Please be careful and come back safe." He hesitated at the door, a look of intense pain on his face. "I knew your uncle very well and I miss him. He had a lot of friends in the Bureau. If I'd been there when that punk shot him, I—" Exhaling loudly, Wilson shook his head. "Well, anyway, he was a good man and a good agent. He'll probably haunt me from the grave if you get caught or killed on this mission."

"I don't plan to do either," Levi assured him. "Don't

worry. This is nothing I haven't done before."

Touched by the man's words, he watched Wilson close the door. Uncle John *had* been a good man. Levi missed him, too.

"What's going on?" Jonas demanded the moment they were alone. "Why didn't Wilson want to tell us there hasn't been a ransom demand?"

Levi wasn't surprised Jonas had held his questions until Wilson was gone. It paid to be careful what you discussed in front of the FBI, no matter *how* friendly the agent was. "You'd better have a seat, Jonas. You're not going to like this." Pacing back and forth in front of the fire, the old man looked so tired and frail Levi was concerned for his health. He was sixty-three, after all. When Jonas reluctantly settled himself in a chair by the window, Levi continued, "Kidnapping's an expensive business. Not only do you have to pay any helpers, but you have to provide food and shelter for the victim for as long as it takes. What that means is you don't kidnap someone unless you have a *very* good reason. Now, there are only three reasons I can think of to kidnap someone—money, sex, or leverage. And since there hasn't been any ransom demand, we can rule out money."

"Are you saying they took her for sex? That poor—"

"No. Most snatchings for sex involve children. And while a lot of women who are kidnapped are also raped, it's usually a perk for the criminals, not the purpose of the crime. I'm not saying that adult females are *never* kidnapped for sex. But I don't think that's the case here, and neither does Wilson." Levi hesitated. There really wasn't any way to say this that would make it easier for Jonas to hear. "What the man didn't want to tell us, and what he was trying to say without actually using the words, is that she was taken for leverage."

"And what does that mean?"

"It means you have a problem in your organization. The most likely scenario is that someone is trying to use Andi to get her father to do something he doesn't want to do. But if whatever they're trying to get him to do was in your best interests, you'd already know about it. Wilson obviously knows more than he's telling, but this little tidbit he gave up is plenty worrying enough."

"I see." Jonas surprised Levi. Now that he understood the problem, his agitation disappeared and his manner became all business. Suddenly, he didn't look frail at all. Crossing to his desk, he buzzed his secretary. "Gloria, please schedule some time for you to meet with me this morning. We'll need about an hour of uninterrupted time, if you can fit it into my schedule."

"I can bump your eleven o'clock with Jeff. Reschedule that for tomorrow."

"That would be fine. Thanks."

"What are you planning?" Levi asked as the intercom clicked off.

"You get the girl and keep her out of harm's way while I start an investigation on Darren Merritt and his people in Springfield. If you have Andi, she can't be used as leverage, and I know she'll be safe with you." He waited for Levi to nod. "Meanwhile, I need to find out what's going on down there and decide what I want to do about it. Now, what do you need from me to accomplish your assignment?"

Levi picked up a satellite photo. "From the look of these pictures, I'll need a ghillie suit—that's a camouflage suit for snipers."

"Yes, I know what they are."

"Good. A ghillie suit specific to this terrain and the snow; night-vision goggles; my usual, double load of plastic explosives; a high powered rifle, with a scope and a really good silencer; at least two handguns; and plenty of ammunition. Oh, and a parka for the girl. We can't be sure she has one." When Jonas nodded, Levi asked, "Who do you have in Oregon or Washington that can get me some vehicles?"

Before Jonas could respond, Jeff came in with another tray of coffee. He set it down on the coffee table, picked up the one from earlier, then crossed to the desk to collect the used coffee cups. Garry was nowhere in sight.

Levi watched as Jeff's eyes zeroed in on the map Wilson had left. The hairs on the back of his neck stood up and he moved instinctively to block Jeff's view. Jeff was okay, wasn't he?

Or was Levi just paranoid? *Sure, I'm paranoid, but am I paranoid enough?*

Jonas intervened, obviously having noticed both Jeff's scrutiny and Levi's reaction. "Thank you, Jeff," he said. "I appreciate the gesture, but it's really not necessary for you to do this. Levi and I can call down to the kitchen if we need anything."

Jeff shrugged. "I realize this isn't in an attorney's job description, Jonas, but this meeting seemed to be rather hush-hush. So I didn't want a lot of unauthorized people coming in." He smiled. "We're much too free with information around here as it is. I believe I've mentioned that once or twice before."

"Yes, I believe you have," Jonas agreed without offense. "But this meeting's just about over." Jeff nodded then excused himself. When he had gone, Jonas looked at Levi. "Is it that you don't like him, or that you don't trust him?"

"He's an attorney." Levi shrugged. "What's to like *or* trust?"

"They do come in handy, occasionally," Jonas said with a chuckle. "Now, what vehicles do you need?"

"An off-road vehicle that can hold two people—and

is as quiet as possible—and an inconspicuous car that's fast."

"How fast?"

"Fast enough I can outrun any pursuers, including the law."

"What are *you* planning?"

Levi grinned. "The usual—kill the bad guys, grab the girl, blow the cabin to destroy any evidence, hightail it out of there with an ATV and a fast car, and not get caught." He ran his finger over the map. The cabin was located in the Cascade Mountains east of a hamlet called Trout Lake, Washington, inside the Yakima Indian Reservation. "I'll go in early tomorrow morning, stay off the reservation roads, and take the logging trails through this little draw here. If I head back toward Mount Adams until I get to this point, I should miss all the tribal police. Once I get the girl and get back to this spot here, I'll ditch the ATV and take the car. The VIN number on the ATV should probably be removed, unless your man wants to claim it was stolen—or else he can come and pick it up after I'm done."

"Where do you want the vehicles left?"

"Have him leave the ATV here," Levi said, pointing to a spot on the map. "If he wants to pick it up after I'm done, that's where it will be. The car needs to be at the Columbia Gorge Regional Airport in Dallesport. I'll have my plane drop me off there."

"Drop you off? You don't want it to wait for you?"

"No. Planes have to file flight plans. Once I get the girl, I'm going to have to hide her until we know who's behind this. I can disappear easier in a car than a plane."

"I see. Well, I can have everything you need at your plane in an hour," Jonas said, settling into his desk chair. "Go pack a bag and head to the airport. Unless you can think of anything else."

"Yeah, duct tape and handcuffs."

"*What?*"

"From what I read in the file Wilson showed me, the beautiful Andi Merritt is a spitfire. If she knows she's being used as leverage, she may not come quietly. I'll try not to use either the tape or the cuffs, but I want the option. I don't like manhandling women, but I don't want my eyes scratched out while I'm trying to rescue her, either."

"I see." Jonas gave him a long look. "Please try to remember that she's the victim here."

"I know. Don't worry. I'll be as gentle as possible. But if you want her kept out of harm's way, I may have to do it against her will." Levi started to leave then turned back. "I should probably have a couple of credit cards that aren't in my name if you think I'm going to be out for a while." He had several old, unused CIA alternate identities—with IDs and credit cards—but he hated to use them if Jonas had another option. "I don't want to be tracked via credit cards in my real name."

"Good point." Jonas went to his safe, took out two small envelopes, and tossed them over to him. "These two haven't been used before."

Levi scanned the envelopes' contents then cocked an eyebrow at Jonas. "John Adams and Joseph Black. Original. What's my limit?"

"Unless you're planning to buy a new yacht, you should be covered. Anything you need that can be billed to me, such as something from our regular suppliers, do that. Use the credit cards for everything else." When Levi nodded and headed for the door, Jonas added, "And, Levi, make sure you both come back safe."

"Consider it done."

CHAPTER 3

Friday, March 30th, 2:35 a.m., the cabin on the Yakima Indian Reservation:

Andi woke up to the sound of arguing in the other room. She heard them shout "the package" several times, but knew they weren't calling her—they were fighting about her.

Not a good sign.

As she listened more closely, fear pooled in her stomach and froze the blood in her veins. "Oh, please, no," she breathed, her throat suddenly dry and burning. They were arguing about who got to do her first. *No!*

Terrified, exhausted, and physically drained, she jumped to her feet and looked around for some place to hide. But she couldn't fit under the bed and the closet door was locked. A weapon then. She wasn't going down without a fight.

Her purse lay on a small, square table beside the bed. Andi slipped the purse strap over her shoulder then picked up the table and hefted it. It was heavier than it looked and fairly solid. She might be able to put someone's eye out with one of the legs or crack open a skull with the edge. Having nothing else available, she took the table and backed into a corner, just as shots were fired and all hell broke loose on the other side of the door.

Forty-five minutes earlier:

Levi found the ATV right where he'd asked for it to be. Jonas had outdone himself. The thing was so quiet, Levi could barely hear it. He drove it to within several hundred yards of the cabin. Then, donning his ghillie suit, camo paint, and night-vision goggles, he grabbed his pack, rifle, and pistols and worked his way through the woods. The goggles made the forest almost as bright as a cloudy day.

When he got close enough to the cabin, he crouched behind a tree to survey his surroundings. There were six men—three on guard outside and three inside. The inside three were arguing so loudly he could hear their voices from his position, though he couldn't make out the words. Those three wouldn't notice anything until it was too late. But he'd have to take down the three outside guards first, so he could rig the cabin with plastic explosives before he went for the girl. That way, he wouldn't have to risk her running off into the woods while he was up to his ears in plastique.

Still watching the cabin, he noticed the outside guards whispering to each other, their gazes repeatedly shifting to the surrounding woods. Levi caught only a few words, but what he heard turned his blood to ice. He was *expected*? Quiet as a thought, he crept closer, inch-by-inch, until he could hear every word.

"So when's the boss man coming to get her?" one man asked.

"Don't know," answered another. "There's a bad

snowstorm on the East Coast. All flights out of Washington, DC, have been canceled."

"Then what the hell do we do with the package?" the first man asked.

"We guard her, you dumbass. And we keep our hands off," the second man replied with a glance at the cabin window behind him.

"Where's the fun in that?" sneered the third man.

"Dammit, Carter, we're not here for fun. If the Ghost rescues her, or anyone lays a hand on her, we don't get paid. And I, for one, want my friggin' money."

"Don't get your panties in a twist, Johnson," Carter grumbled. "I'll do my frickin' job. I just assumed there'd be perks, what with her being such a looker and all."

While Carter and Johnson argued, the last guard nervously scanned the clearing. "If this Ghost is as good as you say, he could be out there right now, ready to pick us off one-by-one."

"The boss is sending more men," Johnson replied. "Should be here any minute."

Levi winced. *Bloody hell, how many of these bastards are there?* The *Ghost* was obviously a reference to him. He'd been called that before. So the *package* must be Andi. Not a person, just a thing. *Dirty buggers.*

Since they knew he was coming, the job would be trickier. But if he waited, he'd have *more* of these bastards to deal with. He really had no choice. He had to make his move now, even though he'd lost the element of surprise. A time or two, he'd worked a blown mission for the CIA and managed to pull it off. This would be no different.

The outside guards were being careful. They kept in sight of each other at all times, so if he dropped one, the others would notice. He could take two without a problem, but the third would be able to sound the alarm before he could get to him. He needed to separate them.

He looked around for some inspiration. It was cold. *Sound travels farther in the cold.* The forest smelled fresh, like pine needles and snow, and was so quiet, it was eerie. Even though the men outside were talking in whispers, their voices seemed loud, due to the lack of all other sound. Levi knew a single misstep on his part would alert them to his presence. He missed the camouflaging noise of traffic, boom boxes at full blast from apartment windows, and barking dogs in the city. Here, so early in the morning, not even the birds were awake.

Since the guards were anticipating something, Levi decided to give it to them. Using the quiet of the forest to his advantage, he reached into his pack for a timer switch, detonators, wire, and some plastique—just enough to make noise. Leaving the rest of his equipment where it was, he inched his way through the trees to the other side of the cabin, placing each foot so as not to make a sound. He positioned three small dabs of plastique in a row several feet apart, wired them up, and set the timer for a half second interval between detonations, starting in six minutes. Then he worked his way back to his original position. Once there, he lay on the ground, snugged his rifle to his shoulder, lined up his sights, and waited.

In the dark, with his ghillie suit and rifle camouflage cover, he was invisible. Even if the men looked right at him, all they would see was snow-covered forest vegetation.

Finally, from the other side of the cabin came a series of popping noises, too soft to be heard inside the cabin over the heated argument. But the outside guards had obviously noticed.

"What was that?" Carter whispered.

"Don't know," the third man said. "It could be the guy they said was coming."

"Can't be," Carter insisted. "He's supposed to be a ghost."

"Whoever it is," Johnson hissed, "if the package gets rescued or killed, we don't get paid." He jerked his rifle in the direction the sounds had come from. "Go check it out, Jones. We'll cover you."

Perfect.

As soon as Jones was out of sight around the corner of the cabin, Levi took his first shot. By the time Johnson started to fall, the second bullet had found its mark and Carter crumpled beside him. The silencer on the rifle was so good there was barely a whisper of sound. Levi would have to remember to thank Jonas later.

All Levi had to do now was to wait for Jones. He figured he'd only have two or three seconds of shocked silence before the guy would start making noise, but that'd be enough.

Jones came back to report, stared down at the bodies of his friends, then joined them in death before he'd even had a chance to make a sound.

Levi gathered the three bodies and stacked them up against the side of the cabin, along with their weapons. They'd all disintegrate when the cabin blew up, but he'd plant an extra charge there just to be sure. He wasn't a man to leave anything to chance.

Now for the explosives. He rigged a double charge at all four corners, put one under the bodies and guns, and set the timer for fifteen minutes. That should be enough time to kill the others, grab the girl, and hightail it out of there.

Setting his pack and rifle beside the front door, he dropped his night-vision goggles down around his neck, pulled one of the pistols out of a pocket in his ghillie suit, and quietly opened the door. The three men were still arguing and didn't even see him come in. Finally able to hear what they were saying, Levi saw red. He took down the first one and had already lined up his sights on the second before anyone knew he was there. Number three lunged for a gun lying on the table, but didn't make it in time. He went down with a bullet to his forehead, crashing onto the table and breaking it into kindling. Normally, Levi didn't like to kill, but this time it felt good. *Damn* good.

Only thing left was the girl. According to Wilson, she was being kept in a small bedroom off to the right. He put the pistol away, stepped over the bodies, and knocked on the door. "Andi?"

When she didn't respond, he eased the door open and peeked inside. Oh yeah, she was a looker, all right. Her picture didn't do her justice at all. Even backed into a corner holding a small table out in front of her as a weapon, dressed in jeans and T-shirt with no shoes, her hair mussed, and her eyes wide with fear, she was breathtaking. Still, Levi was surprised by the flare of arousal he felt. Beautiful women didn't usually have such an effect on him.

From the look on her face, he figured she'd heard what the men were arguing about, too. "It's all right, luv," he said gently. "I'm Levi Komakov. I've come to get you out of here."

"Liar! You can't be him!" she screeched. "You just shot three men. Everyone knows Levi's not a killer." She paused but only for a quick breath. "I don't believe you're him. You don't act anything like him."

He rolled his eyes. "Everyone's a critic. And it was six men, not three." He tried reason next. "Look, luv, I'll be happy to show you my identification when we get back to the car, but this place is going to blow up in about ten minutes, so we really need to get out of here."

"And I'm just supposed to take your word for it?"

she snapped. "Well, I'm not going to. I don't know who you are, and I'm not going anywhere with you. You're probably the one they were waiting for—the one they said was coming to get *the package*."

He stepped into the room with a sigh. He really couldn't blame her. Dressed in a ghillie suit with camouflage paint on his face, he probably looked like a monster. "We don't really have time for this, luv," he said, walking slowly toward her with his hands raised, "so we can do this the easy way or the hard way. It's up to you. I don't want to hurt you, but you're coming with me one way or the other." When she tried to hit him with the table, he figured she'd chosen the hard way. "Bugger this!" he growled and lunged.

The file hadn't lied. She *was* a handful.

Throwing the table at his face, she kicked at him then tried to dash around him for the door. He swatted the table out of his way, dodged her foot, and snagged her around the waist as she ran past. Then he tossed her over his shoulder with her legs against his chest, held in place by his arm, and headed for the front door at a run. Stopping only long enough to pull his night-vision goggles back over his eyes, he grabbed his rifle and pack with his free hand and took off into the woods.

Andi screamed bloody murder.

"Keep the noise down, luv," he ordered, running full speed through the trees. "Or I'll duct tape your bloody mouth shut."

"You wouldn't dare."

"Wanna bet? I'd rather not, it's true. But believe me, I will if you don't keep quiet. We're not out of this yet, and if you don't want to be dead, instead of just leverage, I'd bloody well advise you to shut up."

"You're one of them, aren't you?" she whimpered. "Those men you killed were talking about leverage, too.

Who are you guys and what the hell do you want with me?"

"I'm *not* one of those guys. I don't know who they are or what they want with you, but Jonas is trying to find out. All I want to do is keep you safe and away from them until he does. Now, are you going to cooperate?"

"I'll think about it," she growled defiantly, but she did stop screaming.

Levi laughed. "You do that, luv."

He liked her, he decided. The girl had spunk. Babysitting her could be fun.

He lunged through the forest, trying to put as much distance between them and the coming explosion as possible. Suddenly, the world blew apart behind them.

"Checkmate," he said with satisfaction.

Andi gasped. "You were telling the truth."

"I've been known to on occasion," he confirmed without breaking stride. When they reached the ATV, he set her down on the seat. "Now, don't run. If you do, I'll have to chase you. And while it might be fun for me, it won't be for you when I catch you. Are we clear?"

"You really are an ass."

"I'm not denying it." He tossed her a parka. "Here, put this on so you don't freeze."

She glared at him as he stripped out of his ghillie suit and stowed his gear. Then he grabbed some pre-moistened wipes, cleaned the camouflage paint off his face, and put on his own parka.

When he was ready to go, she still hadn't put hers on.

He shook his head in exasperation. "Andi, are you *trying* to be difficult? Do you want to freeze? Because if you do, believe me, I'll let you. Now, put the bloody parka on and let's get out of here before the other bad guys show up."

"There's *more* coming?" she gasped, struggling to put on the parka.

"They're right behind us," he lied. He really didn't know *when* they were coming, but if it got her to cooperate, he'd use it. When she was ready, he turned, took her chin in his hand, and pulled her face up so he could look her in the eyes. She struggled, but he held her fast and forced himself to think about the mission and not the very tempting mouth just inches away from his. "Now, this is important, luv. You need to hang on to me tight. If you don't, at the speed we're going to be traveling, you'll fly right off and crack your head open on a tree. Are we clear?"

She tried to push his arm away with both hands. "Let go of me," she ordered.

"Absolutely," he said, enjoying himself immensely. "As soon as you answer the question. Are we clear?"

"Yes," she snarled.

"Good, then let's go." He climbed on in front of her, put his night-vision goggles back on, and started up the ATV. As he did, he heard shouts, gunshots, and men running behind them. *Bloody hell, they* were *right behind us. Probably heard Andi's screams.*

"What's that?" she whimpered.

"The other bad guys. Hang on."

As he took off through the trees, Andi wrapped her arms around his waist and held on. Tight. Just like he'd told her. He had to admit, if only to himself, it felt good to have such a beautiful woman holding him like that. He told himself to keep his mind on his job, but he couldn't stop the grin that curved his lips.

At the speed they were going, Levi couldn't help a few near-misses as trees popped out of the darkness. Andi screamed several times but he didn't reprimand her, figuring she probably couldn't help it. By the time they got to the car, they'd lost whoever was behind them—at least for the moment. Levi took off his goggles, stowed his gear in the trunk, shoved Andi into the passenger seat, and told her to fasten her seatbelt. When she didn't, he let it go. She would soon enough. He started the car, slammed it into gear, and raced down the winding road toward Trout Lake.

Halfway through the first curve he looked over and saw she was struggling with the seatbelt.

He grinned at her. "Good show."

She was silent for several long minutes. Then she said, "What kind of car is this?"

"It's a Subaru—custom." When he glanced over and saw the confusion on her face, he added, "It's a Subaru and looks like three out of four cars on the road in this area, but it has a very special engine along with some frame and suspension modifications, so it's very fast. I can get it up to two-twenty-five on the flats." He flew around a hairpin curve. "And it corners like a bloody wet dream."

She snorted. "I'd ask how a wet dream corners, but I'm sure you'd have an answer for that, too." She paused to stare at him a moment. "Are you really Levi Komakov?"

"I am."

"But people say you're *nice*." When his only response was to burst into gales of laughter, she protested, "No, really. I've heard all about you—about how you don't kill people and what a gentleman you are."

"What can I say, luv?" he asked when he could finally control his laughter enough to talk. "I've never claimed to be a gentleman, though I can be when the mood strikes. And it's true that, for the most part, I don't kill people if I can avoid it. However, I make an exception for kidnappers and terrorists." He glanced over at her. "Did you want me *not* to kill those guys? Didn't you hear what their argument was about?"

"Yeah," she whispered, shuddering. "They were fighting about which one got to rape me first." She sighed. "I'm actually glad you killed them. I was just surprised."

"Well, I can't say that I wouldn't have killed them if I hadn't heard their discussion," he admitted. "But I probably wouldn't have felt so justified." His grip tightened on the steering wheel. "What they were saying made my blood boil."

"It made you angry?" She sounded genuinely curious. "Why?"

As he took another tight corner at break-neck speed, he wondered how to explain it so she'd understand. "There's a code of ethics *all* men are supposed to live by. And it basically says that you don't hurt innocent people. Which means, among other things, that you don't murder civilians, you don't rape, you don't kidnap, and you don't plant bombs in airports and shopping malls. The only reason I work for Jonas is because he adheres to that same code." He rolled his head to stretch his tense neck muscles. "I killed six men tonight, and I don't regret it for a minute. They crossed the line."

"Would you kill a mugger who tried to steal your wallet?"

"No, but I'd make him wish he'd chosen another target."

"I'll bet." She frowned at him when he chuckled. "You're certainly not what I expected Levi Komakov to be."

Before he could respond, he saw two sets of headlights flash in his rear view mirror, coming up too fast to be just early morning traffic. "Bloody *hell*," he roared.

"What is it?" she asked, glancing behind them.

"We've got company, luv. I don't know who or why, but *somebody* wants you bad." He shifted gears and shot her another grin. "Sit back, shut up, and hang on," he ordered. "And whatever you do, don't distract me."

CHAPTER 4

Andi locked her door and cowered against it as Levi stepped on the gas. The car shot forward, flying around the curves, taking some—she could've sworn—on less than four wheels. She was glad it was still dark. She wasn't sure she wanted to see all the things they could hit if Levi lost control.

Something pinged off the back of the car. Then again and again.

Oh shit! They're shooting at us! Andi clenched her teeth together to keep from screaming.

Levi sped up. She glanced over at him and was shocked to see him *grinning*. Without a doubt, he was the sexiest and most fascinating man she'd ever met, even with the tiny bits of camouflage paint still clinging to his face.

The instant they came out of the curves and hit a straight stretch of road, he floored it. When Andi looked back, she saw that the other cars had fallen far behind. But more curves were coming up. Scooting around those at an unbelievable speed, he suddenly stomped on the brakes and made a sharp right turn—on two wheels—into a long driveway, pulling up behind some trees. When the car came to a stop, he turned off the ignition and took his foot off the brake. Then he palmed the top of her head with one hand and shoved her down, slumping her over in the seat before ducking down with her.

A few seconds later the lights of a car went flashing by. Andi started to raise her head, but Levi held her down.

"Let's give it a few more seconds, luv," he whispered.

"What are we doing?" she whispered back.

"We're disappearing into thin air," he told her with a chuckle. "Used to do it all the time in the CIA." Another set of lights went by. "That should do it," he said, letting her up.

He started the car, backed out of the driveway, and headed back the way they'd come.

"We're going back?" she asked in disbelief.

"No, not back. Just away," he said. She must have looked confused because he added, "We're not going back to the reservation. We're just taking another route away from here to anyplace else, where they hopefully won't be looking for us." Once back through the curves and the straight stretch, he turned right at a fork in the road. "I won't let them get you, but you're going to have to trust me. Do you think you can do that?"

Trust him? Could she?

In addition to being sexy and fascinating, he was also gorgeous—just under six feet tall, with dark hair, a ro-guishly handsome face, dreamy blue eyes, and a hard, strong body. It was all she could do not to drool. His Brit-ish accent and rakish grin made him almost irresistible, as did the way he called her "luv." He was practically a leg-end in the Family. And he had a reputation for being kind to women. Or was it all an act? Rumors said he didn't kill people, either, although the way he'd explained killing those six creeps earlier made sense. But could she *trust* him? She didn't know but sensed he was waiting for an answer.

"I'm having some issues with trust right now," she said finally. "And listening to those guys talk about how someone in the Family gave them everything they needed to grab me doesn't help."

"Been there, done that, and got the T-shirt," he quipped.

"What's that mean?"

"It means I can relate," he said, suddenly serious. "I know you've had a hard time, Andi, and I know you're hurt, scared, and feeling betrayed. But sometimes you just have to go with your gut. What do your instincts tell you?"

She glanced over at him. His expression was gentle—and unexpectedly tender. The look in his eyes made her want to throw her arms around his neck and cling to him.

Swallowing her urges, she looked away. "They tell me that if I stay with you, I probably won't get raped," she conceded. "And I think I can trust you not to let the other guys get me. I even think I can trust that you are who you say you are. But that doesn't mean I'm just going to automatically trust everything you say. I'm still not sure that I can trust you not to use me as leverage, too."

"Give it time," he told her with a smile. "I suppose I'd be disappointed in you if you were a pushover. Now, I don't imagine you got much rest in that cabin, so why don't you close your eyes and try to sleep?"

Andi leaned her head back on the headrest and closed her eyes. But how was she supposed to sleep with this virile, male animal sitting so close to her? Feeling the comforting weight of the opal pendant around her neck, she had to stifle a gasp as she realized she hadn't thought of Donald even once since she'd met Levi.

When Andi's breathing became slow and regular and he was sure she was asleep—and the road behind him was clear of traffic—Levi pulled out his Bluetooth, put it in his ear, and speed-dialed Jonas.

"Levi," the old man exclaimed. "Is everything all right?"

"Yeah. I got there just as they were arguing about who got to be the first to rape her, but I took them all out before they got a chance."

Jonas sighed, his relief obvious. "Is she okay?"

"Basically. Exhausted, bruised, and feeling betrayed, but other than that she's all right." He hesitated, but Andi hadn't moved. "She told me the men said something about using her as leverage. Have you found out anything on your end?"

"Not yet, but I've got everyone I can trust working on it."

"Work on this, too," Levi told him. "Apparently, whoever nabbed her had deep inside information. They were also *expecting* me. So somewhere you've got a big bloody leak."

"*Dammit*!" Jonas exploded. "You hire good people and pay them well, and you still can't get loyalty."

"Don't blow a head gasket, old man. You know what I always say—don't get mad, get even."

"Humph," Jonas snorted, but he took a deep breath and calmed down. "What do you mean, they were expecting you? They were expecting *you* specifically?"

"Well, they didn't mention my name, but they were expecting someone they called the Ghost. Who else could it be?"

"So what are you going to do now?"

"The only thing I can do," Levi said. "I'll have to

protect her and keep her out of the hands of the people who want to use her until you can figure out what's going on. But whoever's behind this is well staffed. We got chased off the mountain by two vehicles full of people shooting at us. Not sure if they were trying to kill us or just blow out the tires. Though, at those speeds, we might not have survived a crash."

"Are you okay?"

Levi glanced over at Andi's stunning face and felt a grin curve his lips. "Never better."

After they disconnected, Levi continued heading into the rising sun. As he watched her sleep, he realized that some of the pain in his own heart had been eased by her spunk. Normally, he avoided personal contact with women. But, for the first time in a long time, he was enjoying himself in the company of a female. Though she was a sheltered "poor little rich girl," with as much as she'd been through, she hadn't been bitchy or whiney, or really much trouble at all. And there was no denying her attraction. He could get hard just *looking* at her.

The sun had fully risen when she stirred and drowsily asked, "Where are we going?"

"Not sure. We'll stop up the road apiece and get a bite to eat. Then we have to find somewhere to hide. My uncle left me a cabin in the mountains. That might be a good place."

"Can't you just take me to an airport so I can make my own way home?"

"You can't go home, Andi. Until we know who took you the first time, we can't prevent it from happening again."

"You can't just keep me prisoner. That's as bad as being kidnapped," she insisted angrily. "I do have rights, you know."

He chuckled. "Of course you do. You have the right

to cooperate, the right to behave yourself, and the right to let me protect you. All other rights have been suspended for the time being."

"I also have the right to tell you to go to Hell."

"Aye, that you do, luv." He shot her a grin. "And if it makes you feel better, feel free to say it as many times as you want—for all the good it will do you."

Her chin lifted defiantly. "I'm sure the Family has other bodyguards available, Levi," she growled. "It doesn't have to be you. I would be protected at home just as well."

"Not until we find the leak," he said, trying to ignore the thrill he got when she said his name. "They betrayed you once. They'll do it again."

Andi flinched, but she didn't give up. "I'm of legal age. And you are holding me against my will. That's false imprisonment, and it's against the law."

Laughing that the daughter of a crime family member was threatening him with the law, and unable to resist, he reached over and stroked her cheek. Her skin felt so soft he had to stifle a groan.

When she glared daggers at him, he dropped his hand. "So are you saying you'll report me to the authorities?"

"Yes. I'll get a restraining order if I have to." When his chuckles only increased, she snarled, "You can't force me to stay with you, Levi. I *will* get away."

"Not a chance, luv," he told her as the car raced eastward. "The bad guys would get you before you'd even gone a mile. You're stuck with me for the duration."

"Does anyone ever win an argument with you?"

"Not often," he said, trying to suppress a grin. The calculating look on her face was so adorable, it made him want to kiss her. "Don't try it, Andi. I can see what you're thinking. It won't work and you'll regret it."

But he could tell she wasn't convinced. Oh yeah, this was going to be fun!

7:53 p.m., a motel in Payette, Idaho:

Andi was determined to get away, if for no other reason than that Levi was so damned sure she couldn't. She was tired of being treated like a child, tired of being used. It was *her* life, after all. But he just chuckled when she glared at him. Nothing she did seemed to bother him at all. He was a strange man—so different from the way she'd imagined after all the things she'd heard about him. She'd expected more of a strong, silent, menacing type— not this amusing, irresistible Englishman. When he'd stroked her cheek in the car this morning, he'd turned her on so much it was all she could do not to jump across the console and onto his lap. Everyone always talked about him with so much respect. Of course, they also said he was nice and he didn't kill. But she knew better. Not that she was complaining. Like he said, those pigs deserved to die.

Levi stopped for the night at a rundown motel, easily convincing the desk clerk that they were lovers on a road trip. After they left the office and she'd protested about sharing a room, he told her not to worry, that he was there to protect her, not to take advantage of her.

Arrogant prick!

The moment he'd opened the door to their room, she'd told him she wanted a shower and had gone into the bathroom alone. He'd agreed, reluctantly, but advised her "not to lock the bloody door."

She defied him and locked it anyway. Then she saw her chance to escape. Their room was on the second floor and, thankfully, the bathroom window not only opened but was large enough for her to fit through. She turned on the shower—as much to fool him as to muffle the sound of her escape—opened the window, and crawled out with her purse hooked on her shoulder. It would be a long drop, but there was grass below.

She'd never gotten her shoes back from the kidnappers, but if she could get away, she'd just buy a pair. Twisting to face the building with her hands on the window frame, she lowered herself until she was hanging by her fingertips and prepared to drop.

Levi knew she was up to something. She'd been pretty quiet since their argument in the car earlier and when she'd gone into the bathroom, she'd looked downright calculating. He found himself grinning, wondering what she'd try.

Then his trained ears heard shuffling noises beneath the sound of running water, and he realized she was crawling out the bathroom window. *Damn, she certainly is a clever little shit.*

He tried the bathroom door, not at all surprised to find it locked. Chuckling at her antics, he shot out the door of the room and around to the back of the motel. By the time he got there, she was hanging from the window frame. He waited in the shadows. When she dropped, he stepped forward and caught her in his arms.

"Going somewhere, luv?"

She squirmed and growled at him, but he just held her tighter.

"You know, I did bring duct tape and handcuffs," he said, "but I'd really rather not use them."

"Put me down," she ordered.

"Certainly," he agreed. "As soon as we get you back to the shower."

"The shower?" she whimpered in horror as he carried her back into the motel room. "What are you talking about?"

"Since I can't trust you to behave yourself," he told her, thoroughly enjoying himself, "I'll have to stand guard in the bathroom while you take your shower."

"Not on your life!" she screeched.

"Trust me, luv," he purred. He kicked the bathroom door open, breaking the lock, and set her on her feet in front of the shower stall. Steam had already begun to curl above the floral shower curtain. "Here's how it's going to work, Andi. I'm going to close the window and lean against the wall, and you're going to take off your clothes and get into the shower."

"I'm *not* taking my clothes off with you in here."

Her stubborn tone told him she wasn't about to comply without a fight. He didn't care. He was having too much fun. "You shouldn't have run, luv," he said. "I did warn you not to try it. So turn your back to me, take off your clothes, and get into the shower." When she continued to glare at him, he asked, "Would you like me to do it for you?"

"You're supposed to be *nice*." Her voice broke and tears filled her eyes.

He almost relented when he saw her tears, but he had to get her cooperation somehow. "I can be," he said. "And you needn't worry that I'm going to watch you undress or shower. But I'm not letting you out of my sight, either." Making twirling motions with his index finger, he said, "So what's it going to be?"

"Fine," she fumed.

Throwing her purse on the floor, she turned her back to him and started removing her coat, jeans, and T-shirt.

Levi turned his head away, not watching, just as he'd promised, though it was harder to do than he wanted to admit. She really was delightful and very easy on the eyes. He breathed a sigh of relief when she stepped into the shower and pulled the curtain closed, removing the temptation for him to break his promise. When she finished and shut off the water, he handed her a towel then her clothes behind the shower curtain so she could dry and dress herself out of sight. She came out dressed, but glaring, the towel wrapped around her head.

He sighed. "Andi, if I let you go, you'll be back in the bad guys' hands by tomorrow night. Is that really what you want?"

"You don't know that," she insisted, as she removed the towel, pulled a comb from her purse, and started running it through her damp hair.

"Don't I? They want you for leverage, probably to force your father to do something he doesn't want to do. They went to a lot of trouble to nab you in the first place. Do you really think they're just going to give up? That a few extra bodyguards stationed around your house will deter them? Have you even asked yourself who knew where you'd be so they could give that information to your kidnappers?" He crossed his arms over his chest. "Somebody close to you set you up, trust me." He saw a look of intense pain flash across her face. "What is it?"

When she just shook her head and turned away, he couldn't stand it any longer. *She's hurting, dammit.* He went over to her and put an arm around her shoulders. Expecting her to pull away, he was surprised when she suddenly turned toward him and threw her arms around his waist, bursting into tears. He hesitated, not sure what to do. Then deciding, *The hell with it*, he wrapped her in a hug and pulled her against his chest. "Tell me what's wrong, luv," he murmured, pressing his cheek to her hair and just enjoying the feeling of holding her. "I can't help you if you don't talk to me."

"It's because I'm Darren Merritt's daughter, isn't it?" she sobbed. "Every guy I date, every person I meet, even the people who kidnapped me—it's not about me, it's about *him*! I'm not the least bit important, except as a tool to get to him." She stared up at him, tears sparkling in her lovely golden-brown eyes. "You wouldn't even be here if I wasn't Darren Merritt's daughter."

Looking down at the anguish in her eyes, Levi thought his heart would break. He cupped her face in his hands and wiped her tears away with his thumbs. "You're right and you're wrong, luv," he said. "I agree that you were abducted because of who your father is. I also agree that a lot of the guys you meet are probably going to court you because of your father and what he can do for them." He kissed her forehead then, releasing her face, put his arms back around her, and pulled her close again. "But I don't agree that you're not important or that you're only a tool. Your father is a handicap in your relationships because you'll always wonder if someone really wants you or just wants to use you. I understand that. But give yourself some credit. You're beautiful, intelligent, and fun, and that has nothing to do with who your father is." Tightening his embrace, he smiled against her hair. "You're special in your own right. And yes, I *would* be here, regardless." He grimaced then added honestly, "Personally, I don't even *like* your father."

He'd managed to coax a laugh out of her and she smiled up at him. "Thanks," she said. Releasing him, she dried her tears on a towel and headed for the other room. "I didn't mean to fall apart on you."

"Anytime," he replied as he followed her out of the bathroom. "Does this mean you'll cooperate from now on?"

"Perhaps," she said with a wicked little giggle.

Laughing, he checked that the deadbolt was locked and shoved a chair under the doorknob—just in case—thinking how adorable she was and how sad it was that people could look at her and see only a pawn to be used against her father. Next, he went to the window and checked to be sure there wasn't any suspicious activity in the parking lot. Satisfied that everything was secure, he turned back and saw Andi staring at the bed, a look of horror on her face. "What is it, luv?"

"There's only one bed," she said, obviously aghast. "We aren't sharing it, are we?"

Not sure whether to be amused or insulted that she was so horrified at the thought of sharing a bed with him, he settled for amused. "You're a little slow tonight, aren't you?" he teased, tickled by the hesitant way she was standing there, her eyes wide and staring. "Crawl in between the sheets. I'll sleep on top of the blankets." When she still hesitated, he sighed. "Andi, luv, if you know anything about me at all, you should know you're safe. I promise, I'm not going to molest you. Get into bed, but leave your clothes on."

Her look of horror only intensified. "Why?"

"If our friends show up in the middle of the night, we may not have time to get dressed."

"But how could they possibly know where we are?"

"I'm not saying they do, luv. I just want to be prepared. Attention to detail can often make the difference between success and failure."

She sighed, nodded, and crawled into bed. When she was settled, he took off his shoes and stretched out beside her on top of the thin bedspread. Tomorrow, he told himself, he'd have to get her some sneakers.

She shocked him by snuggling up close to him, laying her head on his shoulder, and throwing one slender arm across his chest. Her scent entranced him, the flash of desire so sharp it threatened to make him forget he was only there to protect her. When her soft sigh tickled the side of his neck, he had to grit his teeth to keep from moaning.

Bloody hell, he was in for a very *long* night.

Andi cuddled against Levi, breathing in his scent. Boy, he smelled good. He'd said she was special and that he didn't want anything from her father. She was probably foolish to let that thrill her so much, but she couldn't help it. It had felt so good when he'd held her, even though she knew it was just to comfort her. She couldn't remember the last time someone had held her like that, asking nothing in return. Did he really want to protect her, regardless of who her father was?

Maybe she should have told him her suspicions, but she was so embarrassed. If her own father had tried to get rid of her, would Levi still think she was special?

She wondered if he could ever be interested in her or if he was already seeing someone. As gorgeous as he was, he probably didn't suffer for feminine companionship. His wife had died two years ago, she knew. She also knew he didn't talk about it. People said his wife was beautiful and he'd really loved her. It must have been terrible to finally find someone to love only to lose them so soon.

The fact that she hadn't given a thought to Donald since Levi walked into her life told her that was another relationship going nowhere. Would she ever find someone she could love who would love her just for herself? She'd be twenty-six in just a few months and it felt like her life was heading down a dead-end road.

Lying here next to Levi, she wished she could just stay like this forever and never have to be Anderson Merritt again. She sighed. What had those men really wanted with her? If they'd expected her father to pay a ransom or to do something he didn't want to do in order to get her back, they'd have gotten a very rude surprise. Even if her father hadn't been in on her kidnapping, the only emotion he'd have felt at her disappearance was apathy.

Why couldn't he love her like fathers were supposed to love their daughters? What was so wrong with *her* that her only value lay in her looks or her use as a pawn in the deadly games he was so fond of playing?

She was so damn tired—sick of being used then cast aside like so much trash when the user got what he wanted. The ache in her chest made her shudder.

"Stop thinking, luv," Levi whispered, kissing her hair. "Just go to sleep. I'm right here."

Yes, but for how long? And what will happen to me when you discover I'm not worth it and move on?

CHAPTER 5

Tuesday, April 2nd, 6:18 a.m.:

Levi woke to whispered voices outside the motel room door and the sound of someone fiddling with the lock. Instantly alert, he shook Andi awake, putting a finger to her lips before she could make a sound. Slipping from the bed, he put his coat and shoes on and went into the bathroom to look out the window. There was no one there.

Andi put her coat on and followed him into the bathroom, her purse on her shoulder, her eyes wide. "What do we do?" she whispered.

"Do you remember your little trick last night?" When she nodded, he said, "I'm going out the window first. When I'm down, you jump and I'll catch you like I did last night. Okay?"

She nodded again. He eased the window open, crawled through, and jumped, landing crouched on the balls of his feet. It was a fair distance, but nothing he hadn't done in the SAS. He looked up to see Andi crawling out the window. She didn't hesitate; she just dropped.

Levi stepped up, catching her as she fell. "Perfect, luv," he whispered. He couldn't resist giving her a quick squeeze before putting her down. Hooking a finger under her chin, he lifted her face until their eyes met. "Now, I *can* trust you not to run, can't I, Andi? I need to know."

She swallowed and nodded. "I won't run. I trust you."

"Thanks, luv," he whispered, planting a kiss on her forehead. "That was a good idea you had last night. Make a note: always try to escape. We may have to know how to do it later." When she chuckled softly, he gave her another kiss on the forehead. "Now, as quietly as possible, follow me."

Levi's attention to detail had ensured that the car was already loaded with everything but them and not parked in the motel parking lot, but on a side street a couple of blocks away. He took her hand and led her across the back lawn of the motel and down the street.

As they passed a dark blue van parked by the curb, the side door opened and four men piled out. Three surrounded Levi while one grabbed Andi. She screamed as Levi went ballistic.

Andi started to struggle against the man holding her when she was suddenly freed. She looked around her in shock. Levi had moved like a blur, so fast she could hardly tell what he was doing. Using hands, feet, elbows, and head, he'd annihilated their attackers, all of whom had been armed. She saw the guns lying on the sidewalk *in pieces*. He'd not only taken the guns away from the bad guys, he'd taken the guns *apart*. All before she could blink.

Just as the fourth guy crumpled, the driver came around the end of the van.

"Look out!" she yelled.

But Levi was way ahead of her. Using the follow-through from the hit on the guy he'd just felled, he swung around and planted his foot in the driver's face. The man went down without making a sound.

Levi took her elbow and hurried her away. "We need to move it, luv," he insisted as he unlocked their car and hustled her into the passenger seat.

"But they're all out of commission, aren't they?"

"The ones at the van are, at least for a while, but there's still whoever was at the motel." He started the car and headed for the freeway, weaving through the streets like a formula one driver. "And since they know we're here, there could be more coming."

"But *how*, Levi? How did they know where we were? Have I got a homing beacon on my ass?"

He laughed. "I don't know, but I'd be happy to check, if you like." He shot her a rakish grin, making her heart throb and her knees quiver. Then he fell silent. Suddenly, he slammed his palm down on the steering wheel. "Bloody hell! *Technology*. Damn you, Wilson."

"What's wrong?" she cried in alarm. "Who's Wilson?"

He glanced over at her but remained silent for several minutes with a frown on his face, almost as if he was deciding whether or not to tell her. She held her tongue and waited.

Finally, he sighed. "Wilson is an FBI agent," he said. "And he's the reason I came after you in the first place." When he reached the freeway, he headed east. "I don't know how Wilson found out that you'd been kidnapped, but when his bosses decided that they couldn't send a rescue team for you because of the politics between the tribe and the feds, he contacted Jonas. When I met with them, Wilson told me where you were being held—the exact cabin and room. I asked him how they knew so precisely, and his answer was simply 'technology.' It didn't dawn on me at the time that the technology he was referring to was actually *on* you."

"I don't understand."

"You're bugged, luv. You've got a tracking device somewhere on your body, probably sewn into your clothes."

His words made Andi feel tainted and unclean. She shivered. "What do we do?" she whispered in terror.

"Don't panic, luv," he said, reaching over and giving her shoulder a squeeze. "I've been here before, and it's nothing I can't handle. Okay?" When she nodded, he said, "Good girl. Now, I haven't been out this way for a while, but if I remember correctly, there are quite a few small towns along this stretch of the freeway. One of them has to be big enough to have a clothing store. We'll stop and buy you new clothes from the skin out. I have to get you some shoes anyway."

"But can we wait that long? What if they catch us on the freeway?"

He grinned but she couldn't tell what he was thinking, and his next words didn't seem to fit. "The fact that we were there for several hours before they caught up with us leads me to believe the tracking device isn't one that can be tracked while in motion. It has to be stationary for the satellite to get a fix. Either that, or the bad guys don't have immediate access to the tracking information. They have to wait for it." He shrugged. "Either one works—pay your dime and take your pick. And the fact that no one followed us yesterday morning after we lost the first group out by Trout Lake tells me I'm right. So we can't stay long in any one place until we get rid of the bug, but I think we can buy you some clothes if we don't take all day."

"Okay, I can do it in a hurry." She glanced over at him. "But why were you grinning? Did I say something funny?"

He gave her another heart-stopping grin. "I was just trying to decide if I should tell you my theory or suggest you toss your clothes out of the car now and go nude."

When she laughed at that, she caught a flicker of surprise in his eyes. "Oh. Well, I guess I can stop freaking out then," she mused. "If you're thinking about things like that, we can't be in any immediate danger."

"That's one way to look at it," he said with a chuckle. "Keep your eyes open for a town where we can find a clothing store."

As she watched the scenery, she felt excitement bubbling up inside her. If this gorgeous hunk was trying to think of ways to get her naked, maybe she should consider helping him.

Levi was impressed. She hadn't gotten angry or offended when he told her what he'd been thinking. She'd *laughed* about it. The more time he spent with her, the more he liked her. But when she squealed and pointed out the window at a Walmart sign, he was shocked.

"You seriously want to go to a Walmart?" he asked. "They don't have much in the way of designer clothing there."

She rolled her eyes. "Right now, I think I need to get rid of the bug a little more than I need designer clothing, don't you? Brand names won't help me much if I get kidnapped again."

"Point taken," he said, pulling onto the exit. "I agree, but I was trying to be nice."

She shot him a wicked grin. "I almost think you do a

better job of being nice when you're actually trying to be an ass."

"Oh, you do, do you?" He fought a smile and lost. "Andi, luv, have you ever even *been* to a Walmart?"

"No, but I've seen their commercials and I know they have clothes." She lifted her chin defiantly as his smile widened. "How bad can it be?" When he burst out laughing, she growled at him. "You don't have to come with me, if you don't want to. I can go in by myself, you know."

"Not a chance, luv," he said, still grinning. He pulled into the lot and parked the car then ran around to help her out. "I wouldn't miss this for the world."

He watched her out of the corner of his eye as they walked into the store and wasn't the least bit surprised when she stopped dead and stared, her mouth hanging open. His chuckles caught her attention and she edged a little closer to him. He put his arm around her shoulders.

"I have no idea what I'm supposed to do," she whispered.

He gave her shoulders a squeeze. "I'm not surprised. There aren't any personal shoppers here." When she didn't respond, he asked, "Do you want to go somewhere else?"

"No, this will do if you'll help me."

Pleased at her reply, he kissed her temple. "Certainly." He pointed up. "See the signs hanging from the ceiling? Those tell you where things are. Women's clothing is over this way."

Snagging a cart, he led her to the women's department. On the way, he noticed her eyes were sparkling and realized she was having fun. She'd led a very sheltered life to this point, but he had a feeling she wouldn't allow herself to be sheltered any longer, now that she'd seen some of the outside world. And that was probably a good thing. And if he had anything to say about it, she wouldn't be such an easy target next time, either.

In the women's department, Levi led her over to the jeans stacked in bins on the wall. Her eyes lit up at how they were arranged.

"It's quaint," she said and made him laugh.

You'd think she was in a foreign country.

She quickly found her size, but looked at him with questions in her eyes when he grabbed five more pairs.

"I don't know how long it's going to take to get things settled," he told her. "So let's be prepared. If you don't wear them, you can always take them back."

"No way. These are my trophy jeans. I'm keeping them. I've earned them."

"That you have, luv," he agreed. "Now what size shirt?" He pointed at the racks of T-shirts. "Get ten. And don't forget, you still need shoes."

When she'd selected ten different T-shirts and found two pairs of tennis shoes in her size, she asked, "What about under things? You said from the skin out."

Pointing out the racks of bras and panties, he said, "Get three bras and ten pairs of panties." He hesitated. "Do you know your size?"

With a mischievous little giggle, she grinned up at him. "Why? Are you offering to help *measure*?"

Levi cleared his throat, fighting the urge to grab her and kiss her. "No, luv, but I *was* offering to see if I could find you a female clerk."

"Oh. No, I know my size."

She actually looked disappointed, and Levi had to remind himself *again* to keep his mind on the mission.

After selecting her new undergarments and ten pairs of socks, she turned to him. "Now what?"

He led her over to the purses. "I don't know where the bug is," he said. "So we're changing everything. They don't have anything to equal what you have now so just pick one you like."

She surprised him again by saying, "A purse is a purse." In about thirty seconds she'd selected one roughly the same size and style as the one she had. "Done. Now what?"

"Come with me." He grabbed a black backpack for her on their way to the checkout, paid for everything, then led her over to the women's restroom. Pulling a pair of jeans, a T-shirt, a bra, a pair of panties, and a pair of socks out of the bags, he cut the tags off everything and handed the clothes to her, along with a pair of sneakers. "Run into the loo, take off your old clothes, and put the new ones on. Leave your old clothes in the loo."

She nodded and took off. When she came back out, he decided she didn't need designer clothing. She looked good enough in the Walmart clothes to do their commercials. Trying to control his arousal, even though it felt as if something inside him was breaking free, he took her out to the car and put everything but the new purse in the trunk. "Let's go through your purse and, as we transfer stuff, we can make sure nothing's carrying a bug."

She complied without question, pulling everything out and handing it to him item by item. He examined each one, and when he declared it clean, she put it in the new purse. When she handed him a packet of pills, however, he gave her a surprised grin.

"Two months' worth of birth control pills? You were expecting to get *laid* on this junket?" As soon as the words were out of his mouth, he thought about the men arguing in the cabin and could have kicked himself.

She shuddered but forced a laugh. "Attention to detail. A girl has to be prepared." Then she shook her head. "The doctor prescribed them to regulate my periods. My maid picked those up at the pharmacy for me and handed them to me just as I was going out the door—right before those men grabbed me. I stuck them in my purse because I didn't want to go back to my room. I was in a hurry to see—"

She blushed and he wondered what she'd been going to say, although he wasn't sure he really wanted to know.

"Let me guess," he said instead. "You've never been to a pharmacy, either."

She gave him a sexy smile. "No. Have I missed much? You want to take me?"

Oh yeah, he wanted to take her, all right, but not to a pharmacy! Telling himself to focus, he said, "Maybe some other time. Right now, let's finish this."

After they emptied the old purse, he tossed it in a corner of the parking lot. It had probably cost her over five hundred dollars, but she didn't even blink. Levi had to hand it to her, she sure was a trooper.

"Now, do you have anything else that you brought with you from home? Anything at all?"

"Other than what was in my purse?" She thought for a moment. "No, I don't think—" She gasped. "Yes, my necklace."

"Let me see it."

She took it out from under her T-shirt, unfastened it, and handed it to him. He turned the opal over and immediately noticed something suspicious—something that looked like a defect in the gold backing, but wasn't.

"Where did you get this?"

"A guy I went out with a few times gave it to me. Why?"

"What's his name, luv, and how well do you know him?" he asked, trying to keep the rage out of his voice.

"His name's Donald Carson and I've only known him for about three weeks, so I don't know him well." She looked up and met his gaze. "He's the one, isn't he?"

Levi could see the pain in her eyes. "He's something, all right," he growled. "I don't think he had anything to do with the kidnapping, but I'm not sure. This technology isn't available on the civilian market, but the FBI has it." He noticed tears form in her eyes and pulled her into a hug. "Is this necklace important to you?" She shook her head against his chest, so he tossed the opal into the bed of a nearby pickup. "I'm sorry I put you through that, luv. I should have checked the necklace first." When she chuckled, he looked down to see her smiling up at him. "Do you want to go back in and get your old clothes out of the loo?" he asked.

"Are you kidding? I like my new clothes. This is the only fun I've had since this nightmare began...well, Mr. Toad's wild ride down the mountain was fun, too, but not as much as this."

"That's my girl," he said, opening the car door for her. Driving back to the freeway, he called Jonas. "I need Wilson's number," he said when Jonas answered.

Jonas gave it to him then asked, "What's going on?"

"I'm not sure. Let me find out and I'll get back to you."

Jonas grumbled, but agreed. Levi hung up and immediately called Wilson. When the agent came on the line, Levi demanded, "I guess there were a few more things you didn't want to tell me, weren't there?"

"Such as?"

"Is Donald Carson one of yours?"

"What makes you think that?"

"You just answered my question. To answer yours, he gave Andi an opal necklace with a GPS locater system embedded in it. A system that only certain federal agencies have access to."

"Mr. Komakov—"

"Can it, Wilson. I need some straight answers and

you need some information. That's how this works. I think in law it's called quid pro quo, isn't it?"

Wilson sighed. "Very well. I guess I don't really have a choice. You got the girl out, I presume."

"Yes."

"Good. What do you want to know?"

"Did Carson have anything to do with the kidnapping?"

"No. He's in love with her, actually. He infiltrated Merritt's organization and heard a rumor that the girl is being sold to some Middle Eastern billionaire. A kidnapping was assumed, as that is usually the way these things are done." When Levi gave a shocked grunt, Wilson said, "Yes, the girl's kidnapped so the family looks blameless when she's sold and disappears forever. I'm surprised you didn't know that. Anyway, Carson gave her the necklace, hoping to offer some protection. As it turned out, it's a good thing he did. He was also the one to let us know she'd been kidnapped. Her father never did call us."

As Wilson talked, Levi tensed until he was squeezing the steering wheel so hard, he was afraid it might break. He forced himself to take a deep breath and relax his grip. "What do you mean 'being sold'?" His voice was rough with shock and rage, and he was sure Wilson could hear it.

"I mean the guy's paying twenty-five million dollars to add the girl to his harem," Wilson told him. "Why does this surprise you? I've seen her pictures and you've seen the girl. These Middle-Eastern oil barons have nothing but too much time and money on their hands. The FBI couldn't reveal how we knew where she was without blowing Carson's cover, which is why I asked you to step in."

"Why is she being sold to an oil baron?" Levi heard

Andi gasp in the seat beside him but had to ignore it for now. "And are they the only ones after her?"

"What do you mean, the *only* ones?"

"Some gunmen shot at our car as we were leaving the reservation. I thought they were trying to blow out our tires, but looking back on it, it seems like they were trying to kill us, rather than just reclaim Andi."

Wilson huffed out a breath but didn't answer.

"Dammit, Wilson! Talk to me," Levi snarled. "I'm in a hurry."

Wilson sighed. "As far as we've been able to determine Darren Merritt owes millions in gambling debts and saw his beautiful daughter as a marketable piece of property. The loan shark he owes the money to doesn't want the loan repaid. They want a piece of his action. If he sells the girl, he can pay off the debts. So you have one side trying to sell her and the other side trying to keep her from being sold. Either way, it doesn't work out well for her."

"So you basically have a tug-of-war with Andi in the middle," Levi snapped. He glanced over to see tears streaming down her cheeks.

"Yes," Wilson admitted. "Anything else you want to know?"

"What does the FBI think happened at the cabin?"

"They don't know. They suspect that someone in the Demopulus Family hired some mercenaries to go and get her, but the plan failed. As far as the FBI's concerned, the girl, the mercenaries, and the kidnappers are spread all over the Cascade Mountains. They don't want to look too closely, so they're letting the tribal authorities handle the cleanup and investigation." He cleared his throat. "You made quite a mess, by the way."

"I usually do. Is Jonas in trouble with your guys?"

"No. One of his attorneys convinced my superiors he

had nothing to do with it, so he's covered and so are you. Now, what do you have for me?"

"One more question and then I'll tell you. Is anyone from the FBI looking for us?"

"Not that I'm aware of. I told you they think you're all dead. Why do you ask?"

"I really wish you'd told me about the necklace on Thursday, because if no one in your organization is looking for us, you have a *big* problem." Levi took a deep breath, trying to control his temper. "Someone, probably the loan shark, had guys arriving at the cabin just as Andi and I left. We were also tracked via that necklace to a motel in Idaho this morning. It wasn't official FBI personnel because they didn't knock on the door or identify themselves. So if it wasn't another *unofficial* FBI operation…"

"It wasn't," Wilson confirmed.

"Well then, you have a leak in whatever department is tracking that necklace because both the oil baron and the loan shark are getting that information. And that shit's not supposed to happen!"

"You're right. It's not. Thanks for the heads up."

"One other thing. Pull Carson out. Do it now."

"Now, look," Wilson protested. "We're not after Demopulus, we're after Merritt. He's into extortion and forced protection, plus a lot of other things I *know* you and Jonas don't believe in. It took us forever to infiltrate his organization. I need Carson where he is." He hesitated. "You think Demopulus will hurt him?"

"Use your head, Wilson. Carson's blown. I figured it out. How long do you think it will take Merritt's people to do the same? And news travels fast in the Family. Jonas won't do anything to him, other than show him the door. He doesn't hurt cops. But he can't control everyone in his organization. Besides, Carson isn't technically *in*

Jonas's organization. He's in Merritt's. And it sounds like Merritt doesn't really care what Jonas thinks. I'm sure killing a fed won't bother him in the least. So if you want Carson to live, pull him out."

"If you knew how long—" Wilson began, then he sighed again. "Yes, you're right. It's not worth his life."

"And don't worry about Merritt," Levi said in a voice as cold as liquid nitrogen. "He won't be a problem much longer."

He heard Wilson sputtering as he disconnected.

CHAPTER 6

Andi listened to Levi's side of the conversation in growing horror. Here was more proof, if she needed it, that she only existed as a tool. She was being *sold*! She felt used, cheap, and degraded, as if she were damaged goods. *This must be what hookers feel like. It really sucks.*

She couldn't stop the tears that ran down her cheeks, even though she knew Levi could see them. What would he think of her now that he knew how unimportant she *really* was? He pulled the Bluetooth device off his ear, tossed it in the console, and drove in silence, confirming her fears.

At the next exit, he veered off and drove into a small town. He stopped in the empty parking lot of an old church and got out. Then he came around to her side, pulled her out of the car, and wrapped her in a hug.

"Bloody hell, I'm so sorry, Andi," he whispered. "I would've shielded you from hearing that if I could have."

"I hate being lied to," she sobbed. "I'd rather know the truth, even if it hurts."

He kissed her hair. "At least now we know what you're facing."

"That I'm just a piece of meat to be sold to the highest bidder?" Her sobs increased and he tightened his embrace. "It's my father, isn't it?" She swallowed, trying to stop the tears. "Those kidnappers mentioned him. I should have told you before, but I didn't want to believe it." She clung to him. "Why, Levi? Why couldn't I have a father who loved me?"

"Sometimes life just isn't fair, luv," he said. "If you weren't so bloody beautiful, you wouldn't have these problems. But you are, and there's not much you can do about it."

"Sorry," she muttered sarcastically, though the effect was probably lessened by her tears. "I don't consider being sold a compliment. How much is a twenty-five-year-old woman worth these days? I mean, what's the going rate?"

He hesitated. When she glanced up and met his eyes, he asked, "Do you really want to know?" She nodded and he sighed. "Twenty-five million dollars."

At that, her tears ceased and she started to laugh, though she realized it was partly hysterics. She couldn't help it—it just sounded so ridiculous. Pulling away from him, she wiped the tears off her cheeks with her fingers and fought for control. She looked back to see him watching her with questions in his eyes.

"What?" she scoffed. "You don't think that's the most ridiculous thing you've ever heard? Why would I be worth twenty-five *million* dollars? Looks don't last forever, you know. And even if they did, they're only skin deep." She took a deep breath. "Sorry, I just thought the price was a tad high."

"I don't know, luv," he said with a wink. "I think it's a bit low."

The look on his face as he stared at her took her breath away. She walked back to him, put her arms around his waist, and hugged him. "Thanks, Levi. That's probably the nicest thing anyone's ever said to me." It felt so good to hold him, she snuggled closer. "Why is he doing this?"

"Your father's trying to pay off his gambling debts."

"What else is new?" She sighed again. "What am I going to do?"

"Well, first of all, I'm going to let Jonas know what's going on. Then, if you're willing, I'm going to get you some technology that will let me find you wherever you are."

"Of course, I'm willing."

"After that, I'm going to take you to my cabin in the Bitterroot Mountains and see if I can teach you some self-defense tactics. Then I'll see about getting you a new identity, if you want."

"Really?"

"Really. I hope there was nothing you wanted from home, because you can never go back there." He cupped her face in his hands and raised it until her eyes met his. "You know that, don't you?"

"I know. And no, there's nothing I want there. There hasn't been anything I wanted there since my mother died. She was the only one who never lied to me. I've spent so much of my life trying to make my father love me. And for what? So he could sell me as chattel?"

"I'll be having a talk with your father eventually," Levi promised, his eyes so cold they made her shiver. "But right now, you're my first priority."

Thrilled that he'd just called her his first priority, she almost missed his next questions.

"What about Donald? Is he important to you?"

She looked him straight in the eyes. "I didn't hear the other side of the conversation, but I gathered that Donald's FBI and he had nothing to do with the kidnapping."

"Yes. And from what Wilson told me, Donald fancies himself in love with you. He heard rumors about the kidnapping and gave you the necklace for protection. He couldn't do more because he had to be careful not to blow his cover."

She gave a short bark of laughter, but it held little humor. "In *love* with me? If he loved me, he would have warned me I was going to be kidnapped." She shook her head. "But of course, he couldn't because that would've jeopardized his *cover*. So he cares more for his job than for me." She sighed. "I'm grateful for what he did, but no, he's not important to me."

"You're sure?"

She forced a grin, despite the pain from Donald's betrayal. "I suppose I'm flattered that he thinks he's in love with me, but he still used me to get to my father, just like everyone else. I know I've led a sheltered life, but I have enough common sense to know that's not love, or if it is, it isn't the kind I want." She laid her head back on his shoulder. "I'm through being used. I want to fight back."

When Levi hugged her so tightly she could scarcely breath, she figured she'd said the right thing.

After he got back on the freeway and Andi had drifted off to sleep, Levi updated Jonas on everything Wilson had told him, including the fact that Wilson was after Merritt and not him. However, Levi refused to give him Donald Carson's name.

"Wilson's pulling him out," he said when Jonas argued. "But if anything happens to him before he does, I don't want you to get in trouble. You're safer not knowing."

"Humph. Fine. I'll let it go, but only because I trust you. So what are you going to do?"

"Right now, I'm heading to Boise. Andi and I are flying to Miami to see Pierre. And then I'm taking her someplace safe until you can get the threats removed. Probably my uncle's cabin." He hesitated. "Are you okay with footing Pierre's bill? If not, I'll do it."

"I have no problem with whatever you spend to protect the girl, Levi. Even if I was planning to pay for it myself, which I'm not, I wouldn't have a problem with it."

"If you're not paying, who is?"

"I'm drumming her father out of the Family. Regardless of the danger he's put the Outfit in by his compulsive gambling and by committing crimes that have gotten the FBI interested in him, what he's done to the girl is more than enough for me to evict him. When I settle up with him tomorrow, I intend to take enough money from him to pay for your salary and expenses, as well as enough for the girl so she'll never have to work a day in her life if she doesn't want to. If she'll take it. She may not, you know."

"I thought he didn't have any money. Isn't that why he's trying to sell Andi?"

"He doesn't have a lot of liquid assets, but he has a lot of property, which I plan to take and convert to cash. It's not so much the money as I think he needs to be taught a lesson."

"Bless you, old man. You're brilliant," Levi said with real gratitude. He looked over at Andi still dozing in the passenger seat, totally drained. "But she can never go home again, even if you take care of her father. I have a feeling that Middle-Eastern element is going to be a constant threat. And I'm not sure what to do about it."

"You can't protect her forever, Levi, even if you want to."

Jonas was right, but that didn't make it easy. Levi

didn't just *want* to protect her, he *needed* to. She'd grown into his soul. Holding her had felt so right. There had to be a way to make her safe. "She doesn't deserve to be sold to some foreigner as a sex slave, Jonas," he insisted. "She's a sweet kid, as beautiful on the inside as she is on the outside. What am I supposed to do? Abandon her?"

"I'm not suggesting you abandon her, Levi. But eventually, when I get things straightened out here, you're going to have to make a choice. Either let her go her own way or marry her."

"*What* did you say?"

"You heard me. I've known you a long time, son," Jonas reminded him with a chuckle. "And I probably know you better than anyone, with the possible exception of Tess. I've seen you fall in love only twice before. And I hear the same tone in your voice when you talk about Andi that I heard in it with Tess and Leanne. Lie to *me* if you want, but don't lie to yourself."

Wednesday, April 3rd, 10:11 a.m., the shop of Pierre Bedeau, Miami, Florida:

As they walked into the little shop in Miami, where black ops people the world over bought the *really cool* stuff their parent agencies couldn't—or wouldn't—provide for them, Levi gave Andi's shoulders a squeeze. She glanced up at him. He smiled down into her lovely eyes, still wondering if Jonas had been right—and what the bloody hell to do about it.

"What are we doing here?" she asked.

"Did you see the movie, *Mission Impossible Two*?"

"Yes. Father rented it for our private theater."

"Do you remember the tracking device Ethan injected into Nyah? The one that only he could track?"

She gasped. "They really have stuff like that and it's available to the general public?"

"Yes, they have stuff like that. And no, it's not available to the general public." He winked. "But it *is* available to certain people *if* they know where to go."

"Levi?" called a voice from the other room. "Is that you I hear out there?"

"I can neither confirm nor deny," Levi called back, guiding Andi through the door into the next room.

Pierre, a small, elfin Frenchman sat on a high stool, fiddling with a gadget on his workbench. His eyes lit up like Christmas tree lights when he saw Andi.

Levi made the introductions. "Andi, Pierre. Pierre, Andi."

Pierre hopped down from his stool and came to meet them. He took Andi's hand and pressed it to his lips in such a sensual manner, she blushed. "You're exquisite, my dear. Absolutely exquisite." To Levi, he said, "You've outdone yourself this time, my friend."

Levi tugged Andi's hand out of Pierre's as he seemed reluctant to let her go. "All right, you old pervert," he scolded. "Give the lady back her hand."

Laughing, Pierre invited them to sit. "What brings you to Miami?" he asked Levi. "Does Jonas have you doing black ops now?"

"In a manner of speaking. Andi's been kidnapped once, and I have good reason to believe they may try it again. I found her the first time because she was wearing a tracking device. It was in a necklace. But I want something more permanent, so if they get lucky and take her again, I can get her back."

"Of course, of course. You wouldn't want to lose someone so lovely. And what about you, my dear? Are you willing to let this man know where you are at every moment for the rest of your life?"

Andi looked up and stared into Levi's eyes for so long he wondered if she was having second thoughts. Finally, she turned back to Pierre. "Yes, I trust him. I'm willing to cooperate."

Levi gave her shoulders another squeeze and kissed the top of her head. "You mean I'm *finally* going to get some cooperation?"

She laughed. "I said I was *willing* to cooperate. I didn't say I *would*."

Pierre chuckled as Levi groaned, "I should have known."

Going over to a set of shelves against the far wall, Pierre took down a blue box the size and shape of a small paperback novel. He set it on his bench then beckoned to them. When they walked over to join him, he held up a tiny transmitter. "This will be inserted under your skin, my dear. It will transmit your location to a receiver on a frequency that is rarely used for such transmissions." He pointed to something in the box. "That receiver will pinpoint your location to within two feet."

"And only that receiver can pick it up?" she asked.

"No, my dear," Pierre corrected. "That only happens in the movies. Other receivers can pick it up if they happen to be on the same frequency, which is unlikely, but possible. And it has a type of shielding, one that won't keep the receiver from picking it up but that helps prevent an RF Detector—"

At the look of confusion on Andi' face, Levi whispered in her ear, "That's a 'bug' detector."

"—from recognizing it," Pierre continued as if Levi hadn't spoken. "But again, it is still possible for it to happen. However, the transmissions are encrypted, so unless a receiver has the encryption program already installed, the transmissions won't make any sense. In order to understand the signal, you need to have the receiver that is specifically encoded for your transmitter. Another receiver won't work."

"I'm impressed, Pierre," Levi said. "When I bought one of those for Tess, you didn't have that feature. You were still working on it."

"I perfected it about six months ago. I'm very pleased with it. The unit is expensive, but I assume I will just bill Jonas for it."

"You assume correctly."

"Well then, my dear, if you will just step over here."

Levi watched as Pierre swabbed Andi's lower leg with alcohol, injected a local anesthetic, and inserted the transmitter just above her ankle. Her eyes widened a time or two, but she never flinched. She seemed to handle anything that came at her with poise and humor.

Was Jonas right? Was he falling for her? Levi couldn't decide. There was no question he wanted her—bad—but did he *love* her? He couldn't remember ever being in a position where his personal feelings were in danger of becoming involved while on a mission. He was a professional, and professionals like him were supposed to be immune to that sort of thing. Then again, it had happened to his friend, Max, when he met Tess—and if it could happen to Max, it could happen to anyone.

Finished with the procedure, Pierre had one final word of caution for Andi. "The right equipment *will* jam the transmissions, my dear. So do not tell anyone what we've done. If they know what you have, they may be able to render it useless." He picked up the blue box and turned to Levi. "There are two receivers in here." He held one up to show him. It was about the size of a wallet. "Either one will interpret her signal and translate it into an exact location."

He put the receiver back and handed the box to Levi.

"If you lose the receivers, I can replace them as long as I have the codes written on the box. But if you lose the box, it will be impossible."

"Thanks, Pierre."

Levi shook the Frenchman's hand and turned to put his arm around Andi's shoulders, but she shrugged away from him, went over to Pierre, and brushed a kiss lightly across his lips.

"Thank you, Pierre."

Pierre's eyes glazed over. It was a look Levi recognized—probably the same one he had in his own eyes now and then when he looked at Andi.

"Now, you've done it, luv," he teased. "I'd better get you out of here before he proposes."

Andi giggled. "Who's Tess?" she asked on the way back to the airport.

"Tess is my best friend. Jonas and I would do just about anything for her. You'd love her. She's married to my friend, Max. He works for the CIA, and we were concerned there might be a threat to Tess because of his job. So, as a wedding present, I bought a system like yours for her, so Max could always find her."

He remembered how much he had loved Tess and how hard he'd fought to protect her, too. Tess, Leanne, and now Andi?

Was it possible? And if so, why was he fighting it so hard?

Tuesday, April 9th, 9:24 p.m., the Sydarian Embassy:

"Dammit, where is she?" Jamar growled into the phone. "It has been over a week and the buyer is getting impatient. He has his people working on it, too, but so far they have not come up with any more than you have."

"If I knew where she was, I'd already have told you. All I know is that she's with Komakov. He hasn't been to his office at the estate since the rescue at the cabin, so he has to be protecting her." The man on the other end of the line sighed. "I did warn you he was very good. As long as he's with her, I doubt we'll ever find her."

"Then we have to find a way to separate them. Surely you can think of something. Maybe you could cause trouble for Jonas. Would that flush him out?"

"Probably, but causing trouble for Jonas could be *very* dangerous. However, I do have a plan. That's why I called."

Jamar rolled his eyes. "Then why the hell did you not say so?"

"I just did."

"Well, what is it?"

The sound of a throat clearing came down the wire from Boston. "It's going to involve some risk on your part. But I think it's viable."

Out of patience, Jamar snarled, "What. Is. Your. Plan?"

"There's a faction of the Outfit called the Sons of Zeus—a vigilante group dedicated to keeping the mafia out of the public eye. Jonas is a member of this group, and Komakov owes them a favor. I think if—"

"How in the hell can that help us?"

"If you'll let me finish, I'll tell you. Komakov is known as a man of his word. If we can do something to threaten the Outfit with publicity, the SOZ—the vigilante group I mentioned—would have to call in their favor and Komakov would be obliged to help them. And he'd have no choice but to stash the package somewhere while he does."

"Oh, yes. That is a fantastic plan, you idiot," Jamar

sneered. "Except for the fact that if it would be dangerous to cause trouble for Jonas, it would be even more dangerous to cause trouble for the Outfit as a whole."

"Not necessarily. Komakov's loyalty is to Jonas, not to the Outfit. The only way he'd avenge them is if Jonas asked him to. And if we're careful, that won't happen."

"What would we need to do?"

"We just have to steal a certain document and threaten to make it public. If we put it somewhere only a black-ops specialist can get to it, the SOZ will have to call him in."

The idea had real possibilities, Jamar decided. "But to do that we would have to let them know where it is. Will that not look suspicious?"

"Not if we handle it right. We can demand an outrageous ransom and use the location as a taunt, as if to say that we're guarding the document so well, they'll never get it back if they don't pay up."

"What is it? And why would they want it back so badly?"

"It's a manuscript by one of their underbosses from Pittsburgh who turned state's evidence. Apparently, it was found in his apartment after he disappeared into the witness protection program. He spilled his guts on paper and was planning to publish it, I guess. But the Outfit found out he was talking to the FBI and the Justice Department had to do an emergency extraction. The snitch didn't get a chance to go home and pack. The Outfit kept the manuscript as a reference in case he ever tried to publish it under a pen name so they would know it was him, but it's not something they'll want made public, believe me."

"And you are sure the mafia leaders will contact this SOZ group, who will in turn contact Komakov? It seems an awfully big assumption to me."

"From what I understand, The Commission in Tarpon Springs, Florida, will do just about anything to keep the Outfit's name out of the news."

Jamar thought for a moment. "How difficult will it be to steal this document, and where would we stash it?"

"I have an informant in Florida who works for one of The Commission. He can steal it for me and stage it to look like an outsider broke in. But as to where we should stash it—" A dark chuckle traveled down the line. "How good is your security there at the embassy?"

"My embassy? We cannot put it here. That would tie us into the package's disappearance!"

"I realize that. But we could stash it in another embassy. Don't all embassies have the same tight security?"

"Yes, I suppose you are right." Jamar pursed his lips. "Did you have a particular one in mind?"

"How about the Russian embassy? The Russian and Greek Mafias have never been easy allies. So it's perfect. You're friends with the ambassador there, and the Russians love that kind of cloak-and-dagger double dealing shit, so your friend should have no problems agreeing to help. You can call it a practical joke if you like."

Jamar was impressed. "That might actually work."

"Of course it will. If Komakov breaches their security and retrieves the document, no problem. If he doesn't, or if he gets caught, also no problem. Either way, we'll separate him from the package."

Wednesday, April 17th, 1:28 p.m., a cabin in the Bitterroot Mountains of western Montana:

Andi shook her sore hand and stuck her tongue out at Levi.

"Pay attention, luv," he growled. "Try it again, only this time hit me like you mean it. Now, attack me."

She sighed. They had been here for almost two weeks and she loved it. It was peaceful and so beautiful. And quiet, except for birds singing and Levi yelling, "Attack me," all the time. The air smelled of evergreens and wildflowers. She could have happily lived here forever. But sooner or later Jonas would want Levi to come home, and Andi didn't know what she'd do without him. She'd fallen hopelessly in love with him. Every night she had to resist the urge to go crawl into bed with him. The rustic cabin had a kitchen, a bathroom, a living room, and two small bedrooms. Levi slept in one. She slept in the other.

She tried to hide the attraction she felt for him, though every time he focused those incredible blue eyes on her, it was all she could do not to make a fool of herself. Not having the faintest idea how he felt about her, she kept her own feelings secret, hoping he would make a pass or give her some indication he wanted her. But no, he was always a perfect gentleman.

When they first arrived, she'd discovered that he'd planned for them to eat out most nights in the small town about thirty miles away. "It just so happens I can cook," she'd told him. "And if we're hiding, doesn't it make more sense to eat here?"

He hadn't looked convinced, but he'd taken her to the grocery store—a mind-boggling experience—and seemed pleasantly surprised with the results.

He kept in touch regularly with Wilson and Jonas and, while both were closing in on discovering who the traitors were in their respective organizations, they hadn't quite gotten there yet. Still, she was pleased to hear that her father would suffer for trying to sell her, although, she wasn't sure she wanted the money Jonas was getting her. She didn't want *anything* from her father. She also didn't want Jonas to hurry his investigation. As long as she had Levi here alone, she had a chance to make him love her. Once they went back to Boston, she was certain she'd lose him.

Every morning before breakfast she went with him on his daily run. She'd gotten good enough now that she could *almost* keep up with him. He was in excellent shape—just *looking* at him turned her on. Trying to build up the strength in her upper body, he also had her doing pushups and lifting weights. As he didn't have any dumbbells handy, he used progressively heavier rocks. After breakfast, he would give her stalking lessons until she could move through the trees almost as quietly as he could. He'd also taught her bird calls she could use as signals if necessary. Before long she could make them as well as he did.

But her rigorous training didn't stop there. Just before lunch every day, he gave her lessons on how normal, everyday items could be used as weapons—such as how a set of keys could be used to put out an attacker's eyes, or how a tube of lipstick or a roll of coins could be held in her fist to give it more punching power.

"It's not as good as brass knuckles, luv," he'd told her. "But it will help in a pinch."

He'd also taught her how to make bombs out of diesel and fertilizer—and detonators out of every day household items you could find in any kitchen. Then he showed her how to make a timing switch out of an old-fashioned clock, a length of wire, and a battery. Apparently, these were just some of the handy little tricks he'd learned while in the British SAS and the CIA.

He explained how to anticipate an attack by watching her opponent's body language and facial expressions.

"Especially his eyes," he told her. "If he's going to attack you, you'll see it there first. So you'll have some warning. Not much, granted, but every little bit helps."

In the evenings after dinner, he described different scenarios to her and asked her how she would escape from each one, seemingly delighted by her creativity. Then he'd tell her little tricks to help her—how to protect her hand by covering it with a shirt or a towel before using it to break a window; how to stage a scene to make it look like she went in a different direction than she really did; or how to use a broom, a tree branch, or whatever was handy to sweep out her tracks.

Most afternoons they spent out in the yard, with Levi covered in padding, while she used her elbows, knees, feet, head, and fists to attack him.

"If you only remember one thing I tell you, luv," he'd said, "remember this. Never hesitate. You're lost if you do." He claimed to be pleased with her progress, but he still kept pushing for more. "Come on, luv," he'd yell at her. "Attack me!"

She wanted to *attack* him all right, only she wanted to do it nude, and she didn't want to use her fists. There was just something about his rampant sexuality and hard body that screamed, "Incredible Lover." He was probably as good at that as he was at everything else, and she wanted to know what she was missing. It was high time she took a lover. Screw her father and his high-minded ideas on chastity. The bastard only wanted her to remain a virgin so he could get more for her when he sold her!

If I can ever get up the nerve, she decided, *one of these times when Levi's showing me a new move, I'll make one on him that will knock his socks off!*

His amused voice broke into her thoughts. "You want to share, luv?"

"Share? Share what?"

"What you're thinking. You were a million miles away. Where'd you go?"

Oh, *hell* no, she did *not* want to share what she was thinking. "I was just reviewing techniques," she lied.

He knew she was lying. She could see it in his grin.

"Oh, you were, were you?" he challenged. "And do these *techniques* have anything to do with what we're doing right now?"

"Of course."

Laughing, he beckoned to her. "You're a lousy liar, luv. Now, pay attention. Attack me!"

She growled, drew back her fist, and propelled it forward—keeping her wrist straight and locked and her thumb outside her fist, just like he'd taught her—slamming it into his solar plexus.

"Well done," he said with approval. "I actually felt that one. Now again."

And so it went, on and on. She knew why he was doing it. He wanted to give her a fighting chance when he wasn't with her anymore. Maybe that was why she was resisting. She didn't want him to leave her.

At about four o'clock every day, Levi put his pads away and brought out the guns. But they scared her so much she couldn't hit shit. Every time she pulled the trigger, she closed her eyes. Levi insisted all she needed was practice, but she wasn't so sure.

He set up the targets and she took her usual place. Her first shot went wild, slamming into the trunk of a nearby evergreen tree.

He pinched the bridge of his nose with a thumb and forefinger. "Tell me you didn't close your bloody eyes again when you pulled the trigger, luv."

She grinned at him and, mimicking his accent, said, "I didn't close my bloody eyes again when I pulled the trigger, luv." Pausing for effect, she added, "And even if I did, I bloody well aimed first."

He chuckled. "Aiming's good. But it helps if you

keep your eyes open so you can see what the hell you're aiming at." He came up behind her. "Okay, aim your weapon."

She did—at least she *thought* she did.

"No, no, luv," he corrected. "Like this." He stood directly behind her with his chest against her back and his cheek on her hair. Then he stretched his arms around her and steadied her hands. "Now, a little to your left."

She moved the gun.

His laughter tickled her ear. "Your *other* left, luv."

Right, left—how the hell am I supposed to concentrate like this? It was all she could do not to tremble.

Suddenly, her physical and emotional needs just took over. Almost as if she was watching it rather than doing it herself, she felt her arm lower the gun and her body turn to face him. As their eyes met, her toes lifted her up until her lips pressed firmly against his.

Levi froze, his eyes widening in surprise, but only for an instant. Then he reached down, took the gun from her hand, and laid it on the wooden crate they'd been using as a worktable. Wrapping his arms around her, he pulled her close and took command of the kiss, changing the angle and deepening it.

So he wasn't as immune to her as he'd seemed. *Thank heavens!*

She slipped her arms around his neck and melted against him. When her lips parted on a moan, his tongue slipped inside. Desire stole her breath, turning her brain to mush. Soft moans escaped her as he did things to her mouth she'd never experienced before. Damn, he was good at this! If his slow, plundering kisses did this to her, she couldn't wait to see what came next.

"This is dangerous, luv," he murmured, breaking the kiss at last. "You're playing with fire, and it's likely to get you in trouble."

She exhaled a stunned breath. "Ask me if I care."

"All this just to get out of shooting the gun?" he teased, pausing for another kiss. "I'm supposed to protect you, not seduce you."

"I believe *I'm* the one who kissed you. And anyway, I'd bloody well advise you to shut up and kiss me again, luv," she ordered. "Or I'll duct tape your lips to mine."

Laughing, he kissed her again then rested his forehead on hers. "Ah, Andi, luv. I'm not sure what's right here."

"This *feels* right. Are you telling me it doesn't feel right to you?"

"You've got me there, luv. It *feels* dead right. But that doesn't *make* it right."

His erection pressed against her thigh, so she knew he wanted her, too. His lips moved to her neck and she shivered. "Well, you can't tell me you don't want me, because I won't believe you."

He chuckled softly. "Yes, I'd say wanting you's a given. But I'm supposed to be stronger and more professional than this." She wriggled her hips against his groin and he groaned. "Pushing yourself into me like that's fighting dirty." Reaching his hands down, he cupped her ass and pulled her tighter against his growing need. "Does anyone ever win an argument with you?"

"Not anymore, thanks to you." She grinned. "So you may as well stop fighting me."

"As you can probably tell, luv, I'm not fighting all that hard." Bringing his lips back to hers, he kissed her again. Then he raised his head and waited until she met his gaze. "Are you sure about this, Andi?"

She stared into his eyes. They were hungry, filled with desire. Oh yeah, he wanted her all right. "And if I am?" she whispered, her throat so tight with longing she could hardly speak.

"Well, if you're willing to *cooperate*," he said with a grin and a wink, "I'll pick you up, carry you into the house, tear your clothes off, and make love to you."

"In that case, I'm definitely cooperating."

"You mean I'm *finally* getting some cooperation?"

"You might get more than that if you'd just shut up and get on with it."

He laughed and slipped an arm under her knees—only to suddenly drop her back on her feet. Shoving her none too gently to the rear, he placed himself in front of her and hissed, "Stay behind me."

CHAPTER 7

2:17 p.m., a diner near the St. Petersburg College campus, Tarpon Springs, Florida:

Bartholomew Graves waddled across the main room of the cafeteria-style diner and, reaching the far back corner, settled his five-foot, three-hundred-pound frame onto a chair at the table where Adrian Jackson sat waiting for him. "What can I do for you?" he asked without preamble.

Jackson didn't answer, didn't even look up from the pile of documents he was reading. Graves frowned. *Has one of the missions gone wrong?*

Jackson served as the liaison between the vigilante group known as the Sons of Zeus—of which Graves was the head—and The Commission, the ruling body of the Greek Mafia in the US. He was Graves's immediate supervisor and the man mainly responsible for keeping the Outfit out of the evening news. Something he took very seriously—as Graves knew only too well.

From their plush mansions in Tarpon Springs, Florida, the ten old men who made up The Commission ruled the Outfit with an iron fist. And they wanted none of the publicity that had turned America's citizen against the

Italian crime families and made them a favorite target of the FBI. Determined to keep a low profile, The Commission dealt very harshly with anyone who drew too much attention to them—a fact that kept Graves constantly on edge.

What has gone wrong? he wondered again. Unnerved by Jackson's silence, Graves forced himself not to squirm. "Sir?"

Jackson looked up, finally, and handed him a sheet of paper from the pile. "An important manuscript has been stolen from the home of one of The Commission. It's imperative that we get it back."

Graves stared at the memo in his hand. "Dear heavens! How did this happen?"

"How it happened is irrelevant. What's important is getting it back before it's made public."

"Yes, of course. But from what I see here," Graves said, waving the sheet of paper, "while they're waiting for the ransom to be paid, it's being held in a foreign embassy. We're talking tons of security. What is it you want me to do? Arrange for the ransom to be handed over?"

"Of course not. I want you to get it back."

"Get it back? But how?"

"As head of the SOZ, surely you know someone who can break into this embassy without anyone being the wiser."

Graves cleared his throat. "My men are great if we need someone threatened or intimidated, or…er…taken out." *Like Nick Demopulus in the prison showers. Now, that was a particularly satisfying job.* "But they aren't much good at covert operations."

"There must be at least one SOZ member who's had some military training and could pull off something like this."

Graves leaned back in his chair, the wood groaning

in protest beneath him, as he considered the question. "There's a couple of ex-special forces, but none that can get through that kind of high-level security. As you know, we do not really encourage our young people to serve in the military. Though I'm not sure that even military training would prepare them for something like this."

Jackson sighed. "There must be *someone* who can help us. Surely, with all your contacts?"

Graves shook his head. "I don't think—" When the light finally dawned, it was blinding. "Of course!" he exclaimed, giving himself a mental pat on the back. "I know just the person. And, as it happens, he owes us a favor."

2:23 p.m., the cabin in the Bitterroot Mountains:

Keeping Andi behind him, Levi scanned the clearing. He knew what the sound he'd heard meant. A twig had been broken. It could have been an animal, but he didn't think so. From the sound of the snap, whatever had broken it was no lightweight.

"What is it?" Andi breathed. "Did you hear something?"

"Yeah. A twig snapped. Something, or some*one*, stepped on it."

"I don't see anyone."

"Neither do I, and that's what worries me." And he'd been kissing her when he should have been paying attention to her safety. Cursing himself, he started to ease her back toward the cabin.

"Oh, look!" she whispered, her voice filled with awe.

His gaze followed her pointing finger. A herd of elk stepped out of the forest. Five does, two fawns, and one huge buck. Relieved beyond measure, Levi slipped an arm around Andi's shoulders. "Magnificent, aren't they?"

"I'll say. What are they?"

"Wapiti, also called elk. The largest species of deer in the world."

"Damn, I wish we had a camera."

"There's one of those disposable ones in my uncle's desk."

She glanced at him over her shoulder, her lovely eyes sparkling. "Get it for me, please."

"And leave you alone?" He shook his head. "Why don't you come with me?"

"Because I've never seen elk before, and they might leave before you get back. Please, Levi."

He looked around the clearing again but saw no danger. The elk were certainly big enough to have snapped a branch that hard and, with a group that large, they were more than likely the source of the noise he'd heard. But still—

"Please, Levi," she begged again.

He sighed. How could he refuse her? "All right, luv. But you stay right here. Don't move any closer to them. Promise?"

She nodded. "What do I do if *they* move closer to *me*?"

"I doubt they will, but if they do, haul ass for the cabin."

"No problem."

"Good. I'll be right back." He gave her a quick kiss. "Try to stay out of trouble while I'm gone."

Andi watched him go for a moment before turning back to feast her eyes on the elk. Such gorgeous animals. Damn, she loved it here at his cabin in the mountains, but she didn't know how much longer they would stay. Levi seemed to be getting nervous. He said something *had* to be happening because everything back home was too quiet.

Now that her father no longer had a position with the Demopulus Crime Family, the loan shark had settled for what he could get. Jonas had offered him fifty cents on the dollar, telling him, "Take it or leave it."

But Levi was concerned that the oil baron guy wasn't going to give up. He said the man had seen her picture and was determined to have her. Andi wasn't worried, though. She knew Levi would keep her safe. But he wanted her to be able to defend herself as well. That was why he was working so hard to teach her self-defense and how to shoot. She felt a sudden rush of shame that she'd been so reluctant to learn. After all, he couldn't be with her twenty-four/seven, even if he wanted to. She heard the cabin door close and picked up a gun from the wooden crate, thinking about how much she loved him.

He hadn't been inside more than a few seconds when the elk snorted and stampeded, fleeing along the edge of the clearing, as two men with rifles charged out of the trees. She recognized one of them—the driver of the van at the motel in Idaho.

Screaming "Levi," she raised her gun. "Stop where you are and drop your guns!"

The men didn't stop.

Remembering how he'd told her never to hesitate, she took aim and fired, hoping to hell she didn't miss this time!

Levi heard her scream his name then he heard the gunshot. He didn't stop to think, just dropped the camera, and dove for the door, snagging his rifle as he went. Dropping to his stomach on the deck of the front porch, he snugged his rifle into his shoulder.

Andi was standing where he'd left her, one man down, another with his hands raised and his rifle on the ground. Levi held his breath. If she wanted to shoot the bastard, he wouldn't interfere.

She said something, obviously giving the man an order, but Levi couldn't make out the words. The man shook his head then said something back to her. She backed up a step. He suddenly pulled out a knife and lunged for her. She fired just as Levi put a bullet in the bastard's head. He knew she couldn't hear the shot because of the silencer, but when the guy's head exploded, she turned and ran toward Levi. He rushed to meet her. When they reached each other, she jumped into his arms, wrapping hers around his neck.

Safe. Relax, she's safe, he told himself, trying to calm his racing heart.

She was scared and shaking, but she hadn't faltered.

He held her tight until her shudders ceased. "I'm proud of you, luv. You did just what you were supposed to." He kissed her temple. "Did they hurt you?"

"No." She shook her head, her breath finally returning to normal. "When I shot the first one, the second one stopped and dropped his rifle like I'd told him to. I didn't think about a knife."

"Well, taking a knife to a gun fight wasn't the brightest move in the first place, so I say he got what he deserved."

"I wanted to bring him up here for you to deal with, but he wouldn't go."

"I was going to let you handle it, but when I saw some man trying to put the moves on you, I lost it." She giggled as he'd intended, and some of the tension left her body, so he asked, "Shall we go and see how we did?"

He didn't really want to subject her to this, but she had to face the reality of her actions—killing and dealing with the aftermath—if she was truly going to be able to defend herself.

Nodding, she released him, took his hand, and walked with him back to the bodies.

When he examined the corpses and saw what she'd done, he could hardly believe it. "Bloody hell, luv! You got this one in the carotid artery," he said, gesturing at the man's neck. "Was he moving when you shot him?"

"Yes, he was running right at me. You always say 'don't hesitate,' so I didn't."

"I'll be damned." The second shot wasn't quite as sweet, but almost. She'd gotten him in the liver, as evidenced by the black bloodstain on his shirt. It would have been fatal, but the guy would've suffered in agony for several minutes first if Levi's bullet hadn't shut down his brain. It'd been more luck than skill, he knew, but it had served her well, nonetheless. "This one's a kill shot, too. I don't know what you were aiming at, but what you hit worked just fine."

She took a deep breath and swallowed. "At least I kept my eyes open this time."

"I'm impressed. Pretty soon you won't need me anymore."

She shook her head. "I'll always need you because you make me strong."

He hugged her tight, resting his cheek on her hair. "You killed two men today. Are you okay with that?"

"Considering that they weren't just after my wallet but were trying to haul me off to be a sex slave for some zillionaire—yeah, I think I am. If they'd stopped when I told them to, I wouldn't have shot them. But they didn't." She gazed up into his eyes. "If you're worried I'm going to have nightmares, don't. I read in a book once that you shouldn't kick a tiger in the ass without having a plan for dealing with its teeth. If they didn't have a plan for my 'teeth—'" She made air quotes with her fingers. "—that's not my problem. I told you, I'm tired of being lied to and used. I want to fight back."

He stared at her. She constantly amazed him. "I'm so proud of you, Andi."

She blushed. "Thanks. So what do we do now?"

"Now we get out of here. Run up to the house and start loading the car. If there's any food in the kitchen that will spoil, bring it with us. We won't be back for a while. I'll be up to help as soon as I take care of the bodies."

"What are you going to do with them?"

He hesitated. "Rig them with explosives and blow them to pieces."

"Oh. Okay." She kissed his cheek and ran for the house.

He stared after her, stunned once more. He'd thought she'd be horrified about what he intended to do, but she'd surprised him yet again. Still, as much as he cared about her—and wanted her—he was going to have to tell her they couldn't be intimate. He couldn't afford to get distracted by becoming personally involved. They'd been lucky this time, but he couldn't risk it happening again.

Cursing, he checked the men for identification, but they weren't carrying any.

Figures.

After dragging the bodies onto a clear patch of ground, he went to get the explosives. Andi had already cleaned out the fridge and was almost done loading the car. He pulled the plastique and equipment from his pack in the trunk just as she came out with another load.

"In the third drawer of the desk in the living room is

my uncle's old FBI badge," he said. "Will you get it for me and put it in the glove box?"

"Sure."

He went back to the bodies and rigged them with enough explosives to make hamburger—chopped fine. The local scavengers would eat well for a while. If they could find the pieces.

Setting the timer for twenty minutes, he gathered up the weapons—his and theirs—and headed for the car. Andi had already finished loading it and locked the cabin, waiting for him patiently in the shotgun seat. Levi stuffed the guns and knife into the trunk and climbed behind the wheel.

"Where are we going?" she asked as he started the car.

"I'm not sure where we'll end up eventually, but right now we're headed for Missoula. Tomorrow morning I need to find out who accessed the property records to find this place. If I can do that, we might have a chance at finding out who's behind this."

"That's why you need the badge, isn't it?"

He nodded. "I need to look official if I want to get the information and keep it quiet."

"I would have thought they'd take those badges back when an agent dies, just to prevent what you're planning to do."

"They do. My uncle was killed in the line of duty and for some reason that I can't fathom, he didn't have his badge with him that day. I found it in his apartment a couple of weeks later when I cleaned out his things." He shrugged. "I thought I might have a use for it one day, so I kept it. No one from the FBI has ever asked me about it. So maybe they think it got lost when he was killed."

"If the badge doesn't work, just get me to a computer. I can find out all kinds of stuff for you."

"Really? You're that good with computers? I didn't know that."

"I'm one of the best hackers around," she said proudly. "There wasn't much to do at an all-girls college, so I spent a lot of time on the computer. My roommate was a hacker, and she taught me the basics. After that it was just practice—and an instinctive sixth sense when it comes to code."

"That's good to know," he said, tucking that little tidbit away in the back of his mind for later use. "But for now, let's keep it under our hats, shall we? Especially, in my uncle's hometown."

"His hometown? Wasn't he English like you?"

"No. My dad was American. After college he went to England for a sabbatical before going to law school. He fell in love with my mother and stayed. He died in a hunting accident when I was two, and—" He swallowed. "—my uncle tried to make up for it. He was always there for me."

"How would he have felt about you working for Jonas Demopulus?"

"He actually liked Jonas. In fact, I met Jonas through my uncle. Uncle John helped him clean out the murderers and violent thugs in the organization after Jonas's father died. Jonas doesn't believe in hurting innocent people. And he's not at all opposed to letting someone go to jail if they start terrorizing civilians."

They'd made it halfway down the mountain road when they heard the explosion behind them. Levi glanced over and gave Andi a smile. "You did good, luv. I'm proud of you."

"Thanks. And thanks for all the training." She grinned. "Maybe someday I can do black ops, too."

He sighed. "Be careful what you wish for, luv."

6:12 p.m., the Hilton Hotel, Missoula, Montana:

Andi looked around the spacious suite while Levi tipped the bellboy. When the man left, she breathed a sigh of relief. Maybe now, she and Levi could finally finish what they'd started this afternoon. When he didn't come to her and take her in his arms immediately, she began to worry. Had he changed his mind about wanting her? Was that why he'd gotten a two-bedroom suite?

She watched him cross to the window and look down at the street. "Everything okay?" she asked.

He didn't turn around. "Everything's fine. I'm just a little restless."

"I can fix that." She walked up behind him and put her arms around his waist. "Why don't we go into one of the bedrooms and pick up where we left off this afternoon?"

He turned to face her, but instead of kissing her as she expected, he pushed her gently away. "We can't, luv. We—" He sighed. "We just can't."

Hurt and confused, she stared at him. "Why *can't* we? We're both healthy, unattached adults. I want you, and you want me. What's to stop us?"

"My wanting you almost got you captured or killed this afternoon. I can't do my job if I'm personally involved."

"*What?*" She crossed her arms over her chest and glared at him, fighting back the tears that threatened to fill her eyes. "Well, this is a fine time to tell me since I just happen to be in love with you!"

Levi raked his hands through his hair. "No, luv, you're not. You just think you are."

"*Excuse* me? Are *you* trying to tell me how *I* feel?"

"Look, it's rather like the Stockholm Syndrome, if you know what that is. Your safety and protection depend on me. Plus, we're spending all our time together and you can't really leave, so, in a way, you're being held captive. It's natural for you to think you have feelings for me. Once this is all over, you'll see that I'm right."

Aghast, she gaped at him, pain and rage fighting for domination. Rage won, hands down. "You arrogant bastard!" Unable to resist, she raised her hand to smack him but managed to pull her punch at the last possible second and slammed her fist into the high-backed chair beside him instead. "How dare you! If you've changed your mind about wanting me, the least you could do is say it outright. But don't give me some bullshit about the *Stockholm Syndrome*, for Pete's sake. This situation has nothing in common with a kidnapping. Been there, done that, remember? And I don't particularly appreciate having my feelings for you compared to the fear and disgust I felt for those *pigs*!" She took a deep breath, cursing the tears that escaped her control and rolled down her cheeks. "Either you call Jonas and tell him to get me a different bodyguard immediately, or I will. I don't want your protection anymore."

Disgusted with herself, with Levi, and the whole damned situation, she picked up her backpack, grabbed one of the bags of food they'd brought from the cabin, and fled into the nearest bedroom, slamming the door behind her.

Levi watched her leave, fighting the urge to go after her. *Better to let her cool off some*, he decided. He'd hurt her and, though he hadn't wanted or intended to, it was probably better this way. As long as she was hurt and angry, she'd keep her distance. And if he was going to do his job, that was imperative. He didn't like it any more than she did, but it couldn't be helped.

She loved him. He almost smiled, remembering how she'd *spat* the words at him. He'd been stunned by her declaration and had wanted to take her in his arms, kiss away the fury that darkened her amber eyes, and tell her…

"Tell her *what*?" he muttered under his breath. That he *cared* for her? Had *feelings* for her? *Oh, yeah, that'd go over well*, he mused, raking his hands through his hair again. He couldn't deny he'd handled it badly but…yeah, it was probably for the best.

Still, if she seriously thought he'd call Jonas and arrange for someone else to protect her, she was going to be sadly disappointed. No way in hell would he let anyone else get near her. Not until—

His phone rang, disrupting his mental tirade. He checked the caller ID before answering. Jonas. "What's up, old man?"

Jonas hesitated. "You sound upset. Is everything okay?"

Levi winced. "Yeah, Andi and I just had a bit of a tiff."

"A lovers' quarrel?"

"Don't even go there," Levi ordered tersely. He refused to get into a discussion about his feelings for Andi when *he* wasn't even sure what they were. Of course, as angry as she was, *his* feelings might be completely irrelevant. "Why'd you call? Are you okay?"

"Yes, I'm fine. But I just had a visit from Bartholomew Graves."

"Damn. What's he want you to do this time?"

"Not me. You. He's calling in that favor you owe them."

"Bloody hell! *Now*? Didn't you tell him I was tied up at the moment?"

"Of course, I did, but he says it's urgent, and he needs your particular expertise."

"Tell him to take a number."

"You know I can't do that, Levi. Not unless you want to be looking over your shoulder for the rest of your life. You've actually gotten off easy. It's been three years since the SOZ took care of Nick and, honestly, I expected this a lot sooner. I did buy you *some* time, however, as I told him it would take me a while to get a hold of you. So he's not expecting your phone call until sometime around noon tomorrow."

"And just what am I supposed to do with Andi while I'm off doing whatever it is they want me to do?"

"I don't know. I was hoping you'd have some suggestions. Do you want me to send someone to guard her while you're gone?"

"No! Not until we find the leak." Levi paced between the window and Andi's bedroom door, the hairs on the back of his neck prickling. "Tell me, Jonas, doesn't the timing of this seem a little suspicious to you?"

"You're not suggesting the SOZ could be behind the attack on Andi, are you? Because, I assure you, I'd know about it if they were."

"No, that's not what I'm saying. But it seems to me that the kidnappers are always a step ahead of us, and I'd like to know why."

"What do you mean a step ahead?"

"Someone found us at Uncle John's cabin, and I almost lost her. We had to move again."

"Oh, no! Are you both okay?"

"For now. But my gut tells me this isn't a coincidence. Did Graves say what it was he wanted me to do?"

Jonas cleared his throat. "As a matter of fact, he did.

He wants you to break into a foreign embassy in Washington, DC, and retrieve a manuscript that was stolen from The Commission before it's made public by the thieves. Graves doesn't think The Commission will get it back even if they pay the ransom."

"Break into an *embassy*? What the hell does he think I am? Some kind of super spy?"

Jonas gave a strained chuckle. "Apparently, he's been listening to the rumors about you and believes what they say."

Levi closed his eyes and shook his head. "Perfect. Just bloody perfect."

Thursday, April 18th, 2:03 a.m.:

Her tears long dried, Andi lay on her bed, staring at the ceiling. She felt like a fool. She'd been so sure he wanted her as much as she wanted him. Why had he changed his mind? Had she done something wrong?

It couldn't be the fact that she'd killed those men. He'd said he was proud of her afterward. And he never said things he didn't mean. At least he hadn't *yet*, not to her. Which meant—

She bolted upright in bed. He *did* still want her. He just thought it was unprofessional or…something equally stupid. What had he said? Oh, yeah. He couldn't protect her properly if he was distracted. What bullshit! What if she'd been his wife, Leanne? Would he have been unable to protect *her* if the need arose? Not likely.

Slipping her legs over the side of the bed, she stood up. She was nearly twenty-six and still a virgin. Now she knew why her father had been so insistent she remain chaste, why she'd been so sheltered—virgins were worth more on the human-trafficking market. Well, screw that! That was the best possible reason for her to take a lover. Besides, she was tired of being sheltered, of not knowing what life was all about. She wanted Levi, and if he wouldn't take her, she'd just have to take him. And since she was already on birth control pills to regulate her periods, she didn't even have to worry about getting pregnant.

She'd heard part of his phone conversation earlier and knew he was needed somewhere else. Apparently, he'd be finding someone else to protect her after all. Just like she'd told him to—not that she'd meant it. But if this was their last night together, she certainly wasn't going to waste it lying in bed, feeling sorry for herself.

The suite was eerily quiet. For a while, she'd heard Levi moving around in the room next door. But he'd settled down about an hour ago and was probably asleep by now.

Well, we'll just see about that.

She stripped then dressed in the hotel robe she'd found in the bathroom. Then, her heart in her throat, she headed for Levi's room.

Unable to sleep, Levi lay on his bed, glaring at the ceiling. He felt like a fool. He needed to come up with a plan to appease Graves while still protecting Andi, but all he could think of was her lying in bed in the room next door.

His stomach roiled with guilt at the hurt he'd caused her.

He heard his door quietly open and his senses sprang to full alertness, even as his body stilled. Andi walked softly in and closed the door behind her.

Levi didn't move. Didn't dare. Need coiled inside him like a nest of vipers.

"Don't pretend you're asleep," she snapped. "I heard your breathing quicken."

"You should be in bed."

"My thoughts exactly." She opened her robe, slipped it off her shoulders, and let it fall so that it pooled around her ankles. "Move over."

He blinked. Then he clenched his teeth, his fists, his eyes shut—anything to garner some control over his ever-increasing lust. "Get out."

"Make me."

He cursed and pushed himself up to a sitting position on the edge of the bed, keeping the blankets bunched over his hard-on. "Andi, I've already explained why we can't do this, and—"

"And your explanation was just so much bullshit," she interrupted. "I refuse to believe that making love to me would suddenly render a trained expert like you total-ly incapable of performing your duties."

Why did it sound so ridiculous when *she* said it? It had sounded much more reasonable and logical when he'd argued with himself, but now…

He felt like a teenaged idiot—horny and embarrassed about it—and kept his eyes trained on his lap. He didn't dare look at her again, or he'd be lost. He had to get her out of his room, and fast. "Get *out*!"

She heaved an exaggerated sigh. "Now you're start-ing to repeat yourself."

Sidling up next to him, she put her hands on his shoulders, pushed him back down on the bed, and cov-ered his body with hers.

He stiffened, his hands clenched at his sides. It was all he could do not to grab her, roll her over, and take her with one, hard thrust. "Andi, don't do this."

"Sshhh," she murmured. "Don't be afraid. I'll be gentle."

A strained chuckle escaped him. "I don't *want* you," he managed through gritted teeth.

"Liar," she countered and ground her pelvis on his erection. "I can tell just exactly how much you want me."

He tried again. "Andi, you have to understand why we can't do this."

She ran her teeth along the edge of his jaw and nipped lightly. "So let me see if I've got this right. Are you saying that if your *wife* had needed protection, you would've had to hire someone else to do it because, since you'd made love to her, you were no longer capable of protecting her yourself?"

A stab of pain pierced his heart, giving him the strength to push her off of him. She rolled over onto her stomach and glared at him.

He sighed, closed his eyes, and shook his head. "No, that's not what I am saying—exactly."

"Then what *are* you saying?" Before he could answer, she raised a hand, stopping him. "Because I fail to see how sex could suddenly make you incompetent. And if this is our last night together, I don't want to waste it arguing."

Neither did he. And she did have a point. While he knew that making love to her was unprofessional, it would *not* keep him from protecting her if the need arose. Like most men with his training, he could compartmentalize when he needed to. But he *would* be taking advantage. And that was unacceptable.

Then she ran her fingers up his back.

He turned to face her, looked into her eyes, and was defeated. She reached up, wrapped an arm around his neck, and pulled his mouth down to hers.

As he sank into the kiss, he tried one last time. "This

is a mistake," he murmured against her lips.

She only moaned, long and slow.

He craved the flavor of her, the feel, the scent. They filled him up, shattering his resistance. Before he even realized that he'd moved, he'd pushed her onto her back, covering her and taking the kiss deeper, in danger of swallowing her whole. *Control*, he told himself, *you must exercise control*. But when her curious fingers found his erection, he lost the ability for rational thought.

He wanted to ravish. Plunder. And conquer. It was all he could do to force down his raging need and pull back long enough to ask, "Are you sure about this, luv?"

"Yes. Oh *yes*."

CHAPTER 8

Andi was swamped with wave after wave of sensations, so many she couldn't wrap her mind around them all. When he'd asked her if she was sure, she didn't know how to tell him the only thing she was sure of was that she couldn't bear to have him stop. She opened her mouth, trying to answer, but didn't know if she'd even managed to get the words out.

Levi teased, tempted, and taunted her mercilessly, stimulating erogenous zones she didn't know she had. Full of contradictions, his loving was predatory yet gentle, tender yet rough, giving yet demanding, disciplined yet out of control as he slowly drove her insane. He tasted her everywhere, nibbled at the sensitive skin of her inner thighs, and set her every nerve ending on fire.

"Oh, please," she moaned, arching against his hand as it moved between her legs. She strained for something just out of reach. Not quite sure what she was reaching for, she knew if she didn't get it, she'd likely die. "Oh, please, Levi, I can't—I can't…"

He flashed her a wicked grin. "Sure, you can, luv. Let me show you."

His kisses grew increasingly carnal, harsh, and strangely desperate, making her tremble with need. She could scarcely breathe from wanting him. The heat flared up, burning out of control, as the blood swam in her head until she was crazy with lust. "Please…"

Then his mouth was on her, his tongue teasing the sensitive nub of flesh at her core. Her senses went wild, threatening to blow her body to bits. She grabbed at the bedding, futility trying to find an anchor, but it was no use. The pleasure tightened into an almost-agonizing ecstasy and then exploded, the pressure shooting her into orbit. Her body convulsed, the terrible ache inside erupting into a sweet, but brutal, release.

When the shudders eased, she opened her eyes to see him grinning.

"Again," he said.

"Oh, please, n—" She started to tell him she didn't think she could handle any more, but he silenced her with a long, deep kiss. She could taste herself on his tongue and found it strangely erotic. As he started the process all over again, she arched against him, eagerly reaching for what she now knew was to come. Still, she hungered for something more. She wanted him inside her. She didn't know why it seemed so important, but she didn't question it. "Please, Levi, I need you inside me. Now."

She heard something ripping, like paper only thicker, then he spread her knees and positioned himself between her legs. Trying to hurry him up, she writhed beneath him until he choked out a laugh and grabbed her hips.

"This'd be a lot easier, luv, if you'd not squirm so much."

She stopped wriggling and arched toward him in welcome. But when he drove into her, she couldn't quite muffle a small gasp at the pain.

He froze. "Bloody hell!"

She didn't know why he'd stopped—or why he'd cursed—and she didn't much care. She only knew she wasn't about to let him quit, now that the pain had subsided. Shoving her heels into the mattress, she thrust her hips upward.

"Shit!" he groaned. "Andi, luv, if you don't stop that, I'll never get control of myself."

"Who the hell cares? It's not your control I'm after." Wrapping her legs around his waist and her arms around his neck, she rose up and kissed him. "Please, Levi. Make love to me."

He groaned again but kissed her back and, finally, began to move, thrusting deep inside her.

"Oh, *yes*. Please, Levi. *Please*."

She matched his thrusts in perfect harmony. Her breath rushed out between her teeth as he built the pressure slowly and sensually, taking possession of her with strong, hard thrusts while nibbling on her lower lip, throat, and shoulders. Burning alive, she cried out his name as the flames engulfed her, sending her over the edge again in wave after wave of ecstasy.

As her trembling subsided, she noticed that he'd stopped moving and was watching her face. She smiled up at him and received a heart-stopping grin in return.

"You're so beautiful," he whispered.

Then he started building the fire again, slowly at first, then faster and faster, bringing her back to the peak, thrusting into her deep and hard, and crushing his mouth to hers in long desperate kisses.

When she went over the edge this time, he went with her, growling low—deep in his throat—and calling out her name.

As she shuddered in his arms, she knew in her heart that she had been irrevocably changed by this incredible man. And was forever lost to him.

Shame enveloped Levi like a blanket, smothering him. She'd been *innocent*. How could he have been so stupid? He closed his eyes and shuddered, not knowing how he would face her. She trembled beneath him, and he prayed she wasn't crying. He'd hurt her. He *must* have. And he didn't know how to soothe her. Everything he thought to say sounded trite. Gathering his courage, he pushed himself up and looked at her. Blinked. Then stared. No, she wasn't crying. Her eyes were closed, her lips swollen from his kisses, but her cheeks were bone dry. In fact, the expression on her face could only be described as "cream-fed cat."

"I didn't hurt you?" he asked as some of the guilt and shame drained away.

"Hmm?" she asked dreamily. "Hurt me? No, you didn't hurt…well, okay, maybe for a minute." She opened her amber eyes and those swollen lips curved into a smile. "But it was definitely worth it."

He groaned and rolled off of her, shaking his head. Wrapping an arm around her, he pulled her into his side and nestled her head on his shoulder. "You should have told me you'd never had a man before," he scolded. "At least then I could have been gentle with you."

Her laugh, strained though it was, went a long way toward dispersing the dregs of guilt and shame and made him feel clean again.

"Are you kidding?" she demanded. "I nearly had to beat down your defenses with a sledge hammer, as it was. If I'd let it slip that I was still a virgin, I'd have needed a nuclear missile to get through."

He buried his chuckle in her hair. "I wouldn't go *quite* that far, luv, but I daresay you'd have had more of a struggle on your hands." He kissed the top of her head. "Still, I took advantage, and I might have been able to stop myself if I'd known."

"Took *advantage*?" she growled, jabbing him none-too-gently in the ribs. "Whose bedroom are we in? And who came to you, stripped naked, and refused to leave until I got what I wanted? Seems to me, I'm the one who took advantage."

"Well, in that case, I feel so *used*," he quipped. "But as the older, more-experienced member of this—"

She responded by jabbing and pinching any part of him she could reach.

Laughing, he grabbed both her hands before she could do serious damage to his anatomy. "Stop that now, or I'll duct tape your hands to the bed."

She giggled. "Ooohhh, *that* could be fun."

Torn between a laugh and a groan, he released her, sat up, and, stripping off the condom, dropped it into the trashcan beside the bed. Perhaps he *hadn't* taken advantage as much as he'd feared. When he turned back to face her, his heart stuttered. She was so breathtaking, lying there, flushed from their love-making, with her lips swollen and her hair a tangled fan around her head.

He stroked his fingers across her cheek. "You are so beautiful," he repeated. "Inside and out."

"Inside?"

"Absolutely." He drilled a finger into her navel and made her laugh. "Even after all you've been through, you're still sweet, loving, and completely unspoiled."

"Sweet and loving, maybe." She shrugged. "But—" With a wicked little giggle, she pushed him down and rolled over on top of him. "—*unspoiled*? Not so much after tonight."

CHAPTER 9

8:12 a.m., County Courthouse, Missoula, Montana:

Andi waited in the car while Levi went inside to get the information he needed. When he came back out, his face was devoid of any emotion. Only the storm clouds in his eyes gave away his feelings. It was a look she'd never seen him wear before. He looked dangerous. She could tell why people respected him—he wasn't a man you wanted to piss off.

"What's happened?" she asked. "Whatever it is, I don't think it's good news."

He glanced over at as he started the car. "You know me so well you can tell when I'm mad, can't you?"

"It doesn't take a genius. I think I would recognize a look like that even if you were a stranger," she said with a smirk. "Now, stop trying to change the subject, because it won't work. What's wrong?"

"You're a delight. Do you know that, luv?"

Though she was thrilled at his words, she refused to be put off. "Again, thanks, but you're stalling."

He finally laughed and shook his head. "When Wilson wrote in your file that you were stubborn, he had no idea how right he was." He sighed, his humor fading. "What's wrong, Andi, is that we have a rouge FBI agent out there, and I'm going to have to go deal with him."

"The guy who got the information on your cabin was an FBI agent?"

"Yes. Special Agent Travis McCarty from Springfield. He called the clerk's office here and asked who owned my uncle's cabin now. My uncle used to loan it to any agent who asked, so it was well known in the Bureau. I'd guess that this guy did some background work on me, discovered that I was John's nephew, and put two and two together. My last name's not common."

"But why would they be looking for you? Do they know you're with me?"

"I guess there's a rat in the wood pile somewhere that we still don't know about. Since Wilson didn't tell anyone about my operation to rescue you, that's the only way they could know. That means McCarty is in touch with the guys who are trying to take you."

"Maybe he just wanted to use the cabin and wanted to know who to ask. I mean we were there for two weeks."

"That's a possibility, except he asked the clerk to have someone in the sheriff's office secretly check to see if there was anyone there. Told her he was working on a special case. Apparently, someone came out to check from the ridge across the way and saw us."

"Oh. What are we going to do now?"

"I'm going to call Jonas and have him find out where this guy lives and then you and I are flying to Boston. If that's okay with you?"

"As long as I'm with you, I don't care where we go," she told him. When he glanced over at her, she was surprised at the look in his eyes—pride, love, and burning desire all rolled into one. By the time he turned his eyes back to the road, she could hardly breathe. "If you look at me like that again," she whispered, barely able to speak, "you're going to have to pull over and kiss me."

His laugh was filled with lust and the muscles in her belly clenched. "I was thinking the very same thing." Easing the car onto the shoulder and parking, he leaned over and kissed her until they were both breathless.

"We don't have to go to Boston today, do we?" she murmured against his lips. "It will take Jonas some time to find McCarty, won't it?"

"Are you trying to say there's something you'd rather do than fly home today?" he murmured back.

"Yes." Her voice was husky with a longing she made no effort to hide. "I want you. Anytime and anyplace."

"Damn, you are *so* bloody sexy when you say things like that," he whispered, dragging in a ragged breath. "Tomorrow works just fine for me." He pushed himself away from her with obvious reluctance and pulled back out onto the road. Then he stuck his Bluetooth in his ear and called Jonas. "I need a favor," he said. Jonas must have agreed because Levi said, "FBI agent Travis McCarty from the Springfield office. I need his home address and his schedule." A pause. "No, I don't want Wilson to know about this. I'll tell him after I'm done. Don't we have someone there who can identify him and follow him to find out his schedule and where he lives? Or do you have someone who can hack into the FBI's system?" Another pause. "You're right, that would be better— much quicker—but I won't be there until tomorrow. I have something to do here that won't wait." He grinned over at Andi and she giggled. Then he sighed. "No, I haven't called Graves, yet. I still have a couple of hours before my time's up." He listened for a moment. "I know. Thanks, old man."

As he hung up, she leaned over and put her head on his shoulder. "He sounds like a sweet old man."

"He is. And he's going to love you."

She sighed happily. "You know, someday I'm going to have to thank my father. If he hadn't had me kidnapped, I would never have met you."

"Well, I think you *should* thank him, luv," he agreed, laying his hand over hers for a moment. When he spoke again, his voice was so cold she shivered. "Right before I cut out his heart."

11:55 a.m., the Hilton Hotel:

Levi sighed, raked a hand through his hair, and dialed the number Graves had given Jonas.

"Hello?" asked a familiar voice.

"Levi Komakov, Mr. Graves. Jonas said you needed to talk to me."

"Yes, thank you for calling." Graves hesitated, cleared his throat. "Jonas said that you were protecting another young woman at the moment, so I apologize for calling in our favor. But this is an emergency."

Stifling a sigh, Levi waited for him to go on.

"A manuscript has been stolen from The Commission," Graves continued after a slight pause. "The thieves are demanding a ransom and threatening to publish the document if we don't pay. We're willing to pay, but we don't believe that we'll get it back, even if we do. So we need you to retrieve it for us."

"That's not going to help you."

"W—What?" Graves stammered. "What do you mean?"

"Even if you retrieve the original document, the thieves will have likely made a copy, so whether you pay the ransom or not, your document is probably going to be made public."

Graves sighed. "Yes, you're probably right. But what else can we do?"

"Beat them to it. Publish it yourself."

"You don't understand. The document is damning. It's a manuscript written by a whistle blower who turned state's evidence. It contains a lot of lies and half-truths, probably included for dramatic effect, and makes the Outfit appear to be monsters. It is exactly the kind of publicity The Commission so wants to avoid."

Levi shook his head and stifled another sigh. "Look, whoever did this is not a friend of the Outfit, so you need to assume that the document is going to be published. Period. Accept it. Now, knowing that, you can handle it one of two ways. You can either pay the ransom and then cringe and stutter when the document is published, or you can take the offensive and beat the thieves at their own game."

"But—"

"Tell me, Graves, do you think it will look worse for the Outfit if The Commission makes the document public, explains what it is, stresses that it's full of half-truths and lies, or if the thieves publish it and the Outfit is forced to defend itself?"

The line went silent for a moment. "You do have a point," Graves said at last. "But we will still need you to retrieve it, as I am not sure that we even have a copy."

"Oh, come on, Graves. Are you telling me that you didn't make a copy of the manuscript?"

"I don't know. We may have, but it is hardly be a document that we would be desirous of saving. We only kept it so that if it was published under a pen name, we could find our snitch." Graves cleared his throat again. "So are you telling me that you *won't* retrieve it?"

"That's *not* what I said, Graves, and you know it. But

you had better discuss it with your superiors and make sure that they want me to."

"Why wouldn't they?"

"Tell me this. How did you find out where this manuscript is being held?"

"We received a recorded message from the thieves, telling us that they had the document and wanted to ransom it. They also told us that it was being held at the Russian Embassy, so we needn't bother trying to retrieve it as the security there was top notch."

"And this didn't seem the least bit suspicious to you?"

"What do you mean?"

This time, Levi didn't bother to hide his sigh of frustration. "Think, man! First of all, these thieves have some pretty powerful contacts, or else how would they get the document into the Russian Embassy in the first place? So it's quite possible that they have another agenda than simply extorting money. And secondly, why would they bother to tell you where it was unless they were *hoping* that you'd try to get it out. This could be a very elaborate trap. If you think the scandal will be bad when the document's made public, imagine how much worse it will be if the Outfit gets caught trying to get it back."

"I was actually hoping that you *wouldn't* get caught," Graves said tersely. Then he sighed and continued before Levi could respond. "But I do see your point. And even if you didn't get caught, once the document was back in our possession, the thieves could make their copy public and claim the Outfit got caught trying to get it back, which was *why* it was being made public. That would add credence to the document that it wouldn't otherwise have."

"Precisely. So that makes it all the more imperative that you publish the copy immediately or, at the very least, make its theft and its contents known. Explain what it is, where it came from, and that what it says about your organization is mostly untrue."

"Very well," Graves conceded. "I will speak with my superiors and see what they want to do. However, if they still want the document retrieved, can I count on you to get it?"

Levi closed his eyes, shook his head. What could he say? He'd promised to return the favor when Graves had taken care of Nick Demopulus and saved Tess's life three years ago. It wasn't Graves's fault that the timing really sucked. "Yes, you can count on me."

Friday, April 19th, 1:21 a.m., the apartment of Travis McCarty, Springfield, Massachusetts:

Having told Graves to contact Jonas when he had an answer from his higher-ups, Levi decided to take care of McCarty in the meantime. After they had flown back to Boston, he'd left Andi at the estate with Jonas and gone to Springfield alone. He didn't like leaving her and missed her already. While he knew Jonas would protect her, Levi had been with her every minute for almost three weeks, and he wanted to be with her now. But this was a mission he couldn't possibly bring her on.

Jonas's people had hacked into the local FBI field office's network. Apparently, it was easier to hack into the field office systems than the national ones, for reasons only a hacker would understand. But Levi now had what he'd wanted: McCarty's home address and schedule. So he'd packed his gear and driven his Jaguar down to Springfield.

McCarty had gone to bed about an hour ago. Levi had been watching his apartment since the man arrived home at eleven. He should be deep in sleep enough by now that he wouldn't be coherent for a few seconds when Levi woke him up. McCarty's apartment was on the fifth floor. Levi had gone in through the front door before McCarty got home and jimmied a window. It looked closed and locked, but it wasn't. He'd also reset the alarm system to bypass that one window.

Levi had chosen his wardrobe carefully, wearing dark-blue cargo pants and a dark-red long-sleeved turtle-necked T-shirt. Those colors were as invisible in the dark as black, but less suspicious if he got stopped by a cop. Outside the apartment building, in the shadows of an alley, he put on camouflage paint, night-vision goggles, and his vacuum pack. Flipping on the vacuum's ultra-quiet motor, he started climbing up the side of the building. When he reached the window, he eased it open and slipped inside. Once in the room, he turned off the pack and slid it silently onto the floor, along with the googles. McCarty was asleep in the next bedroom over. Luckily for Levi, he lived alone.

Levi sighed. Although he abhorred violence, he knew that most thugs rarely understood anything else. Still, as much as he hated it, he was damn good at it when he needed to be. And if McCarty wasn't in the mood to cooperate, Levi would do what he had to.

He crept soundlessly through the apartment. He'd scouted it out earlier when he jimmied the window so he had an idea of the layout. Pulling out an eight-inch knife, he slipped into McCarty's bedroom and crossed to the bed. The man was sleeping peacefully. For now.

Levi put the knife to McCarty's throat and pressed, not enough to break the skin, just enough to give him a rude awakening. The man jerked awake, felt the knife, and froze.

Levi could read his thoughts as they flickered on his

face. He grinned. "Don't try it, Special Agent McCarty. Whatever you're thinking, it won't work. You and I need to have a little talk and then you can go back to sleep."

"Who the hell are you?" McCarty demanded, but Levi heard his voice crack.

Good, the man was scared. "Levi Komakov."

McCarty gasped. "You! What are you doing here? What do you want with me?"

"I want to know who you're working for. And don't say the FBI. You collected the information about my uncle's cabin for someone. Tell me who it is, and I won't hurt you."

"I'm not going to tell you anything," McCarty snarled.

"I always love it when they say that," Levi lied. "Tell me, *Travis*, did you know there are twenty-seven bones in the human hand?"

"So what?"

"So, how about we make it fifty-four?"

He grabbed McCarty's hand and squeezed. When McCarty didn't respond, Levi squeezed harder. A crack rang out and McCarty screamed.

"That's twenty-eight," Levi told him. "Shall I keep going?"

McCarty gritted his teeth but kept silent.

Levi had perfected this technique a long time ago and could break each bone in the hand individually. He had a reputation in the Family for being able to get information from any subject, willing or not. And when he had the time to spare in interrogations like this, it was his favorite technique.

There was no bloodshed and the damage was limited, easily repaired, and never fatal. And it worked almost every time.

Another crack. "Twenty-nine." Another. "Thirty. I

can do this all night. And don't forget, you have another hand, as well as two feet."

McCarty groaned and Levi could tell he was trying hard not to scream. Another crack rang out.

Levi chuckled. "Thirty-one bones. Bloody hell! I've got to hand it to you, man. You've got balls. But I have the upper hand, as well as the motivation." Another bone broke. "Thirty-two. That's *my* woman you guys are trying to sell into slavery, and I want to know who's behind it. I'll break every bloody bone in your body, if you don't tell me what I need to know. Don't think I won't." Another crack. "Thirty-three. This is fun."

"All right, all right," McCarty gasped.

Levi instantly let go of his hand, knowing that when he released the pressure, it would hurt even more. McCarty screamed.

"Come on, McCarty," Levi ordered, keeping the knife pressed to his throat. "Or we start with the other hand."

"His name is Mohammed Amal Ahasama. He's in Sydaria. That's all I know."

"Who's your contact here?"

"I don't know. When they want to talk to me, they call my cell phone. But it's a restricted number so it doesn't show up on Caller ID."

"What happens if you need to get ahold of them?"

"I put a piece of black tape on the lamp post on the corner."

"How did you know I was with Andi Merritt?"

"They called and told me you were with her and they wanted me to find out where you'd go to hide." McCarty moved his hand and groaned. "So I did a background check on you and found out John Komakov was your uncle. After that, I took a chance and called Missoula."

"You took a chance, all right. Too bad it isn't working out so well for you right now." Levi thought for a moment. "How do they pay you?"

"Cash comes to my post office box."

"Number?"

"Four twelve."

"Well, you put tape on that lamp post, and when your contact calls, you tell him I said to leave Andi alone. If I have to get the CIA involved, I will."

"You can't do that. You're bluffing!"

Levi's voice turned deadly cold. "I never bluff." He saw McCarty flinch. "And you have no idea what I'll do if Andi gets taken or hurt. I suggest you get that hand taken care of. And find another job. Because if you're still with the FBI by this time tomorrow, I'll make sure federal charges are filed against you. And don't think I can't do that, because I can. The only reason you're alive right now is because I don't kill cops, even dirty ones. After tomorrow, you'll no longer be a cop—" He leaned closer to McCarty, getting right in his face. "—so you'll be fair game. Help these buggers again, and you're dead. If you don't believe me, ask anyone in the Family. They'll tell you that I don't make threats I don't intend to carry out." Levi sheathed his knife and stepped back. As he faded out of the room, he said, "Don't make me come back here, McCarty. You'll regret it."

By the time the lights came on in McCarty's apartment, Levi was on the ground, packing up his gear. He'd call Wilson in the morning and tell him about McCarty. That way if the man decided not to quit, Wilson could handle it.

McCarty was arrogant so Levi doubted he'd resign. But Levi wouldn't go after the agent again unless he found out the man was still helping the Sydarian.

It was time to take Andi to meet Max and Tess, Levi decided. Max had forgotten more about the Middle East than Levi would ever know. If anyone had info on this Ahasama, Max would.

4:51 a.m., the estate of Jonas Demopulus:

Andi had stayed awake, waiting up for Levi, until about up two in the morning. Then she'd fallen asleep in the chair in their room. She hated sleeping alone because even though she'd told Levi she wouldn't, she was having nightmares about the two men she'd shot in Montana. If Levi had noticed, he hadn't said anything, but she was afraid the nightmares would be worse if he wasn't there.

She woke up with a start to find herself being carried to bed in his arms.

"Didn't I tell you not to wait up for me, luv?"

"Yes, but I did anyway."

"Why am I not surprised?" He placed her in the middle of the bed and kissed her senseless. "You could have been all comfortable and warm the whole time I was gone."

"I know, but I was lonely. I don't like being in a bed without you."

"Afraid the boogey man will get you?" he asked, chuckling.

"The only boogey man I know went to Springfield," she told with him a giggle. "Why do you think I was waiting up?"

"You're a bit of a devil, aren't you?" He started removing her clothes. "The boogey man's back now," he murmured. "So the only sleep you're going to get for a while is what you got in the chair."

"Promises, promises," she murmured back. "But first, tell me what happened in Springfield."

He looked surprised. "You really want to know?"

"Of course I do, silly. I know you got the information, because you always do. I know you didn't kill him, because you don't kill cops. Period. So what *did* you do?"

He watched her eyes. "I asked him if he knew that there were twenty-seven bones in the human hand and then asked him if he'd like to make it fifty-four. Then I started breaking the bones one at a time until he answered my questions." When she grinned, he looked stunned. "You think that's *funny*, do you, luv?"

"He's alive. His hand will probably mend eventually. And I bet he learned not to mess with you again." She kissed him. "How many bones did he have in his hand when you left?"

"Thirty-three."

"What a wuss!" she exclaimed. "He gave in much too quickly." She kissed him again, more desperately this time. "That's the next thing I want you to teach me—how to break the bones in a hand."

"And why would you want to learn that, luv?"

"A girl has to know how to defend herself, after all. And you never know when a trick like that will come in handy."

Laughing, he gathered her up in his arms. "You're adorable. Do you know that?"

"Thanks. But what do we do now?"

"Now I make love to you until you can't see straight, and later today we'll go see Max and Tess."

"I like the first part." She gasped as he started nibbling on her neck. "Can we start on that right now?"

"We could if you'd just shut up!"

Delighted, she giggled, but since he didn't stop what he was doing to her, she figured he didn't mind. He kissed her desperately, hungrily, using his tongue to drive her insane. Then he started tasting all over her body, his hands trailing the scorching path laid down by his tongue. She trembled.

"Damn, I love your body," he murmured against her skin. "I wanted you the first time I saw you—when you were standing in the corner, holding that stupid table, and telling me I wasn't me."

Kissing every part of him she could reach from her compromised position, she paused to laugh. "You mean the table I threw at you?" she asked. "I think the first time I realized I wanted you was when those guys started shooting at us on our way down the mountain. I looked over and saw you *grinning*." She nibbled his earlobe and made him groan. "I thought you were the sexiest man I'd ever seen."

"Hmmm. Does that mean if you ever get tired of me, I can just take you on a wild ride down a mountain and you'll be interested again?"

"I'll never get tired of you," she promised. "And you could take me on a wild ride right now if you'd just shut up and do it," she said, tossing his words back at him.

Laughing, he let his lips continue their assault. But he couldn't suppress his chuckles, so his breath felt like a percussive beat on her skin. It was incredibly erotic. Before long the only thing she was aware of was his mouth, his hands, and his tongue. She moaned as his clever fingers did new and unexpected things, his mouth finding first one nipple then the other.

He dipped one hand between her thighs and slowly slipped a finger inside her, then two, while his thumb stroked her sensitive nub. She arched her hips toward his hand until he took his fingers away and replaced them with his tongue. A cry broke from her lips—half moan, half sob.

Levi stoked the blaze until she was dizzy with heat

and exploded into a kaleidoscope of ecstasy. When the fireworks subsided and she opened her eyes, he was watching her face.

"You're even more beautiful when you come," he whispered, starting to build the passion again.

"You're just saying that because you like to watch," she answered.

He chuckled and gave her his heart-stopping grin. "That I do, luv."

Lowering his head, he started administering the carnal kisses she loved so much, his hands everywhere at once. She wanted him desperately. Could never get enough of him. He drove her higher and higher until she begged him, "Please, Levi."

He rolled on top and entered her with one sure thrust, making her complete, claiming her as his own. She arched her body to meet his thrusts until they both could last no longer and surrendered.

She cried out his name as the waves of ecstasy engulfed her.

Wrapping her arms and legs around him in a death grip, she wanted to hold him forever. When he opened his eyes and gazed into hers, the look she saw in them took her breath away.

He shifted onto his back and pulled her into his arms. "I love you, Andi," he whispered. "But I have to warn you. When this is all over and you have to make your decision, if you choose me, I'll never let you go."

Joy filled her heart. She kissed him, long and deep. "I've already made my decision. The only one I want is you. I'll never belong to anyone else."

"I'll make sure you never regret it, luv," he promised. "No matter what it takes."

9:10 a.m., the office of Levi Komakov at the estate of Jonas Demopulus:

Levi stood staring out the window at the estate gardens. He couldn't believe he'd actually told Andi that he loved her. Not that he hadn't meant it. Any doubts he'd had about that had long since fled. Still, telling her was wrong. She needed to be free of this mess, free of him, so she could examine her feelings—without the fear and pressure she was currently under—and figure out how she really felt about him. Right now, she was convinced she loved him. But how much of that was tied up in gratitude, excitement, and lust? Not to mention the fear of being kidnapped again if he wasn't there to protect her.

He could keep her, he knew. Make sure she went on believing she loved him. But that wasn't fair. It also wasn't what she needed, or what he wanted. If she stayed, he wanted her whole heart. Wanted her to love him for what he was, not for fear of what might happen if he left her unprotected. He'd have to let her go. It would likely kill him, but he'd have to cut the ties, once this was all over, and give her the freedom to choose her own way. But if she came back to him, like he'd told her this morning, he'd never let her go—*if* she came back.

Depressed, he gave a small sigh of relief when the buzz of the intercom pulled him out of his thoughts.

"Levi, you there?" Jonas asked.

Levi walked back to his desk and pressed the intercom button. "Yeah, I'm here."

"Graves is on line two. He wants to talk to you."

Levi was just about to say, "Thank you," and take the call, when his training kicked in. "Tell him I'll call him right back."

"Will do."

Levi didn't know why he was suddenly uneasy about

taking the call from Graves in his office, but he didn't question it. His gut instincts had saved his ass more times than he could count, so when his sixth sense said, *Be paranoid*, Levi listened. He grabbed his cell phone and headed for the garden. When he reached a copse of willow trees far enough from the house to be out of earshot, he punched in Graves's number. The call was answered on the first ring.

"So what did they say?" he asked, cutting off Graves's greeting.

"They're taking your advice and will make the existence of the document public, but they still want the original document retrieved. That way, even if the thieves publish a copy, they can't change anything in the original, and if *we* have the original, we can prove what the document actually said, should the thieves decide to change the copy."

"But you said the document was damning, so what's the difference?"

"It is, but it's not as bad as it could be. Or rather as bad as someone could make it be, I guess I should say."

"I see." Levi thought for a moment. "Okay, the timing on this could be critical. When do you plan to make the document public, either by publishing it or by telling the media about it?"

"Why does it matter?"

"Because if I go in to retrieve the document and the thieves find out, you don't want them getting to the media first. Your best shot at damage control is to announce the news first before they get the chance."

"True," Graves conceded. "But on the other hand, if you go in before we announce the news, they may not be expecting that. After we leak it to the media, they may be watching for you."

Levi shrugged. "You could be right. It could go either

way, and since we don't know who took it, trying to second guess them is a crap shoot." He thought for a moment. "Who, besides you, knows that *I* will be going in?"

"No one, with the exception of Jonas. I haven't told anyone else who I would be sending in and I don't intend to. I was told to get the document back. How I do that is up to me."

"Good, keep it that way. And don't talk to Jonas about this again. From this moment on, he's out of the loop." Levi paused. "Get me a substitute copy of something about the same thickness that I can exchange for the one I'm taking. Can you do that?"

"I don't see why not."

"Good. When's the deadline on the ransom?"

"We have to pay by five p.m. Mountain Time on Monday, or they go public."

"Okay, plan to leak your news to the media on Monday morning. I'll go for the document this weekend. But when you tell your higher ups when to leak the news, do not tell them when to expect the document back. In fact, tell them that you want to wait until after the deadline passes before the attempt to retrieve the document is made. Say you expect less resistance in obtaining it that way. I'll tell Jonas the same."

Graves huffed indignantly. "You think someone in the Outfit is a spy?"

"Someone found out about the document in the first place, didn't they? So what do you think?"

CHAPTER 10

6:53 p.m., the home of Max and Tess Maxwell, Williamsburg, Virginia:

Levi led Andi up the path to Max's front door. Jonas had gone overboard on clothes for Andi, and she looked stunning in a soft pink sweater-and-pants set that made her ivory skin glow and brought out the highlights in her red hair. Levi still couldn't get over how beautiful she was. But right now she seemed shy and a little nervous as she held tightly to his hand.

"It's all right, luv," he told her. "They're good friends and nice people. They don't bite."

The door opened to his knock. Tess looked out and stared for just a moment, her eyes wide. "*Levi*?" Then she threw her arms around his neck and hugged him. "Damn, it's so good to see you. I've missed you so much!"

Levi wrapped his free arm around her and buried his face in her hair. He'd missed her terribly. She'd been his best friend for years and knew him better than anyone.

"Are you manhandling my woman?" Max called from behind her. "Or is she manhandling you?"

"I think it's a bit of both actually," Levi said, laughing, as Tess released him and stepped back so they could enter.

Levi made the introductions then Max led them into the library where he poured each of them a glass of wine. Levi had never seen Tess look more beautiful. She was glowing. Her long, golden-red hair poured over her back and shoulders and formed a cloud around her face, while her intelligent, dark-gray eyes sparkled with mirth. He watched her carefully for a few moments then looked at Max. He looked smug, more so than usual.

"Tess," Levi said, "are you pregnant?"

She laughed. "Three months. I figured you'd guess."

She started at him for a moment then, looking between him and Andi, she smiled. As perceptive as always, she glanced at Max then back at Levi with a question in her eyes. Levi nodded, knowing she understood.

She stood up with her wine glass in her hand. "Andi, would you like come with me to see the garden? We've done a lot of work on it. I finally got Max to help me and it looks terrific. Bring your wine."

Levi squeezed Andi's hand for encouragement. She kissed his cheek and stood up. "Thanks, I'd love to."

The two girls went out the french doors, leaving him alone in the library with Max.

"What's up, Levi?" Max asked immediately. "I know you well enough to know you wouldn't show up unannounced unless there was trouble."

Levi watched through the french doors, until the girls were out of sight, then explained about Andi, her father, and the oil baron, telling Max what he'd learned from McCarty.

Max looked grave. "Yes, I know who he is," he said. "Ahasama's not one of my favorite people. He's a clan leader—arrogant, filthy rich, and he thinks he's above the law."

He was quiet for several minutes and, knowing how Max worked, Levi didn't interrupt him.

Finally, Max sighed. "I can contact some people for you and see if we can get him to back off. The problem is he doesn't take threats seriously. He thinks, with his diplomatic immunity, that he's untouchable. I'll bet you good money that Andi's not the first woman this has happened to. She may be the most beautiful, but I'm sure she's not the first." Max studied Levi a moment. "You really love her, don't you?" When Levi nodded without hesitation, Max sighed again. "Then you probably don't want to hear this, but I would say, as beautiful as she is, Ahasama is probably going to use her as leverage."

"Andi heard the same thing from the kidnappers before I rescued her, but even the FBI can't tell me what it means as far as the oil baron is concerned. They thought it might have something to do with the loan shark who wanted in on Jonas's organization."

"Well, I can't tell you what the kidnappers meant," Max told him. "But to me, it has nothing to do with anything in the States. Because she's so beautiful as well as an American, Ahasama's likely planning to offer her to other clan leaders as leverage for favors or power over the other clans. He may even just charge a fee and use her as a prostitute. These perverts seem to think that by raping these women they are somehow 'screwing America,' so to speak."

Levi was stunned. The thought of Andi in a situation like that filled him with rage and anguish. Her laughter floated in from the garden, and he clenched his fists, trying to retain his composure. "She can't be subjected to something like that, Max! It would destroy her. I *have* to keep her safe. I even took her to Pierre's, so that if they do take her, I'll know where she is. But if he takes her to Sydaria, what am I going to do?"

"In a case like that, I think I can get authorization for some drastic action. I'll try to threaten first and see if that works, but don't get your hopes up. Even if you married her, it wouldn't stop him. They'd just kill you before they took her, and then there'd be no one to rescue her."

"And I can't let her make a decision like that now when she needs me for protection," Levi protested. "It would be disastrous if, after this is all over, she feels like she was forced into it because she's afraid."

"Levi," Max scolded gently. "Do you really think Andi is going to change her mind? The way she looks at you and the way you look at her tells me nothing's going to change the way either of you feel. I'm not suggesting that you marry her now, but only because it won't help."

"I know, Max. But it's not ethical to ask her to make a decision like that when she has a gun to her head."

"You and your ethics." Max shook his head. "What about her father? You're going to have to take him out. You know that, don't you?"

"I was planning to have a talk with him at some point, but I didn't think I would actually have to kill him. What makes you think so?"

"He's her father. I'm no Middle Eastern expert—I'm paramilitary, not an analyst—so I could be wrong, but the way I understand it, if Ahasama does grab her and her father's alive and signs the clan papers of marriage, it will be even harder to get her back. If he's dead before Ahasama takes her, then to the authorities in Sydaria, she's a free agent and has to sign the papers herself. I doubt I can get authorization for an operation to go get her if her father's alive and signs the papers, even though she's of legal age and was taken against her will."

"*Bloody hell!*"

"I totally agree."

"How do I tell her that I have to kill her father? She's accepted that she'll never see him again, but this?"

"Do you have to tell her?" Max got up and went to

his desk. He unlocked a drawer and pulled what looked like a large ballpoint pen out of a box of several. "I'm not supposed to have these, but the scientists held a meeting in my office one day when I was teaching a class and left these by mistake." He winked at Levi and tossed him the pen. "It's a lethal dose of fast-acting, non-traceable poison. Even if it shows up at autopsy, it is so unusual they'll probably figure a Russian did it, since they invented it."

"Thanks." Levi examined the pen. Max walked over and showed him how to use it. Levi fiddled with it until he was sure he understood. "I still have to tell her, Max. She's been lied to her whole life by everyone she's ever met. If I start lying to her now, I'm no better than the rest of them."

"Well, that's up to you. But don't wait too long. We don't know when Ahasama'll take her." Max looked at Levi's face. "I know you'll try to stop him, Levi, but even you aren't invincible."

"I need to find a way to keep him from taking her at all."

"Again, I think the only way is to kill him. If he'd never seen her picture, you might accomplish it, but now that he has, he'll stop at nothing. All we can do is to prepare for the worst."

Levi sighed and held up the pen. "Speaking of the Russians, I have another problem. A very important document belonging to the—a client—has been stolen and stashed in the Russian embassy in Washington, DC. I need to find out for certain if it's there, and if it is, I need to get it back. Any help you can give me?"

Max's eyebrows shot up. "You taking on private clients now? That doesn't sound like you."

"No, this is repayment for the favor of stopping Nick Demopulus three years ago when he was putting out contracts to have Tess killed. I couldn't get to him while he was in prison, so I had to ask for help, remember?"

"How could I forget?" Max glanced out at the garden, as if to make certain that his wife was all right. "I almost lost her several times back then." He got up and went to the phone. "Let me see what I can do." He talked to someone for several minutes and, when he hung up, excitement shone from his eyes. "I spoke with our contact in their embassy and—"

"You have a contact in their embassy?"

"Of course. If we hadn't already had one before this mess in the Ukraine started, we'd have gotten one somehow." Max shrugged. "It's the CIA, Levi. It's what we do. You know that. Anyway, the document is there. Or at least, there's a document in the ambassador's office safe that is related to 'some group in organized crime.' I assume that's the one you want."

Levi chuckled. "'*Some* group in organized crime,' huh? Yeah, I imagine that's it. So did this contact suggest any ways of getting the document *out* of the ambassador's safe?"

"As a matter of fact, he did. He doesn't believe Mother Russia's faithful servants should be catering to thieves, especially not when relations between our two countries are so strained. But, as the request to hold onto the document came from the ambassador of an ally, the Russian ambassador didn't feel he could refuse, or so the contact thinks."

"*Another* ambassador is involved? Did your contact say who that was?"

"He doesn't know. The whole thing is very hush, hush. His boss passed it off as a practical joke, but our guy wasn't convinced. He wants the document out of his embassy before this 'organized crime group—'" Max made finger quotes in the air. "—finds out where it is and makes its location public. So if he helps us get it out, we can't tell anyone where it was."

Levi snorted. "Doesn't he know that the thieves told the Outfit where it is? How else did he think we knew it was there?"

"We're the CIA," Max repeated with a chuckle. "We know everything."

"Yeah, right. So what's the plan?"

Hesitating, Max cleared his throat. "Before we get into that, what are you going to do with Andi while you're off 'returning favors'?"

"Take her with me. What else can I do?" When Max blinked and opened his mouth, Levi held up a hand. "The timing's too suspicious, Max. While I don't think the Outfit is involved, I do think someone who *is* involved is pulling their strings. And if this is a ploy to get me away from her so they can snatch her again, I don't intend to fall for it. Besides, she's an expert hacker. She claims that if I can get her some special equipment…a code breaker and a jammer, I think she said…she can hack into the toughest security system and shut it down. Of course, she wasn't talking about an embassy at the time, but it should work for that too."

Max frowned. "I see your point. Of course, you know that if you're wrong and this really *is* just a coincidence, you're taking her into a potentially dangerous situation for no good reason."

"I know. But I don't think so. Not only don't I believe in coincidences, but if we didn't take Andi, we'd have to take someone else to hack into the security system, because the last time I checked, neither you nor I had that as an MOS."

"They teach it at The Farm," Max said, grinning, "but not to paramilitary guys like me."

"I didn't think so. So, again, what's the plan?"

Max's grin widened. "Well, it so happens that the ambassador's giving a reception tomorrow night…"

Sunday, April 21st, 7:15 p.m., the Russian Embassy, Washington, DC:

Andi flipped back the hair of her long black wig and grinned over at Levi. "I can't believe we're going to a reception at the Russian Embassy in Washington, DC," she gushed. "Not only that, but you're taking me with you on a heist."

Levi grimaced as he made the turn into the embassy driveway and stopped at the guard station. He said nothing as he passed their forged invitation through the window for inspection. The man glanced at it, handed it back, and waved the car on.

"Let's just keep that little tidbit to ourselves, okay, luv?" he whispered as they drove away from the guard. "Besides, you said if I got you to a computer, you could hack into anything, remember? Well, I hope you meant that, because we're going to put it to the test. The security surrounding the ambassador's office, not to mention the safe, is first rate."

"If you got me the equipment I asked for, you have nothing to fear," she whispered as they were waved to a stop by a valet.

The valet came around to Andi's side, opened the door, and held out his hand. At Levi's nod, Andi took the offered hand and stepped out of the car. She glanced around at the huge building. "Now what?" she asked as Levi came up beside her and offered his arm.

"Now we go to the party," he said and led her toward the entrance. When they were out of earshot of the valet, he added, "Then we'll meet up with our doppelgangers, and the real fun begins."

Andi swallowed, trying to calm her nerves. She knew that Max and Tess had arrived at the embassy earlier, disguised as employees of the company hired to cater the reception. She also knew she and Levi would be switching disguises with them, but beyond that Levi hadn't shared much of the plan, at least not with her. All he'd told her was that they needed Max and Tess to come in with the catering company employees because Levi thought his British accent would attract too much attention, and he also didn't think Andi could hold it together during the harsh interrogation the Russians would subject the catering staff to when they arrived. Max and Tess were also bringing in the needed equipment. How they were doing this, Andi didn't know. But Levi assured it would be fine. She figured he didn't tell her any more than that because he didn't want to frighten her. But she was plenty frightened anyway. While she trusted him to know what to do, she prayed that she wouldn't let him down when it came time for her part in the scheme.

Once inside, Levi guided her to the reception room with ease.

"Have you been here before," she asked. When he shook his head, she added, "Then how—"

"Blueprints," he whispered. "I memorized the floor plan."

They mingled with a few people and shook hands with the ambassador, making sure they were noticed. Then Levi signaled that it was time to go to work.

"Excuse me," Andi said to a passing waiter. "Can you tell me where I can find the ladies' room?"

"Out the door and down the hall to the right, miss."

"I'll be back in a minute," she told Levi. "I just need to powder my nose."

"I'll wait for you over there by the buffet table," he

said. "Don't be too long."

Giving him a quick kiss on the cheek, she hurried off to the ladies room. A woman was leaving just as she arrived, and Andi hoped the restroom was now empty except for Tess, or this was going to be difficult. When she slipped into the room, the only one there was a blonde maid, scrubbing one of the toilets. A small cart stood in the middle of the room.

The maid looked up. It was Tess. "Thank heavens," she said in a hushed voice. "At last. I feel like I've been scrubbing toilets for an hour." She pulled an *Out of Order* sign from the cart, hung it on the outside doorknob, and locked the door. "Quickly, give me your wig and your dress."

Andi pulled off her wig and slipped out of her dress. She handed them, along with her jewelry, to Tess, who passed her the maid's wig and uniform. Once dressed again, they checked their reflections in the mirror. Andi thought she looked better in the blonde wig than the black one, but Tess seemed to look stunning in anything.

"Your equipment's in the bottom of the cart," Tess told her. "Wait exactly fifteen minutes after I leave, and then head for the fourth floor. Levi will meet you at the third door on the right after you leave the service elevator. If he's not there when you get there, wait five minutes then get back here STAT. If something's gone wrong, there'll be an abort note behind the tank of this last toilet."

"Oh, crap. Do you think it will? Go wrong, I mean?"

"No. Max and Levi know what they're doing. They're good at it. But part of being good at it is having a backup plan in case you have to abort. So don't worry. If you don't want to play maid, you can leave the door locked, but fifteen minutes is a long time and someone might notice."

Andi shook her head. "No, that's okay. I'll scrub the sink and get myself into the part. Levi said he'd meet you at the buffet table. When you get there, he'll go to the men's room and switch places with Max."

"Got it." Tess unlocked and opened the door, handed Andi the sign, and winked. "See you on the flipside."

With that, she was gone, leaving Andi alone. Alone and scared to death. Her heart racing—and pounding so loudly, she was sure the embassy's security guards could hear it—she checked her watch. Fifteen minutes seemed like forever.

Levi waited until Tess joined him at the buffet table. "Perfect," he murmured in her ear as he kissed her cheek. "You look just like her."

"Max is waiting for you in the men's room. Be quick."

He squeezed her hand. Though he knew he should be going, he had to ask, "How's Andi holding up?"

"She's fine. She'll hold it together. Now go."

He gave her hand one last squeeze and raised his voice. "I'll be right back. Wait for me here."

When she nodded, he turned and headed for the men's room. It was empty. He cleared his throat and a stall door creaked open.

"About time," Max grumbled. He'd already stripped to the waist. "Here," he said, handing Levi his waiter's shirt and vest. "Since I'm taller than you, we'll have to wear our own pants."

"Then aren't we lucky the waiters are all wearing similar ones?"

"That's why I chose these for us, dumbass." Max slipped on Levi's shirt, tie, and jacket. "Your hair's a little darker than mine, but since we're crashing the party and no one knows us, I doubt anyone will notice."

"At least the women look the same," Levi pointed out. "And beautiful, so no one will pay *us* much attention."

Max grinned. "Yeah, ain't it a kick? Best cover I ever had." He checked his watch. "You have three minutes to get your ass to the fourth floor and meet Andi." Clapping Levi on the shoulder, he added, "Watch your six, man."

Levi followed Max out and made his way quickly to the service elevator. Andi was just entering the lift.

"Hold the door, please," he called softly.

She turned, but neither recognition, nor the relief she must have felt, showed on her face. He didn't think he could've been more proud.

"Certainly, sir," she replied calmly and put her hand on the door to hold it open.

They didn't speak again until they were inside the elevator with the door closed. Levi scanned the lift, looking for cameras or microphones. Not seeing any, he winked.

But she didn't break character. "Which floor, sir?"

"Fourth."

She nodded and pushed the button. The service elevator slowly moved upward. When the door opened, Andi pushed her cart out into the hall. Levi took her arm and guided her to an unlocked office. Once inside, he closed the door, locked it, and wedged a chair under the handle.

"Whose office is this?" Andi asked.

"I don't know his name, but he died last month and his replacement isn't due in until next week," Levi told her, pulling a dark blue, turtle-necked T-shirt out of the cart and slipping it on over his white waiter's shirt. "You can set up your equipment using that computer on the desk. The username and password have already been entered—or at least they were supposed to have been."

"So does that mean that if our break-in is discovered, no one will get into trouble because the dead guy's username and password were used?"

"What are they going to do to a dead man? Kill him again?"

"They *killed* him?" she asked, horrified.

He shoved his hands through his hair as his breath huffed out in a helpless laugh. "No, no, luv. He died of a heart attack. He was getting up in age some and overweight as well. He also smoked heavily, from what our contact told Max. I only meant that since he's dead, there's nothing they can do to him, even if they do discover that his username and password were used to hack into the system."

"Oh. But don't they do something to a person's family sometimes?"

"Not to worry, luv. They don't do that so much anymore, and even when they did, it was to put pressure on a man by threatening his family. And as this guy is already dead, applying pressure's a moot point."

"I guess that makes sense," she said with a little sigh of relief. Of course it was silly to be worrying about the consequences to some dead guy she didn't even know and never would. But she didn't want anyone to get hurt because of her. "Still, I'd better make extra sure that I slip in and out with no one the wiser."

"That'd be best."

Andi pulled her equipment from the bottom of the maid's cart and set it on the desk. Sitting down in the chair, she attached the USB cable from the code breaker to the back of the desktop computer and plugged the jammer into the code breaker. Then she wiggled the computer's mouse to wake it up. When the computer came to life, she began hacking into the building's security system. As she worked, Levi pulled his gear from the cart and began to assemble it.

"Let me know when you've breached the main security," he said as he put on what he called his vacuum pack. "I don't want to bugger the window until you have."

"Almost there," she said, her fingers dancing over the keyboard as her code breaking equipment cut through layer after layer of complicated security measures. "By the time you get set up, I should have it done."

He looked over her shoulder as he pulled a large bag from the cart and slung the strap across his chest. "Amazing." Shaking his head, he kissed her hair. "You are truly amazing. We could've used you in the SAS."

She flushed with pleasure. No one had ever called her amazing before. "Almost got it. Just a…" She pushed a button on the jammer. "There! The security system is off line. I've bypassed the main systems and just shut down the alarms on the floor the ambassador's office is on. Hopefully that will keep anyone from noticing. And if they do, they'll just think it's a glitch." She held up her hands, fingers crossed. "I hope."

Levi kissed the top of her head again. "I repeat. Amazing."

He moved to the window, took a glass cutter from a small pouch clipped to his belt, and cut a single vertical line in the glass on the left side of the window.

"Why are you cutting the glass?" she asked.

"Like the windows in most high-rise office buildings with air conditioning, these windows don't open. So I'm making a door. Also, but cutting a hole in the window, I won't set off the alarms like I would if the window was opened or broken," he explained as he pulled two hinges from his pouch, stripped off the paper from the adhesive backing, and stuck them over the cut he had made, one close to the top and the other toward the bottom. Next he made two horizontal cuts at the top and bottom of the first cut, followed by one more vertical cut on the right, to form a rectangle. Stripping the paper from the adhesive backing of a small handle and latch set, he stuck that on the glass over the vertical cut on the right side. Then he went all around the rectangle, thumping the glass next to the cuts with his fist. A series of little popping noises sounded as the glass rectangle separated from the rest of the window. Levi turned the handle, eased his "door" open, and peered out. "Perfect." He came back to the cart, removed another little pouch, and opened it. "Here," he said, handing her an earpiece. "Put this in your ear." Putting a second one in his own ear, he added, "Testing, one, two, I love you."

"Three, four, I love you more," she replied with a grin. "Now what?"

He bent down and took her mouth with his, kissing her long and hard. "Now—as much as I would rather stay here and make love to you—I have to go to work." He moved the handcart out of sight of the office door by shoving it into a small alcove between the far corner and a row of filing cabinets. He messed around with it for a minute, but she couldn't see what he was doing. Then he walked back to the desk and, taking her hand, pulled her to her feet. "Come with me to the window and lower the blinds once I'm through. Then once you disarm the security in the ambassador's office, let me know, and I'll break into the safe."

Easing his upper torso backward out the window, he attached the top two feet of his vacuum pack to the outside wall and activated the system. Then he maneuvered the rest of his body out, attaching the two bottom feet of his pack to the wall. With a wink, he pushed the door closed and started climbing.

Andi waited until he was out of sight then lowered the blinds. She looked around the office. With the cart stuffed into the shadows of the corner alcove and the blinds lowered, the only visible evidence of their "invasion" into the office was her hacking equipment on the desk, and the light from the monitor.

She couldn't do anything about the monitor, at least until she was done, but she moved the hacking equipment to the left of the monitor and placed a stack of books in front of it, careful not to loosen the cables. That way, at least, it would be out of sight of the door, and someone would have to come farther into the room before they could see it. She wasn't sure why she was hiding it, but as Levi always said, attention to detail…

Levi climbed the building's wall, moving laterally first until he was well hidden in the shadows around the corner. Then, scaling upward to the ambassador's office, he climbed over the railing of the small balcony with french doors on the side of the office, out of sight of any arriving guests and the valets greeting them. It was unlikely that any of them would happen to glance up, and even if they did, it was dark enough by now that would be almost impossible to see him in his dark clothes picking the lock on the doors. And this way, he wouldn't need to cut the glass and announce the break-in. He knew the gig would be up as soon as the dead man's replacement arrived from Russia and raised the blinds in his office on the fourth floor. But that wouldn't be until next week, by which time any number of people could have come and gone in the embassy building, so the number of suspects would be impossible for the Russians to narrow down.

"Where are we at, luv?" he asked softly.

"Just about there. This one's a little trickier. Give me another thirty seconds. Where are you?"

"Just about to pick the lock on the french doors," he said, pulling a set of lock picks out of his pocket.

"Oh, well…there we go. Motion detectors and infrared sensors inside the office are shut down. I'll wait until you get through and then start the system up again."

"Thanks, luv. I'll be quick."

Levi picked the lock, eased the doors open, and slipped inside the office. According to their contact, the safe was behind the bookcase with the bust of President Putin on the top shelf against the far wall. Levi inspected the bookcase, triggered the catch, and guided the shelves away from the wall on their hinges. Pulling a laser and a spray can out of the pouch clipped to his belt, he sprayed the keypad on the safe then shot it with the laser to see which letters had been pressed numerous times.

"E-F-S-Y," he told Andi, who ran them through her equipment.

"Okay, just a moment. Here we go. Are these words in Russian?" she asked.

"I doubt it. They probably used an American company so the words would mostly likely be in English."

"Well, this makes no sense, then, because none of these are words, just letters.

"What are my choices?"

She read off a series of four letter combinations, ending with, "…Y-E-S-F, S-E-Y-F, and E-S-F-Y."

"It's S-E-Y-F."

"How do you know?"

"That spells safe in Russian."

"Oh."

He keyed in the letters. When the safe clicked, he

swung the door open and ruffled through the stack of documents until he found the one he was looking for. He pulled it out and stuffed it into his chest bag, putting the substitute he'd gotten from Graves in its place.

He'd just closed the safe when he heard voices approaching the door. Shoving the bookcase back into place against the wall, Levi sprinted for the french doors. He heard a key in the lock. Flicking the lock on the french doors, he pulled them softly closed behind him, activated his vacuum pack, and slid over the railing, onto the wall beside the balcony. Scuttling as quietly as possible out of sight underneath it, he held his breath and waited.

Thinking of Andi and, wondering if they were checking that office too, he whispered, "Andi, are you okay?" as the french doors opened with a soft click and footsteps sounded above him on the balcony.

"Levi," she breathed. "There's someone at the door. They've unlocked it and are trying to get in. I guess my hacking wasn't as invisible as I hoped."

The footsteps halted at the railing, and Levi assumed they were scanning the grounds. When the footsteps sounded again then faded, and the door closed with a soft click, he breathed a sigh of relief and began his descent.

"They must be doing an office-by-office search. Shut down the computer, grab your equipment, and meet me at the window. I'm on my way."

"What about the cart?"

"Leave it! The chair I wedged under the handle won't hold them for long, and I don't want you inside that room when they break in."

Fear clutching at his heart, he moved as quickly as he could—and still avoid falling—desperate to reach Andi. If she got hurt or arrested, he'd never forgive himself. *Max was right. I never should have involved her in this.*

When he reached the fourth floor office, he could

hear them slamming into the door, trying to force it open. Andi was chewing on her lip, waiting between the blinds and the window, with the glass door open and her hacking equipment clutched to her chest. He took her gear and stuffed it into his chest bag. "Lean out," he ordered. "Wrap your arms around my neck and your legs around my waist and don't look down."

She looked as if she was about to argue when a crash sounded. The office door shook violently and one of the chair legs splintered.

Swallowing hard, she wrapped herself around him, just like he'd told her, and buried her face in his neck. Levi pushed the glass door closed to buy them some time and headed for the deeper shadows at the corner, before beginning his descent.

Max checked his watch for the tenth time in five minutes. "They should be back by now," he murmured to Tess. "I wonder what's keeping them."

"Uh-oh. Look," she whispered back. "Over there by the door."

Max turned to see a security guard, with one hand to his earpiece, rush out of the room. "Uh-oh is right. Looks like something didn't go as planned."

"What can we do?" she asked, panic coloring her voice.

"Let me think." He scanned the room. All the security guards were heading for the door. "Faint," he hissed.

"What?"

"We need to create a diversion. So moan loudly and faint."

"Okay," she said, sounding a bit uncertain. "But you'd better catch me. I don't want to hurt the baby."

"No sweat. Don't you worry."

Tess sighed. Then, slapping the back of her hand to her forehead, she moaned loudly and started to crumple. Max caught her before she hit the floor.

"Help," he cried at the top of his voice. "Is there a doctor in the house? My wife's pregnant and she just collapsed."

Bedlam erupted. Several men and a couple of women started running toward him, shoving guests and guards out of the way.

The remaining guards in the room were speaking rapidly into their radios, seemingly uncertain as to whether they should leave to help with the security breach or stay to help with the pregnant woman. Meanwhile the rest of the guests—human nature being what it was—were surging forward, curious to find out what was going on, and pushing the guards with them, effectively cutting them off from the door.

"Let me see her," said the first man to reach Max. "I'm a pediatrician." He checked the pulse in her neck and placed a hand on her forehead. "Her pulse is strong and she doesn't have a fever. Has this ever happened before?"

"No, but she's only three months along and her morning sickness has been pretty bad."

On cue, Tess moaned.

"She's coming around," Max said, throwing some desperate relief into his voice. "Honey, can you hear me? Answer me, sweetheart. Are you all right?"

She moaned again.

"She's probably just overcome with the stress of being newly pregnant," the doctor said. "It's rather warm in here as well. I suggest you take her home and put her to bed. And have her seen by her regular doctor as soon as possible."

"Thank you. I will."

Max shifted Tess in his arms and carried her toward the door. The crowd parted before him.

"You can put me down now," she said as they waited for the valet to bring Levi's rental car around.

He grinned at her. "Well, I suppose I could, but why should I? I love holding you like this. Besides," he whispered as the valet drove up in the car. "You're going to be angry about the next part of the plan, so I might not get to hold you again for a while."

He set her carefully in the passenger seat, buckled her seatbelt, and kissed her quickly on the lips.

She glared at him. "What's the next part of the plan?" she demanded as they drove away.

"I'm going to have to park on this side of the gate long enough for Levi and Andi to get to the car from wherever they are right now. Which means you're going to have to create another diversion."

"Oh, no," she groaned. "You mean I have to—" She broke off and buried her head in her hands.

"Yep." Max patted her shoulder. "For as long as it takes."

"You couldn't just tell them we had car trouble?"

"Sorry, babe. But if I told them that, they'd just come and try to help. No, a pregnant woman puking her guts out on the pavement is the best way I know to keep everyone as far away as possible."

CHAPTER 11

When they reached the ground, Levi hugged Andi tightly, immensely relieved that he'd gotten her out unscathed. Then, taking her hand, he pulled her into the cover of some shrubbery. "So far, so good," he said as he took off the vacuum pack and stuffed it into his bag.

"What now?" she asked.

Levi scanned the area. "No guards searching the grounds yet, so they probably haven't figured out that we're not still inside."

"But if they found the little door you cut in the window, won't they come to search outside?"

"They might not have found it yet," he said. "I closed the door and the blinds are down. Chances are good they'll focus on the maid's cart in the corner, once they break through the door, and won't think to look out the window. After all, with the blinds closed, it's not immediately obvious that the window's been breached."

"The cart!" she gasped. "If they check the cart, they'll get our fingerprints. And yours are probably on record with the CIA."

"They are. But that information's classified and won't ping the police or FBI databases. And we don't have to worry about that, anyway."

"We don't?"

"No, luv. I wiped down the cart when I put it in the corner," he said, quickly brushing his lips over hers.

"Oh. So that's what you were doing. Okay, then how do we get out of here? Just walk out the front gate and hail a cab?"

He chuckled. "There are guards at the gates, remember? And a fence around the whole perimeter." He shook his head. "No, we'll have to depend on Max and Tess."

"But they're inside at the party."

"We've been gone too long, luv. Max is bound to know that something's gone wrong. And if the guards have been alerted to search the building, he'll know to get Tess out and wait for us at the gate."

Andi craned her neck, peering through the darkness. "Can you see them? Are they there?"

"Relax, luv. We can't see the gate from here, but they'll be there. And if they aren't, we'll stay out of sight and wait until they come. Now, follow me. Quietly."

Hugging the deepest shadows, they made their way toward the exit gate—and its guards—moving through the vegetation like ghosts. When they were close enough to see the gate clearly through the growing darkness, they both stopped and stared.

"Oh no," Andi gasped. "Something's wrong with Tess!"

Before she could break cover and run to Tess, Levi grabbed her arm, holding her back. "Don't blow it now, luv. We need to make our way over to those bushes close to the car without being spotted."

"But Tess—"

"I'm sure she's fine, luv. It's probably just a diversion." At least he hoped it was. "Let's just get there as quickly as possible so we can find out for sure."

Taking her hand, he started moving again, making

his way across the grounds to the car. When they were level with it, he put his hands to his mouth and made a bird call to let Max know they were close.

"Thank heavens, you're here," Max whispered. "We were beginning to worry."

"'Bout time you got here," Tess growled, straightening up and rubbing her throat. She turned to Max. "How do we get them into the car without them being seen?"

"Well, first I'll open the back door," he said, moving around the car. After opening the rear car door, he crawled onto the back seat. "And pretend I'm searching for a bottle of water. Nope, not here."

He backed out of the car, leaving the door open, straightened, then took Tess's arm, and led her around to the trunk. Opening it, he pulled out a bottle of water and handed it to her.

"Here, rinse your mouth out with this."

"Thanks," she said then made a big production of sipping and spitting the water into the bushes.

Chuckling, Levi grabbed Andi's hand and pulled her in a crouch toward the car. Once in the backseat, he squeezed onto the floor and pulled Andi down with him.

Max closed the trunk and the back door then helped Tess into the front passenger seat.

As he got behind the wheel, he said quietly, "Well, did you get it? Or were Tess and I acting like idiots for nothing?"

"Of course, we got it. What do you take me for? No, don't answer that," Levi ordered as Max drove through the gate and onto the street.

Max chuckled and waved at the guard.

"And *you* may have been acting like an idiot," Levi continued, grinning, "but Andi and I thought Tess was brilliant."

Monday, April 22nd, 3:10 p.m., the Sydarian Embassy:

"Did you see the news from Tarpon Springs this morning?" Jamar snapped into the phone. It was all he could do not to throw the device against the wall.

"Of course, I did. But that doesn't necessarily mean Komakov won't try to retrieve the document. The Outfit can't be sure we won't still make it public."

"The document has already *been* retrieved, you idiot! The ambassador told me this morning that there was a break-in at the embassy last night. Someone took the document from his safe and replaced it with a lookalike."

"You're sure?"

"Of course I'm sure," Jamar snarled. "When I saw the news, I called the Russian embassy and talked with the ambassador. He told me there had been a break-in of sorts, but he thought they had been foiled and nothing was taken. So I asked him to check the document in his safe and call me back. When he did, it was to say that the document we gave him was gone and another had been put in its place."

"But how—when—I mean, what did he do with the package? He didn't leave her at the estate."

"How should I know?" Jamar could hear something cracking as his hand tightened on the phone. He grimaced and forced his fingers to loosen their grip. "He could have taken her with him on the heist for all I know. I only know we *still* don't have our merchandise and Ahasama is getting very impatient."

"All right. All right. Don't panic. She's staying at the estate now, so I'll alert her father. Maybe he can figure out how to get her back into his custody. Give me twenty-four hours."

"Maybe we should just kill this Komakov and be done with it," Jamar suggested.

"No! That's the worst thing you could do," the voice on the other end of the line said in a panic. "Komakov's ex-SAS *and* ex-CIA, and from what I hear, he still has a lot of friends in both organizations. You take him out and you'll have a war on your hands. Believe me, it isn't worth it."

Jamar sighed. If it was not one thing, it was another. "Very well, brother," he conceded. "Twenty-four hours. But I want results this time."

Tuesday, April 23rd, 6:55 a.m., the estate of Jonas Demopulus:

Andi grabbed Levi's hand as he started to get out of bed. "Levi? Wait, please."

"What is it, luv?"

"That's what I want to know. You've been so quiet lately, ever since we said goodbye to Max and Tess on Sunday night. And your face—Tess said you get that blank look when there's something you have to do that you don't want to do, or when there's bad news you don't want to talk about. She told me not to worry, but I do." She ran her fingers down his bare chest. "Talk to me, Levi. Please tell me what's wrong."

"Tess knows me too bloody well," he growled. "And it sounds like she talked to you quite enough already." He leaned down to give her a searing kiss. "What else did she tell you?"

"Quid pro quo," Andi said with a breathless giggle. "Just like with Wilson. If I talk to you, you have to talk to me."

"You won't like hearing it."

"I still want to know."

Levi stared into her eyes for a long moment while she waited, holding her breath. Finally, he sighed. "First, let me ask you a question. If you had to do something to help keep me safe, but you knew it would hurt me if you told me about it, what would you do?"

What's he talking about? Andi wondered. He couldn't be thinking about leaving her because there was no way he could do that and have her not know about it. As long as it wasn't that, she could handle it. She met his eyes and saw the pain he'd stopped trying to hide. But there was more than just pain, there was fear, too.

She didn't understand. What could he possibly have to do that would cause pain and worry in this strong man? Something that would help keep her safe? Something that would hurt—

The light dawned and she gasped. "You're going to kill my father, aren't you?"

She saw the truth flicker in his eyes before he could conceal it.

"Why do you think that?"

"You just confirmed it," she told him. "But what else would cause the pain and worry I see in your eyes?"

"And if I did?"

"Can you tell me why?"

Andi listened in horror as Levi recounted what Max had said. Tears filled her eyes as she realized what a monster her father was. How could Levi really love her when she came from someone so evil, someone who would sell her into a life like that?

When he saw the tears, he pulled her into his arms and held her tightly. "Don't cry, luv. I'm so sorry for all this. I thought about not telling you and just doing it, but you've been lied to so much already. And I just couldn't. I need your trust too much to lie to you."

"That's not why I'm crying," she sniffed. She stared

at her hands, afraid to look him in the eyes. "How can you love me, knowing where I come from?"

"*That's* what's bothering you?" he asked, his voice filled with relief. "Andi, I wouldn't care if *Hitler* was your father." When she kept her eyes down, he said, "Luv, please look at me." He waited until she complied then captured her gaze with his. "I love you. I don't care who your father is. The monster that is now Darren Merritt is not your father. Your father is the man your mother loved, the man who conceived you, the man he was before he became the monster he is now. Your father died when the monster took over." He kissed her tears away. "I love you and I always will. If you never trust me on anything else, please trust me on this."

"I do trust you."

"Then believe me when I say I love you." He kissed her again, setting her on fire.

"I just don't understand how you can feel that way," she breathed when he finally let her up for air.

"Let me see if I understand what you're saying. You don't understand how I could love the most marvelous, beautiful, and fascinating creature I've ever met. You think I should throw her back into the pond just because she has a prick for a father." When she laughed and he flashed his rakish grin, she thought her bones would melt. He kissed her again. "Is that right? Because if it is, I'm going to have to refute that common sense you told me you had."

He stroked her cheek with a forefinger. "I remember the first time I did this on our way to Idaho. Your skin was so soft, it was all I could do not to moan. But from the way you glared at me, I thought you were going to bite me."

"That was when I was threatening to report you to the authorities, wasn't it?" When he nodded, she giggled.

"It was just an act. I didn't want you to know how much you turned me on."

"Does this mean you don't want the restraining order keeping me away from you?" he asked, pushing her back down and lying beside her so he could kiss her neck.

"No way," she moaned. "I love you, Levi."

"And I love you." He rested his cheek against hers and just held her quietly for a long moment. "What about your father?"

She stared at the ceiling. "Like you said, the monster already killed him. I have no problem with you killing the monster. He's evil."

"If there was any other way, luv, I'd take it, but I can't see one. I doubt even threatening or torturing him would stop this. I don't know what else to do."

"Levi, he tried to *sell* me to be some rich Arab's sex slave. He knows me. He knows it would destroy me, that I would probably kill myself rather than submit. He doesn't care. He arranged to have me kidnapped by guys that fought about who got to rape me first. And I don't imagine I'm the first woman from the Family he's sold to human traffickers. What gives him the right to live after what he's done?" She tilted her head and looked him in the eyes. "Even if we sent him to prison, it wouldn't stop him signing the papers or giving permission."

"No, for twenty-five million dollars, he'd still find a way," Levi said.

"Then as far as I'm concerned, it's self-defense. I mean, even if this wasn't about me, he needs to be stopped. Twenty-five million can buy a lot of power and it makes me shudder to think how he'd use it. Killing him's really the only way."

"I'm grateful you feel that way. I was afraid you'd hate me."

"Not a chance."

He pulled her head back to him and started kissing her neck again. "What else did Tess tell you about me?"

Andi hesitated then decided to tell him *almost* everything. "She told me that while she loved you more than anyone in the world except Max, the two of you had never been lovers. She said you were the best friend she'd ever had. That she could see how much you loved me, and she was happy for us. She said if I trusted you, you would never betray me, and that you were the most honorable man she'd ever known. And—" She stopped to moan as his tongue tickled her ear.

"Remind me to thank her for that," he whispered. "And what?"

"And she knew without a single doubt that, no matter what happened, you would overcome any obstacles and do whatever you had to do in order to find me and get me back."

His tongue left her ear and moved onto more erotic territory. "Like I said, luv, Tess knows me very well."

CHAPTER 12

Levi left the bedroom an hour later, a satisfied grin on his face and his mind filled with a fierce determination to find a way to keep his woman safe. Thinking about her, he headed to the kitchen for coffee. He couldn't get over how wonderful she was. Warm, responsive, and giving—so full of love. *Damn, what a great mother she'll make.*

Darren Merritt had the most loving and beautiful daughter, and he couldn't even see it. He wanted to sell her for money like a piece of bloody property. What was happening to people nowadays? It was a wonder Merritt hadn't totally ruined Andi and turned her into a complete shrew while she'd lived at home. Instead, she'd turned out to be this truly delightful creature.

And now he had a mission to plan—to take Merritt out of the picture. He grabbed a cup of coffee and went down the hall to the security office to go over the new security arrangements with Charles, the chief of security for the estate. He was still there thirty minutes later when the butler came in.

"Mr. Komakov, sir, is Miss Andi going to eat breakfast this morning or did she go out?"

"She was dressed and ready to come to breakfast

when I left the room, Ralph. Just knock on the door and ask her."

"I did, sir. I even opened the door and looked in the room. There's no one there."

"Perhaps you missed her and she's at breakfast right now."

"No, sir. No one's seen her."

"*What?*" Levi ran back to his room with Ralph and Charles right behind him. Sure enough, Andi was gone. On the floor near the bed was a small syringe, and the Persian rug was missing.

"I—I saw two m—men leaving with a rolled up carpet," Ralph stammered. "But I just thought Mr. Demopulus was getting a carpet cleaned. He sometimes forgets to tell me about things like that."

"It's not your fault, Ralph," Levi told him, fighting to keep control of his rage. So the bastards had waited for him to leave the room, then they'd burst in, grabbed her, injected her before she could defend herself, and carried her out in the rug. "Don't worry, I'll get her back. But please don't mention this to anyone. Understand?" Levi waited until both men nodded and left the room. Then he went to the dresser and pulled out one of the receivers Pierre had given him. He put in his pocket and headed for the study at a run, dashing in without knocking.

"Jonas, An—"

He came to an abrupt halt.

Jonas was sitting at his desk, going over some papers with Jeff. Jonas took one look at Levi's face and turned to Jeff. "Let's take this up later. If you could excuse us, I need to talk to Levi."

"Of course." Jeff eyed Levi strangely then picked up the papers and left, closing the door behind him.

"What is it?" Jonas demanded.

"Andi's been taken. They ambushed her in our room

after I went down for coffee. I found a syringe on the floor so they likely injected her with something. Ralph saw two men carrying a roll of carpet out of the house." Levi sank into a chair and pulled the receiver out of his pocket, telling himself if he panicked, he'd doom Andi. He shut down his emotions—rage, fear, love for Andi, and thirst for revenge—one by one and locked them away in his mind, as he'd been trained to do, concentrating instead on what needed to be done. "How'd they know she was here?"

"That's a very good question," Jonas said. "I'm beginning to suspect we have a rat in our wood pile." He jerked his chin at the receiver. "Have you told anyone about that?"

"Only Max. He probably told Tess, but I'd trust her with my life and so would you."

"That means only four people besides Pierre and Andi know she has one. You, me, Tess, and Max. Let's keep it that way. If the leak is here at the estate, I don't want the information on her transmitter to get out."

"I agree." Levi looked at the receiver, playing with the dials. "From the look of these coordinates, I'd say they're taking her to Springfield. That means it's probably her father's people. I'm going after her."

"Of course, you are. I wouldn't expect anything less from you. Just tell me what you need and it's yours. Until we find out how they discovered she was here, we need to keep everything about this just between us. Agreed?" When Levi nodded, Jonas continued, "But you'll still have to wait for the right time. You can't do anything until after dark. They couldn't be sure they'd get her today, so they won't have called the buyer yet. They'll wait until she gets to Springfield. The guy couldn't possibly be here before tomorrow. So we have some time." He studied Levi. "Now, tell me—without stopping to think about it—who would you suspect among our people?"

Levi knew Jonas was right. He had to wait for the best time and that was tonight. So there was time to plan. He relaxed a little and shook his head. What had Jonas asked him? Oh, yeah—

"Who, Levi?" Jonas repeated.

"Jeff," Levi said immediately, not even realizing he'd thought it.

"Really? Why?"

Levi blinked. "I don't know. It just popped out." He stopped and thought about the feelings and instincts he had regarding Jeff, trying to form them into words. "There was the coffee service the day Wilson asked me to go get her. Has he ever done anything like that before or since?"

"Now that you mention it, no, I don't believe he has. Of course Garry was with him. But go on."

"And then there was the way he looked at the map and the papers on your desk. Something about his eyes instinctively set off my hackles. But I thought it was just paranoia."

"Yes, I noticed your reaction that day," Jonas told him. "Anything else?"

"Only that when I got to the cabin they were expecting me and they seemed to know something of my abilities. Merritt's people know about me, of course. But I don't think that any of his people had the slightest inkling that you or I knew anything about the kidnapping. They had no reason to suspect I would come after her." Levi paused to think. "There's also the way he looked at me just now. Like he already knew what was wrong." Levi hesitated. "And the fact that he told you that we were too free with information around here."

"Why does that make you suspect him?"

"First of all, because we aren't free with information.

As a rule, our people are very closed mouthed. And secondly, because that's exactly what someone who's guilty, but trying to look innocent, would say."

"Yes, I see your point."

"The leak had to come from here, Jonas. And it had to come from someone who knew I was going. It didn't come from me, Wilson, or you. So who else knew?"

"Lots of people knew you were off on some kind of job for me. I told the guys who gathered up the gear you wanted that it was for you so they'd be sure to get it right, but I didn't tell them where you were going or why. I also didn't tell Jeff. So if he knew, he had to get it off the map, and I don't know if that's feasible."

"Did he know I was with Andi? The guys who came to the cabin in Montana seemed to know. The must have been ordered not to kill me because they waited until she was alone to try and grab her."

"I didn't tell him you were with her, but you were gone for nearly a month, so if he's the spy, he could've easily figured it out. I agree that's not very much to go on. However, if the three of us who knew didn't tell anyone, we can begin to narrow the possibilities."

"Yes, but this is all very circumstantial. I hate to condemn a man based on my instincts."

"Don't you trust your instincts, Levi?"

"You know I do. But I like to have concrete evidence before I destroy someone. If you get rid of Jeff, his career and life in Massachusetts are basically over. I think we need to be sure."

"Do you think he could get enough information to understand your mission just from a short glance at that map? You moved to block him pretty quickly."

Levi frowned. "The only way he could was if he already knew she'd been kidnapped and where she was being kept. If he'd already seen a similar map, then I doubt he'd need more than a quick glance. He's an attorney. He's not dumb."

"No, he's very clever. But he couldn't have known *when* you were going just from looking at the map. You said the kidnappers were expecting you."

"They were, but I don't know if they were expecting me exactly when I got there. However, the loan shark's guys were right behind me, so they also got the information from somewhere, and if not from the FBI, then from the spy playing both sides. And whoever our rat here is, he could have been simply listening at the door." Levi got up suddenly, moved to the door as silent as an idea, and whipped it open. No one was there. He closed the door, locked it, and went back to his seat. "It's suspicious, but it's still very circumstantial. We could be condemning an innocent man."

"I agree. But I also think that we need to make sure he doesn't tap into any more sensitive information."

Levi's head snapped up and he stared at Jonas. "What did you say?"

"About?"

"You said 'tap' into information. What if that is exactly what he's doing? What if it's 'tape' instead of 'tap'?"

"What do you mean?"

"Do you have a tape recorder?"

Jonas opened his bottom desk drawer, pulled out a small tape recorder, and handed it across the desk. Levi took it, checked the batteries, then pushed "record." Getting up from his chair, he started walking around the room, holding the recorder close to furniture, walls, and objects. When he got to the hutch with its decanters of wine, a squeal started issuing from the recorder.

"What's that?"

"Feedback. It means there's a bug." Levi shut off the

recorder and began inspecting the hutch. A tiny microphone was concealed in a notch behind the row of decanters, with wires running down behind the hutch to the floor underneath it. Levi got down on the floor on his stomach, reached under the hutch, and pulled out a tape recorder twice the size of Jonas's. He shut it off and yanked the wires out. Then he turned the other one back on and reexamined the room. Satisfied he'd found the only bug, he returned to his chair to examine it. "Well, it's pretty amateurish. It holds two tapes, but there's no transmission port. That means whoever's spying has to come in when you're not here and collect the tapes." He set the device on Jonas's desk. "We caught a break. If this had been transmitting, everything we said before I found it would've already been heard."

"What should I do?"

"You have a couple of options." Levi held up his index finger. "Set up a camera in here and see if you can catch the spy, or—" He held up a second finger. "—send the recorder to someone and see if they can get prints off of it. If you can do it without anyone knowing, I'd opt for leaving it off and putting it back. Then set up a camera. Just make sure you don't leave this room until the camera's up and running."

Jonas pressed the intercom. "Gloria, please call Steven Pullus and tell him I need him to come out immediately—incognito. Understand?"

"Yes, sir. Right away."

"Good. Thank you."

"That's your tech guy?" Levi asked.

"Yes. For audio and video stuff. He's done this kind of thing for me before. He'll come out here in a three piece suit, posing as a salesman, and set up the camera. He's very good." Jonas put the used tapes in his safe. "Okay. Put it back where you found it." After Levi replaced the machine, Jonas said, "Now what?"

Levi pulled out his phone and called Wilson.

Wilson was laughing when he came on the line. "I've got to hand it to you, man. I saw the X-ray of McCarty's hand. Remind me never to piss you off."

Levi couldn't help but grin. "What happened with him?"

"As you know, everything related to you or the Demopulus Family has to come through me, so McCarty had to come up to Boston to see me. When he did, he told me he wanted to file charges against you for assault." Wilson chuckled. "I got a song and dance routine from him about how you approached him with a bribe, and when he wouldn't accept, you broke his hand."

"Really?" Levi looked over at Jonas and rolled his eyes. "He said I tried to bribe him?"

"That's right. Now, even if you hadn't called me with the real story before he came to see me, I wasn't born yesterday and I'm not a fool. I'm a good enough judge of character to know that isn't the way you work. Your reputation is for creative ways to get information, not for corruption."

"Thank you," Levi said sincerely. "I appreciate that. So what happened?"

"I'd already spoken with both the clerk in Missoula and the deputy sheriff, the one who went to check the cabin, before McCarty came in to see me. I had enough to convince the district attorney to file charges and we had a warrant waiting for McCarty along with a set of cuffs. He was stunned when I told him he was being brought up on federal charges for treason. He didn't realize that helping a foreign national to kidnap a US citizen can be construed as espionage by a creative district attorney friendly to the Bureau." Wilson chuckled again. "McCarty kept muttering something about how he should have believed you. I take it you warned him to resign or you'd have charges filed against him?"

"I did, but I knew he wouldn't resign. He's too arrogant. Has he given you anything yet?"

"He's singing like a canary. He's given us everything he gave you as well as the names of the other agents on this Ahasama's payroll. There were three and one of them was working for the loan shark involved with Merritt as well, so he was basically a double agent." Wilson hesitated. "I'm afraid we're in your debt. Because of you we cleaned out a whole ring of dirty agents in the Springfield office."

"I'm glad. I don't like dirty cops and I'm sure you don't either."

"No, I don't." The condemnation in Wilson's voice was unmistakable. "Was that the only reason you called, or did you need something?"

"Jonas and I found a bug in his study just now. We think that's how the kidnappers knew I was going after Andi." He hesitated, clamping down hard on his emotions again. "Her father's people knew I brought her back here and this morning they kidnapped her again." He heard Wilson gasp. "Don't worry. I'll have her back by tonight. But I need to find the spy. Can you run a check on someone for me? I'd do it myself, but I have to concentrate on Andi."

"Certainly. It's the least I can do. Who is it?"

"Hang on." Levi asked Jonas for Jeff's last name then said to Wilson, "Jeffrey Bradford. He's an attorney. Some things he's done seem suspicious."

"Oh, yes. The attorney who brought in the coffee. You know, at the time I wondered about that. I'll get right on this. I assume you want me to be thorough, so it may take a few days."

"That's fine. And check to see if he has anything to

do with the Yakima Indians in Washington, will you?" Wilson gave an affirmative grunt. "Thanks, Wilson." Levi disconnected and glanced at Jonas. The look on his old friend's face told him something was on his mind. "What is it, Jonas?"

Jonas gestured at the hutch. "How do we know that isn't an FBI bug?"

"Several reasons," Levi explained. "First of all, the technology itself. The FBI has the best technology available. They'd never plant something like that. Then there's how easily I found it. If the FBI had planted this, I would've had to have special equipment like an RF Detector to find it, and they wouldn't have put the microphone in a notch behind a decanter on the hutch." He paused for a breath. "Then there's Wilson. If this had been an FBI bug, Wilson would never have met with us in the study when he asked me to go after Andi. He really went out on a limb for her. If the FBI found out what he did, his career would be over. Now, we know they tap your phones occasionally. That's why you had those devices put on your lines so you'd know when they *were* tapped. But so far they haven't planted a bug. So no, you don't have to worry about that."

"Well, that's something, anyway," Jonas mused. "I'll have Pullus come in with an RF detector and double check anyway."

"That's probably a very good idea."

"Now, what do you need to get Andi back?"

Levi took a deep breath. "I need complete schematics of Merritt's estate, including all the security measures so I can figure out how to get in."

"You think he'll take her there?"

"It's the most secure place to keep her. You gave him two months to vacate the property, so he has four more weeks. And he doesn't know about the transmitter, so he'll expect us to think that he'd hide her somewhere else, if you know what I mean."

"Kind of like reverse psychology?" Jonas asked. "He's thinking that we'd know he'd assume we'd think of the estate, so we'll figure he'd hide her somewhere else, and meanwhile he hides her there, right?"

"Something like that." Levi chuckled at the convoluted statement. "And while we're looking somewhere else, the buyer comes in for the handoff."

Jonas got up and went over to a cabinet on the wall. He pulled out a stack of papers and handed them to Levi. "I got all that information when I took the property to pay expenses and set up the trust fund for Andi." Jonas cleared his throat. He sounded nervous, which was unusual for him. Levi looked up at him. Jonas sighed. "Levi, I know that you don't like to do this, but if you want Andi to be safe, I'm afraid you'll have to—"

"Kill her father, I know." Levi cut him off so he wouldn't have to say it. "Andi and I already discussed it. I planned on it, but I wanted to clear it with her."

Jonas dropped back down into his desk chair and stared at Levi in shock. "You *told* her? Why on earth—" He shook his head. "Well, never mind that. What did she say?"

Levi decided to answer his first question even though Jonas had canceled it. "I told her because everyone she's ever known except her mother has lied to her. I need her trust. If I lie to her, especially about something like this, I'll lose that trust and it's not worth it." He took another deep breath. "There are some things I learned from Max that make it imperative I kill Merritt. I'm not going to tell you what they are because it would only disgust you, and I'm disgusted enough for both of us. I would've killed Merritt anyway, regardless of what Andi thought. But I still had to tell her."

"I see. And she said?"

"She said she understood. She knows she'll never be safe unless I do. She also understands why I told her. She's okay with it."

"My word, son! Marry the girl as soon as you get her back. You'll never find another like her."

"I know, Jonas. But I have to make sure she doesn't have a gun to her head before I ask her. I think she'd be too afraid to refuse me when she needs me for protection, and I don't want to put her through that."

"Yes." Jonas sighed. "I can see why you'd feel that way. Have you told her how you feel?"

"Yes. I also told her that when this is all over I want her to stay with me, if she will, but that I don't want her to make a decision until she's out of danger."

Jonas smiled. "Well, all I can say is I'm proud of you, son. Very proud, indeed."

"Thank you, Jonas," Levi said, touched by the old man's words. "Your opinion means a lot to me. You know that." He gathered up the paperwork on the Merritt estate. "Now, let's see what I'm going to need to get her back."

He and Jonas studied the floor plans together for some time until Levi thought he saw a way in. "See these air-conditioning ducts? If the measurements on the schematics are correct—and they should be as the mansion is over ten thousand square feet—that's my way in."

"If they have the air conditioner on, it will be too dangerous," Jonas argued.

"It won't be dangerous, just uncomfortable. Besides, I can always rig an electrical failure in the unit. But it is still cold up here and the weather there is pretty much the same. So I doubt it will be turned on."

Jonas scanned the schematics again. "They obviously planned for intruders. How will you get over the poisoned-tipped spikes on top of the wall?"

"A blanket. I'll also need a dart gun for the dogs. How many do they have now? Three?"

"The security packet I got said four."

"Then I'll figure on eight dogs. That's one thing they'll probably beef up while she's there. Dogs don't talk."

"You're right. You'll also need a ladder for the wall, won't you?"

"Yes," Levi replied. "A rope ladder with hooks on the end large enough to fit over the wall. Does he have trip lasers? If he does, I'll need a can of spray powder."

"I don't know but you'd better plan for them anyway. He does have cameras on the wall and sonic traps in the front and back lawns."

"I know. I'm planning to stay off the lawns. Get me a can of spray grease to fog the cameras and a can of that spray powder for the lasers, just to be safe." Running his finger over the diagram of the wall, Levi pointed to a certain spot. "This is where I'll go over. David, the man who did Merritt's wall cameras, also did yours. He told me there's a blind spot here for a few seconds. That should be all the time I need." He thought for a moment. "And do we still have any of those things Pierre made for diversions? You know—they're about four inches high and dark blue. You wind them up and they run a few feet away and make noise. I can't remember what he called them."

"Ah, the Diversion Smurfs," Jonas told him with a twinkle in his eye. "I think I have three. I'll include those with your gear. What time do you think you'll go in?"

"Probably around eleven tonight, but I'll have to see what happens when I get there."

"How will you kill him?"

"A fast-acting poison. It's in a new system that Max

gave me. But I can't kill him until I find Andi."

Jonas patted him on the shoulder. "If anyone can do it, son, it's you."

Levi sighed. "I just wish her father was all I had to worry about."

10:51 p.m., the estate of Darren Merritt:

Andi woke up confused and disoriented in her old bedroom at her father's house. *What's going on?* Was everything that happened with Levi just a dream? Then she recalled their conversation that morning and the two men who burst into their room just after Levi left. The last thing she remembered was them injecting her with something. Infuriated, she jumped up. Immediately, the room began to spin. She dropped back down on the bed and tried to control her panic. Levi would come for her. It wouldn't make any difference where they took her. She had the transmitter and he would find her. She believed in him. In the meantime, she needed to remember what he'd taught her.

Slowly and carefully, she eased herself into a sitting position on the edge of the bed. The world finally stopped whirling, but she had an excruciating headache. Forcing herself to take it gradually, she stood up. Since she didn't feel sick or faint, she decided a headache, as bad as it was, was not going to keep her from getting out of here. Already knowing just how much of a prison her father's house was, she didn't even bother trying the barred windows. Instead, she strode to the door of her bedroom and flung it open, only to confront a guard, armed with a rifle, standing in the hallway. As she exited the room, he lowered his weapon and approached her.

"I'm sorry, Miss Merritt, but I need you to stay in your room."

"And if I refuse, are you going to shoot me?" She gave a short bark of laughter. "I doubt the rich Arab my father is selling me to is willing to pay twenty-five million for a corpse." The look on the guard's face was priceless. "Oh, I wasn't supposed to know about that, was I?"

She started down the hall to her father's study. The guard followed her until she got within a few feet of the door, then he stepped in front of her and lowered his rifle like a gate to bar her way.

"You need to return to your room," he told her.

"I'd bloody well advise you to get out of my way," she snarled, in a perfect imitation of Levi's accent. "Or I'll duct tape your ass to the wall."

Momentarily stunned by her comment, the guard's face quickly filled with annoyance. He shifted the rifle to his other hand then took hold of her left arm. Rage surged through her—pouring adrenaline into her system, easing her headache and clearing her mind. Drawing her right arm back, she clenched her fist and shot it forward with all her might, right into his solar plexus. The man staggered backward. Andi reached out and grabbed his shoulders, pulling his head down. Then she rammed her forehead into his nose at the same moment her knee connected with his groin. The rifle fell from his grasp as he collapsed on the floor, groaning in pain. He lay on his side, one hand holding his nose, the other covering his groin. Andi picked up his rifle, walked around behind him, and slammed the butt-end of the stock into the back of his head, just as Levi had shown her.

"I did warn you," she told him as he went limp. "It's not my fault you didn't listen."

Deciding the other guards might find him and interfere with her plans if she left him there on the floor, she slung the rifle over her shoulder, grabbed the front of his shirt with both hands, and dragged him along with her. When she reached the door, she kicked it open, stormed in, then dropped her prize and his rifle on the floor before closing the door.

Her father bolted from his chair, staring at her in shock. "What are you doing here," he demanded. "And what happened to him?"

"I'm here because your goons abducted me again," she growled. "And I did to him what I'll do to you if you don't let me go."

Pulling a pistol out of his desk he pointed it at her, his expression smug.

She just laughed. "Like I told your guard," she said, tilting her head at the unconscious form on the floor, "I doubt your buyer will pay twenty-five million for a corpse." He started to open his mouth, but she cut him off. "And I don't think he'll want me scarred by bullet holes, either. I wouldn't be so beautiful with scars, now would I? So don't even bother threatening me."

"What Arab are you talking about?" he blustered.

She could see the shock in his eyes. He hadn't expected her to find out about this. "Don't lie to me!" she shouted. "You'll just disgust me more than you already do. How many other young women have you sold into slavery, you pervert?"

He sighed, shrugged. "What difference does it make? It's a living. And I never heard you complaining when that money provided the best of everything for you."

She gasped in horror. "Only because I didn't know where it came from! How *could* you?" Appalled, she stared at him. "I can't wait to see what Levi does to you when he gets here."

"Levi? Levi *Komakov*?" The blood drained from his

face and he slumped back into his chair. "What's he got to do with this?"

"Levi loves me and I can only imagine how mad he is right now that you took me away from him. Do you know what happens to people who piss him off?"

"I knew you were staying at Demopulus's estate, but it never occurred to me…" He trailed off then straightened his shoulders, as if girding up what loins he had. "Well, if Komakov does come, I'll send him back to Jonas in a box."

"Oh, *really*?" Andi arched an eyebrow. "Let me know how that works out for you."

Her father scowled. "You don't believe me? If he comes for you, I'll be happy to prove it," he sneered, regaining most of his bravado. "*If* he comes. But why should he? He doesn't love you. You're just a job to him. I wouldn't be surprised if he was just after the money Jonas is putting in a trust fund for you." He snorted. "You're so gullible. He was just trying to get you into bed. Just because a man says the words, it doesn't mean they're true."

If anyone knew about empty words, it was her. But Levi wasn't like Donald or her father. "You're right, when those words are from an evil monster like you. But I trust him and I've learned to follow my instincts. Levi's an *honorable* man. He doesn't use women like you do." Remembering what Tess had told her, she added, "Besides, Levi doesn't need my money. He's got enough of his own. He only works for Jonas because he wants to."

"Did he tell you that?" He shook his head pityingly. "The man lies like a rug."

"No, I found it out on my own. But at least he isn't trying to sell me."

He shrugged again. "Yes, well, I'm sorry about that, but I was in a bind. I didn't see any other option." He didn't sound very apologetic. Standing up, he started toward her, the gun still in his hand. "And I still don't. I need the money more than I need you. And you're right, I won't shoot you, but I don't think Ahasama will mind too much if I mess you up a bit. He'll do worse, I'm sure."

"Bring it on," she crowed, taking the fighting stance Levi had taught her. She'd been wanting to take down her father since the moment she'd learned the truth and now, thanks to Levi, she felt confident she could.

"Believe me, *dearest*, I will," he said, using one of her mother's old endearments. He smiled at the flash of pain on her face then studied her more closely. "You seem different. What's happened to you?"

"Gee, I don't know. Maybe being kidnapped— twice—can change a person. Or maybe it's that I finally found out what a good man is like. Or maybe I was always like this and you never bothered to notice."

"Perhaps. You've surprised me once or twice before. But now you're going to be a good girl and do what I say." Still aiming the gun at her, he reached down, his hand slipping behind the desk, and she tensed. "Ahasama's men will be here for you in the morning and I'm not letting you escape again." He stepped around the desk. "But from the looks of him," he said, glancing at the unconscious guard on the floor, "I'll need a little help."

Four guards rushed into the room and Andi stared at them in shock. She'd only ever fought one-on-one with Levi before, so how was she supposed to handle four at once? She should have taken Levi's advice and paid attention to detail by locking the door. Shooting a glance at her father, she saw his smile had turned smug. The bastard was looking forward to this.

Rage-fueled adrenalin poured into her system, erasing her fear. Would the burst of strength increase her odds enough to take them all? She almost didn't care.

Something crashed behind her, just as the wrecking crew started forward.

CHAPTER 13

Levi arrived at the Merritt estate at ten thirty p.m. and parked on the road out of sight of the gate. The estate grounds lay in ebony darkness, the moon captured behind a layer of clouds. Everything was still and quiet, the only sound coming from occasional traffic on the road.

His night-vision goggles over his eyes, he moved silently through the trees to the wall surrounding the estate. Over his shoulder he carried a blanket, the rope ladder, and the strap of the dart gun. In each side pocket of his dark-blue cargo pants, he carried a spray can. The Diversion Smurfs and poison pen were nestled securely in another pocket. His pistol was tucked into his waistband and a knife was clipped to his belt.

As he approached the point on the wall where he would make his ascent, he stopped and pulled the receiver for Andi's transmitter from his hip pocket, double-checking the coordinates. She was still here.

The multitude of cameras on the wall covered every inch of the grounds, except for this specific spot. Here, when the two cameras got to the far outside limits of their radius and started to turn back, they were blind to this one small area for almost thirty seconds. Levi only knew about it because David had told him. Charles and Levi had supervised every inch of the camera project on the Demopulus estate, which had seemed to impress David. As he worked, he told Levi about how Merritt had built a fountain next to the wall and didn't want the cameras to spoil his view of it. So being arrogant and stupid, Merritt had insisted they be moved. David had been stunned that someone would be dense enough to compromise their security for aesthetics, but right now Levi was glad Merritt was dumb.

When the cameras reached the blind spot, Levi threw the ladder up on the wall and climbed. Reaching the top, he laid the blanket over the spikes, stepped on top of it, switched the ladder to the inside of the wall, and climbed down. Creeping along the shadow of the wall toward first one camera and then the other, he sprayed them both with grease. The guard monitoring the cameras would probably think water from the fountain had been sprayed on them by the wind again—a common enough occurrence, according to David. And with a little luck, no one would come out to check until morning.

Pulling the dart gun off his shoulder, Levi waited for the dogs. He heard them rushing out of the darkness before he could see them—four of them, lunging for his throat. Aiming for the two leading the pack, Levi took the closest one in the shoulder and the one right behind it in the flank. Dodging out of the way of their collapsing bodies, he waited for the others. The remaining two were still coming and closing fast. He aimed and shot—twice. Both dogs went down almost instantly. Whatever drug Jonas had secured, it worked fast.

He checked the dogs for vital signs, while listening and watching for more. Nothing else came. *Only four dogs?* Merritt really *was* dumb. All the dogs were sleeping, their vital signs strong. Levi sighed with relief. He hated to kill animals. He'd have done it if necessary to save Andi, but he was glad he hadn't needed to. He slipped the dart gun back onto his shoulder and pulled the dogs into the shadows of the wall, out of sight.

Skirting the fountain, he glided through the grounds, without even a whisper of noise, and worked his way toward the house, watching carefully for lasers but finding none until he was almost to the back door. While the two laser generators were disguised as part of the wall that ran down each side of the back walkway, Levi wasn't fooled. He'd seen it all before. He couldn't avoid the walk, however, because of the sonic traps in the lawn. Staying far back from the rays of the outside lights, so he wouldn't have to remove his night-vision goggles, he surveyed the area.

Before he could deal with the lasers, he needed to take out those lights. According to the schematics, the circuit-breaker box was in the garage. Detached from the house, the garage was left open—for reasons Levi couldn't fathom—so dowsing the lights wouldn't be a problem at all. He crept down the driveway, quickly killed the lights, and headed back. The guards would notice, but by the time they came to check, he'd be out of sight in the vents.

Back at the walkway, he sprayed the can of powder into the air in front of the laser generator. The light from the laser reflected off the powder, allowing him to see how high the beam was situated. A little above knee-high. Too low to crawl under easily and too high to just step over. Levi jumped, clearing it by several inches, and ran to the porch. Attached to the house, not far from the back door, was the small building that housed the huge air-conditioning system for the mansion. Just inside that was the vent access he wanted. He stashed the dart gun in the bushes by the door and slipped inside. Using his knife as a screwdriver, he detached the giant hose between the air-conditioning unit and the vent to gain access then hoisted himself up and into the metal channel. It was a tight fit, but doable.

He slithered through on his stomach, spreading his weight so as not to flex the metal vent and make noise. Working his way through the house, he listened for voices. They should carry well through these tunnels. But he heard nothing as he slid through what seemed like mile after mile of ducting, checking through the decorative vent cover in every room he came to, looking for Andi.

Finally as he reached a crossroad in the ducting, the sound he longed to hear came faintly to his ears. Andi.

"…and I don't think he'll want me scarred by bullet holes, either. I wouldn't be so beautiful with scars, now would I?" he heard her say, her voice raised in anger. "So don't even bother threatening me."

That's right, luv! You tell him, he told her silently.

Her father said something but Levi couldn't make it out. Turning toward the sounds, he picked up the pace. He had to get to her before Merritt did something stupid. When Levi reached the study and peered through the vent cover, Merritt was aiming a gun at her. Levi almost burst into the room to help her. But Andi didn't seem worried. She was taunting him. And as she'd said, her father couldn't risk shooting her. So Levi decided to wait and see what she'd do. No longer needing them, he slipped his night-vision goggles down around his neck.

As he listened to their conversation, he was filled with conflicting emotions. He swelled with pride when she defended him, shock when she discussed his finances, amusement as she told her father to "bring it on," and rage at her father's reaction.

But when the four guards stormed in and started toward her, Levi'd had enough. He kicked out the vent cover and jumped into the room. Lunging for the closest guard, he took him out then quickly moved through the rest before they could react. When they were all down, he walked over and closed the door, locking it securely. Then he walked back to Andi's side.

"Forgot to lock the door, didn't you?" he teased gently.

She whirled into him, hugging him fiercely. "I knew you'd come."

"I'll always come, luv. Trust me," he murmured, so glad to have her back in his arms it hurt. He looked over at Merritt. The bugger was staring around the room in shock, the gun lax in his hand and his mouth open as if he couldn't believe what had just happened. "I'd put that gun down on the desk if I were you," Levi told him firmly, his voice as cold as he could make it. "Unless you don't mind losing that hand."

Andi chuckled against his chest, and he kissed her hair. Merritt looked sick with fear, yet determined. He started to raise the gun. Keeping his left arm around Andi, Levi whipped his pistol from his belt with his right and fired, taking advantage of Merritt's hesitation. The bullet pierced the heel of Merritt's gun hand. The man screamed, dropping the gun, and tried to stop the bleeding with his handkerchief.

"I did warn you," Levi reminded him. "And so did Andi." He released her and pulled the poison pen from his pocket. But when he started toward her father, she put a hand on his arm.

"Wait," she said. "There's something I need to do first."

He couldn't imagine what she was thinking, but he shrugged and backed off.

Andi walked over to her father, ignoring his whimpers of pain, and put her hands on his shoulders, almost as if she planned to kiss him goodbye. Both men watched in confusion, but her father's face filled with horror when she grabbed hold of his suit jacket, pulled his head down, and slammed hers into his nose. Then she drew back her fist and punched him in the solar plexus before kneeing him in the groin. He collapsed to the floor, groaning.

"That's for trying to sell me, you pig," she declared, standing over him. "And for all those other women you sold as well." Then she turned to Levi and asked matter-of-factly, "How are we going to kill him?"

Fear instantly mixed with the pain in her father's eyes and Levi smiled, knowing that was her intention.

He held the poison pen up to show her. "Max gave me something new."

But as he prepared to administer it, she stopped him again. "Wait. Let me do it."

"Are you sure, luv?" he asked, stunned.

"Yes. Why should you have to violate your ethics by killing someone who's not a direct threat to *you*, when this is *my* fight?" She stared into his eyes as if trying to make him understand. "Besides, the cops will suspect you for sure, but they might not suspect me. After all, I know I'm not in his will. And this way you can honestly say you didn't do it."

"You're doing this for me? To give me an *alibi*?"

"I'm doing it because I *need* to. For you. For us. For myself. For all the other women he's destroyed for the sake of money." She sighed. "I know you'll blame yourself because he's my father. You'll always feel guilty for this, and I don't want that. I need to be the one to kill the monster."

"Are you sure you can?"

She sighed. "No, but I have to try. I'm the reason you're here. And I don't want his blood on your hands. As I said before, this is my fight. When I think of all the women he sold before me…" She trailed off, shaking her head.

Levi didn't know what to say. Amazed at the depth of her understanding, love, and courage, he gave her the pen and showed her how to use it. "In the hair right behind the ear, luv, where it'll likely be missed at autopsy."

He turned back to find Merritt squatting on his haunches, the gun in his uninjured left hand aimed right at Levi. Before her father could fire, Andi grabbed his hair and stabbed the pen into his scalp behind his ear, hard enough to activate the trigger. As her father slumped to the floor, she kicked the gun out of his hand.

Levi watched her face. There was no pleasure or triumph, only sadness, mixed with determination.

"Goodbye, Father," she said sadly. "I'm just glad Mother didn't live to see how evil you've become." She passed the pen back to Levi. "Thank you for having me kidnapped. Otherwise, I would never have met Levi."

Levi gathered her in his arms and kissed her. "Damn, I love you. I'm so proud of you."

"I love you, too." She turned to watch her father writhing on the floor, her face filling with sadness again. "Well, I thanked him. Do you want to cut his heart out now?"

"Actually, luv, I think you already did. Let's get out of here before the guards wake up." As they passed a guard with blood crusted on his face, his nose clearly broken, Levi paused. "Did you do this?" When she nodded, he smiled. "I thought it looked like your handiwork. Good show."

He ushered her over to the vent then hoisted himself up, pulled her in, and led the way back outside. At the door, he retrieved the dart gun and slipped it back over his shoulder. Remembering the height of the laser beam, he lifted her over then jumped.

As they crept through the grounds, he noted with pride that she was almost as quiet as he was. Almost to their destination they heard voices and froze. Guards were searching the area in front of the fountain. Levi reached into his pocket for a Diversion Smurf, wound it up, and sent it scurrying across the ground. When it got about thirty yards away, it stopped and the sound of gunshots issued from the tiny speakers inside it. As the guards ran toward the noise, he and Andi bolted from the shadows.

When they got to the wall, the dogs were just beginning to stir.

"Thanks for saving me again, Levi," she whispered.

He chuckled. "As I once told Tess, it's getting to be a full-time occupation."

"She told me about that, and I know she appreciates your efforts as much as I do." As she climbed the rope ladder, she asked, "How long will it take my father to die?"

"With this new stuff, I don't know. Max didn't tell me and I didn't think to ask. But the poison works quickly." He checked his watch. "He's probably already dead." He repositioned the ladder then, gathering up the blanket, followed her down the other side of the wall. "Now, I have a question for you," he told her as he retrieved the ladder and ushered Andi toward the car. Once he'd stowed his gear and climbed behind the wheel, he started the car and headed out. "Where did you learn about my finances?"

"From Tess, of course. She told me you were one guy I didn't have to worry about trying to marry me for money. Even if you were that kind of guy, which you aren't, you didn't need it."

"I see," he said as he cleaned camouflage paint off his face with a moist towelette. "Maybe, I should speak to

Tess about a non-disclosure agreement," he said with a grin. "I noticed you neglected to include that little tidbit in the things you told me this morning."

"Of course. I wouldn't want you to think I was a gold digger, after all."

"So, how can I be sure you're not after *my* money?"

"I'm afraid you're just going to have to trust me," she told him with a wicked little giggle. "Sometimes you just have to follow your instincts. What do your instincts tell you?"

He laughed. "They tell me I'm a very lucky man."

Figuring they were far enough from Merritt's estate, he pulled the car over to the side of the road and called Jonas to let him know Andi was okay. Then he leaned over and kissed her with everything he had. When he drew away, there was fire in her eyes.

"Where are we going now?" she asked in a low sexy voice that turned him on even more. "Because it had better be close. I'll never make it to Boston."

"Hadn't planned on going there," he whispered, leaning over to kiss her again. "I'd take you in the car right now, but it would be awkward and uncomfortable," he murmured against her lips. "But I did have the foresight to pack you a bag and bring your purse."

"I don't care where you take me, just make it quick," she murmured back. "The only thing I need tonight is you."

Grinning, he pushed himself away from her and put the car in gear. "We'll go to a hotel in Springfield. Then tomorrow, we'll take my plane to California."

"Why are we going to California? Not that I mind. Anywhere's fine as long as I'm with you. I just wondered, that's all."

"We're going to rent a cabin in the desert, luv. I still have things I need to teach you in case that Sydarian bugger manages to get his hands on you."

Out of the corner of his eye he saw her shudder. "Do you really think he will?" she asked. "Even though my father's dead?"

"I hope not, luv. But Max seemed to think so, and he knows those people better than I do." He reached over and grabbed her hand, squeezing it. "I'll do my best to keep you away from him, but I'd be letting you down if I didn't teach everything I could before you needed it."

"Can't we just take him out? Why do we have to wait for him to come after me?"

"Because I can't do it alone. I'd need help from the CIA, and they won't act until he actually takes you."

"That's so stupid! That's the same thing cops tell women who get threatened by men. 'We can't do any-thing until the guy actually breaks the law,'" she said, lowering the pitch of her voice to imitate a man. "But when the guy breaks the law, the poor girl's already dead."

"I know it seems that way sometimes, luv. But in your case, you have to remember we're dealing with for-eign governments and international law. The CIA doesn't want to start a war."

Andi didn't argue, but she didn't look convinced, ei-ther. She was silent for a while, and he wondered what she was thinking. Then she said, "So what will you teach me in California?"

Levi took a deep breath and tried to make his voice sound matter-of-fact. "I need to teach you to fight dirty. So if you're ever facing a man with a gun again, you'll know what to do. I need to teach you how to survive in the desert, in case you have to. If he manages to get you back to his country and you escape, the desert can easily kill you unless you know what to do." He glanced over at her, surprised to see she was excited about that. With a sigh, he gave her the bad news. "And I believe the only way to stop this Ahasama is to do it permanently. So I need to teach you how to kill with your bare hands. After your performance tonight, I think you can handle it."

CHAPTER 14

Wednesday, May 15th, 8:50 a.m., a cabin in the desert east of El Cajon, California:

Andi was fascinated with the desert. During the three weeks they'd been here, the desert had bloomed, thanks to the spring rains. She would never have believed it could look so beautiful. Dressed in greens, blues, reds, yellows, and purples, in shades so delicate and lovely they almost didn't look real, the vegetation seemed to glow in the sun. She'd always thought deserts were barren places, devoid of life, but the amount of plants and animals here amazed her.

Two days after they'd arrived, Wilson called and Levi put it on speaker phone so she could hear, too. The FBI agent didn't sound happy. Apparently, the guards they'd left unconscious in the study had called the police after waking up to find her father dead. They reported that she and Levi had been in the study just before he died. Wilson wanted to know if Levi had anything to do with the murder.

"I didn't touch the man," he replied honestly. "I admit I put a bullet through his hand when he wouldn't drop the gun he was pointing at Andi. What was the cause of death? Did he bleed out from the wound in his hand?"

Wilson sighed. "No, he didn't bleed out. So all you did was shoot him in the hand?"

"That, and I took out the guards then got Andi out of there. Merritt was alive when we left, but I'm sure he had other enemies."

If Wilson didn't believe him, he never said so. Even though it gave her an additional nightmare, Andi was glad she'd done what she had. Levi was a good man. He didn't need her father's death on his conscience.

Then Levi asked Wilson about somebody named Jeff. Wilson said he'd done an exhaustive background check on the man, but could find nothing suspicious. Another department was just starting to go over his finances. Apparently, if this Jeff person had anything to do with her kidnapping, he would have been paid. Wilson reasoned that if he had more money than his legitimate income suggested, they could get a search warrant to dig deeper and find out where the extra money came from. Right now, they had to do the search on the sly.

"What about his assistant, Garry?" Levi asked. "I can't remember his last name, but you can get it from Jonas."

"The one that came in with Jeff when he brought the coffee? I'd forgotten about him. Want me to check him out, too?"

"I guess you'd better."

After Wilson hung up, Levi called Jonas, again putting it on speaker phone, and asked if someone had collected some tapes.

Jonas told him the camera had caught someone in the study at about three in the morning. He said the person on the video almost looked like Levi. The guy had the same sort of special ops moves and was dressed in black with a ski mask covering his face. "He must have realized the tape machine had been found when he saw it was off," Jonas said, "because he hasn't been back since. There's no way to tell who it was."

"I asked Wilson to run a check on Garry as well, so check to see if he or Jeff has had any military training," Levi suggested. "That should help us rule one of them out."

"Will do."

While waiting for news, Levi filled her days with more training. This time, he concentrated on the skills she would need to survive if she was forced to run and hide in the Sydarian desert.

"Max said this guy doesn't actually live in the desert, but where he lives is *desert-like,*' so it's a lot like the area around here. And you're not going to find many rivers or ponds. There will be some, but not many," he'd said on the first day. "But most places like this have cacti, luv, and cacti store water. So come and look at this." He'd dragged her over to one variety of cactus. "If it smells like this, you can't eat it." Then to another. "If it feels like this on your skin, don't eat it." Then to another. "This one you can eat. Go on, luv, break off a piece, but mind the spines."

They went rock climbing everyday on some cliffs a few miles from the cabin and Levi taught her to repel. It was a lot of fun to walk vertically down a sheer wall. Andi took to it like a fish to water. Besides making love to Levi, it was the highlight of her day. Levi told her it was an excellent way to build upper body strength, which would be important if she had to fight someone off.

"If you don't keep it up, you might as well not do it at all," he would tell her whenever her arms felt they would fall off from exhaustion.

He also taught her how to make a ghillie suit by wrapping twine or cord around her body and sticking plants in the twine to break up her outline. From a distance, she'd be almost invisible—as long as she held perfectly still. "Well, not really invisible, luv," he'd said. "But you won't look like a person or like anything that's a threat. And remember, when you're trying to get away and not get recaptured, there are six directions and you need to be aware of what is in your AO at all six."

"Six?"

"Yes, back, front, both sides, down, and *up*. Most people look down and all around them when scanning their AOs, but they rarely remember to look *up*."

He took her out into the desert at night and taught her to navigate by the stars. Some nights they would go out with a flashlight to watch the animals. He taught her how to catch and kill snakes and how to cook them.

"Snakes are good," he'd said with a grin. "They taste like chicken. Just mind the fangs." He just laughed when she shuddered then told her, "Tarantulas are yummy, too, if you can catch them, and spiders get big over there."

Pointing out the markings on snakes and other desert wildlife, he taught her how to tell if animals or insects were poisonous and which ones were safe to eat. "Nature always marks it villains, luv, at least as far as animals are concerned. Things like that bright yellow stripe there tell other animals to stay away. So you take heed."

He taught her how to cover her tracks in the dirt, how to disguise her scent with pepper in case they used dogs to track her, how to protect herself in case of a sandstorm, how to hide from the sun in the heat of the day, and how to conserve water if she had it. He even showed her how to distill urine and turn it into drinking water. "Urine is sterile, luv, and can't cause infection. When it's distilled, it's just water again." Then he showed her how to use a plastic bag to collect water vapor and condense it back into liquid. "In the desert, staying hydrated will be your biggest problem. You can go for a while without food, but not without water."

He taught her so many things, everything she needed to know to survive without him. That thought made her shudder every time it came into her head. But not nearly as much as when he said, "I don't know how long it will take for Max to put an operation together. It may be just a week, or it could be two or three. But however long it takes, I *will* come for you, luv. Your only job in the meantime will be to stay alive."

Then he hugged her to his chest while she cried.

His fighting-dirty techniques amazed and amused her. She'd never realized there were so many things she could do.

"Blind your enemy by throwing a piece of cloth over his face or sand in his eyes," he said. "Ground pepper works good, too. Pepper in the eyes is almost as good as mace, if it's the right kind of pepper. Then, if you're not going to kill him, run like hell."

Some of the tricks were fun. "Anything you can do to distract him, do it, such as dragging one leg so he thinks you're weak or injured. Or hold one arm funny, like you're wounded. Or look like you've surrendered in defeat. Yes, just like that. That's good, luv. Anything to let you close in for the kill, especially if your enemy has a gun."

She practiced faking injuries and surrendering for hours, getting more and more extreme until they both dissolved into laughter.

The distraction he thought she'd do best at was the seduction ploy. "As beautiful as you are, this'll be easy. A man would be seduced just by looking at you, luv. Happens to me all the time," he'd told her with a grin. "If you act like you're going to cooperate, he'll let you walk right up to him. He won't even know what hit him until he's dead. And always remember," he'd said, suddenly turning serious, "*dead* men don't beat you. They don't rape you, and they don't chase after you if you manage to get away."

He taught her how to kill with her bare hands, showing her how a chop to the throat with the side of her hand could kill by crushing the larynx. A chop to the back of the neck could also kill—though this was unpredictable. They constructed a false neck out of plastic and padding and she practiced the techniques over and over until she could get it right every time.

"Now, remember," he'd told her, "if you decide you have to kill someone to save your life, don't hesitate. And give it everything you've got the first time. You'll only get one shot to take him down. If it takes more than that, you've already lost."

Then he showed her how to break a neck while pretending to give a back rub and where the bones in the skull were thinnest and easiest for her to penetrate with a sharp object. While he was teaching her, she sensed he was trying to cram in as much knowledge as possible, as quickly as possible. They still made love at night and sometimes in the morning before they got up, but he never interrupted lessons, always focusing on what she needed to know to survive. His single-mindedness scared her. It was almost as if he knew the future and saw her doom rushing to meet her.

She'd started having nightmares about Middle-Eastern abductors, in addition to the ones about killing, but she kept them to herself. Levi was worried enough about her as it was.

She missed the Bitterroot Mountains and the fun and adventurous weeks they'd spent there. But she knew she needed to concentrate. And she tried. Levi was a patient teacher, never getting upset if she couldn't answer a question or forgot a technique. He just kept reviewing the lessons over and over again.

Their cabin was so isolated they hadn't seen a soul since they'd arrived. Not a single car had driven down the lonely dirt road. Small planes flew overhead on occasion, but other than that they were completely alone. They'd brought a month's worth of supplies when they came, as Levi was afraid to have her seen in town. He planned to go shopping in a few days to resupply and wanted to leave her here alone.

She wasn't looking forward to that at all and persisted in trying to change his mind. "I'll wear sunglasses and a scarf," she offered. "No one will notice me."

"Oh, you think you can hide your beauty with that, do you, luv? Not bloody likely."

"Levi, I'm scared to stay here without you," she told him, finally resorting to the truth. She knew, by the look on his face, that he could see her fear. Tears she couldn't stop welled up in her eyes. "Maybe when the food's gone, we should just leave and go somewhere else."

He wrapped his arms around her and held her close. "Maybe you're right. We'll see how much we can accomplish in a week. But if you're scared, luv, I won't leave you."

"I'm sorry I'm such a wuss," she murmured against his chest. "But every time you leave me alone, I get into trouble."

"That you do." He kissed her hair then wiped away her tears. "Don't cry. We'll figure it out somehow."

5:16 p.m., the Sydarian Embassy:

Jamar paced his office, waiting for the phone to ring.

His bastard brother had called this afternoon while Jamar was in a meeting, leaving a message that he had news and he'd call back around five. *It damn well better be good news,* Jamar thought darkly. They couldn't afford any more mistakes.

When the phone finally rang, Jamar snapped it up without waiting for Bas to screen the caller. "This better be good news."

A chuckle traveled down the phone line. "It is. I found them—or at least their general location. I pulled his phone records. Komakov's cell phone pinged off a tower near El Cajon, outside of San Diego. I imagine they're probably hiding out in the desert somewhere east of there. I suggest we have someone do flyovers in a small plane until we spot them."

"How did you get his cell phone records?"

"How do you think? I bribed a judge and got a court order. But that's irrelevant. How do you want to proceed?"

"You are sure they are there? I do not want to alert Ahasama to their location if he only used his cell phone as they were passing through Southern California on their way to Mexico."

"Yes, I'm sure. I went to the airport in disguise and checked the flight plan filed by Komakov's pilot the day after Merritt's murder. The flight plan was for the San Diego International Airport, which is only twenty-seven miles from El Cajon."

"Very well." Jamar hesitated. "I will alert Ahasama and see what he wants to do. He is none too happy with us at the moment. He is in New York at a conference for the next three weeks, and he called me this morning to tell me he is most displeased."

"Well, if you let him handle it, you'd better tell him that he can't kill Komakov."

"One does not tell Ahasama anything. One can only make suggestions. Besides, what can they do to him? He is a Sydarian clan leader and has diplomatic immunity while in this country."

"Listen, Jamar, I don't care who he is, where he lives, or what kind of passport he has. The CIA and the SAS have a *very* long reach. They don't play by the rules, any more than Ahasama does. And diplomatic immunity won't help the man if they send an assassin after him. Then when they're finished with him, they'll come after us as well."

Jamar frowned. "Do you think it will really come to that?"

There was an exaggerated sigh on the other end of the line. "From what I hear, Komakov has pulled more asses out of the fire than most people can count. A lot of people owe him their lives. Not to mention their careers. Even though he's been retired for years, he's still got a lot of friends in those organizations, friends who would stop at nothing to avenge his death. I wouldn't chance it."

"I see," Jamar said uncertainly. "But still—"

"Let me put it another way. How far do you think Ahasama would go if some rogue agent in the US were to kill one of his family?"

"To the ends of the Earth." Jamar sighed. "Yes, I see your point. I will tell him."

"See that you do. And be very clear. If one of Ahasama's men gets carried away and Komakov ends up dead, I refuse to be responsible for the consequences."

9:46 p.m., the cabin in the desert east of El Cajon:

Levi worried about Andi more than ever that night as

he held her, wondering what else he could have taught her that would make this easier. Max was so sure this Sydarian would take her. To hear him talk, the guy seemed almost invincible.

Andi had been on the run for almost two months now. But for every obstacle Levi had batted out of her way, two more seemed to rise up. Just like the multi-headed Hydra from Greek mythology: you cut off one head and two more grew in its place.

This wasn't any kind of life for her. Still, she never complained. Just trusted that he would protect her. But how could he, when the danger was so elusive? He'd never felt so helpless against a threat in his life. When he'd seen her tears earlier, it almost broke his heart. Of course, she was scared. With all his lessons focusing on worst case scenarios, how could she not be? But she had to know—she had to be prepared. Her survival could depend on this training!

Dammit, why is life so bloody unfair?

She was right. It was time to move on. Besides, the longer they were here, the greater the chance that someone could find them. They needed to leave, and soon. He could take her to Oregon. She'd never seen much of the country and she would probably enjoy that. Or maybe Alaska. She'd love Alaska. He could make it a real adventure.

As he thought about what his next step would be, he slowly drifted off to sleep.

Friday, May 17th, 3:35 a.m., the cabin in the desert east of El Cajon, California:

A loud boom jerked Levi awake and he bolted upright in bed. But he wasn't fast enough. A man with a dart gun shot him with a tranquilizer, the drug immediately paralyzing him. Even the rush of blind panic and rage couldn't help him. There was too much drug and not enough adrenalin.

He heard Andi scream as the world went black.

When the explosion sounded and men rushed through the front door of the cabin, shock and panic had kept Andi silent. But when one of them shot Levi, her scream just slipped out. Before she could react, Levi had slumped back onto the bed.

She reached for him but someone grabbed her from behind, pulling her to her feet. Struggling, she scratched at her attacker and bit his hand. She tried to use the moves Levi had taught her, but the bastard had attacked her before she was fully awake. She felt like she was living in déjà vu as they'd tied her up, taped her mouth, and wrapped her in a blanket. One of the men picked her clothes up from where she'd laid them on the chair beside the bed then they carried her out to a van. Just like both times before.

She hadn't seen any blood, just a dart sticking out of his neck, so she prayed Levi had only been tranquilized. Surely, he would wake up soon and come find her. He'd promised to always come for her. All she had to do was stay alive until he got there. *Piece of cake, right?*

The van drove to a rural airfield and the men pulled her out, carrying her toward a small jet. Beside the jet stood a short, olive-skinned man with black hair and black eyes. From the way the men treated him, she figured this was the oil-baron guy, Ahasama.

"You are exquisite," he said in heavily accented English. "Just perfect." He stroked her cheek with his finger, and she flinched. Squirming, she tried to avoid his touch. That seemed to excite him and a sickening grin spread across his face. He said something to his men in a language she didn't understand then stroked her cheek again. "This is all your fault, woman. If you had come quietly the first time, I would have been there to give you the attention you deserve." His tone of voice made it sound like she had missed out on a special treat. "But now you will have to wait another three weeks until I get home." He ran his hand through her hair, letting the strands slide between his fingers. "So beautiful. You will serve me very well."

Then he turned, got into a long silver limousine, and drove away, the van following behind.

The remaining men carried her aboard the plane and it took off. They waited until the jet was at cruising altitude, then they removed her ropes and gag, threw her clothes at her—no shoes again—and told her in broken English to get dressed.

She went into the small restroom and dressed with only one thought on her mind. *I have three weeks before that pig gets home. More than enough time to escape. Levi should be there by then. I can do this. He taught me everything I need to know. I* can *do this!*

A small sob escaped her, but she forced back her tears and concentrated on her training. This time would be different. She wasn't just a helpless victim anymore. Levi had seen to that.

7:02 a.m.:

Levi woke up to find debris from the mangled front

door scattered all over the small, one-room cabin, the space on the bed next to him empty and cold. Shame and guilt, mixed with the lingering effects of the drug, turned his stomach. He had failed Andi, yet again. He lay on the bed and stared at the ceiling until he was sure the room wouldn't spin when he sat up. Then he got the receiver for Andi's transmitter and checked the coordinates. After that, he took out his cell phone and called Max.

"They took her, Max," he said. He could hear the rage in his voice but couldn't help it. "They tracked us to the desert somehow. Took us by surprise early this morning. She's somewhere over the ocean right now."

"I knew the threats wouldn't work," Max said with a sigh. "Get on a plane and come to Virginia. We have a mission to plan. I'll try to have authorization for the operation by the time you get here. Come straight to the house."

"On my way, Max. And thanks." Levi disconnected and called Jonas. "Our spy struck again, Jonas." As he relayed the events, his rage rose with each word.

"But how could he have known where you were?" Jonas demanded. "I don't even know."

"There's only one way. He found out where my plane dropped us off. We've seen several small planes fly by overhead the last couple of days. I'll bet they flew here and made passes over the entire area until they found us. So either he got a hold of the flight plans somehow, or he talked to one of the flight crew. If we find out who did either of those things, we've got him."

"I'll get on it right away. Oh, and I found out that Jeff and Garry were both in the military. Jeff was a marine, Garry a ranger."

"Well, that's not much help. See if either one talked to any of the flight crew or accessed the flight records. If so, we know he's our man."

"What are you going to do?"

"What do you think? I'm going after her."

"Do you want me to send your plane?"

"No, I don't want the spy to know what I'm up to and give him the opportunity to warn the Sydarian. If he found out we were here, he can find out where I'm going now. I'll fly commercial using one of the IDs you gave me for the Washington mission."

"Do you need anything from me? Any gear?"

"I don't know. I'm on my way to see Max right now. If the CIA can handle it, I'll leave you out of this one. Then no one will be the wiser. But send that picture of Andi to Max's house so the guys on the team will know what she looks like, in case she escapes and we have to find her in the desert."

"I'll send it by express mail today. Good luck, son. Call me as soon as you know anything."

Next, Levi phoned Pierre to check out what new equipment might be available. Then he packed up their stuff and loaded the car, his heart and mind black with despair. He'd taught her everything he could in the time he'd had. Now it was up to her. She was smart and unpredictable. And though she was scared, she had courage. Andi could survive this. She *had* to survive it.

I'm coming, luv. Just stay alive until I get there.

<h1 style="text-align:center">CHAPTER 15</h1>

6:53 p.m., the home of Max and Tess Maxwell:

When Levi got to Max's house, Tess met him at the door. "Max isn't home yet, but he called and told me what happened," she said, throwing her arms around him. "Oh, Levi, I'm so sorry. I know how hard this is on you."

Levi hugged her back and buried his face in her hair, though it wasn't her arms he longed for. "It's harder on Andi. But I'll get her back."

She released him then stepped back to let him in. "Of course, you will. I told her you would. She'll be okay until you get there because she knows you're coming."

Tess served him a glass of beer and offered him dinner. He took the beer, but the thought of food turned his stomach. Thirty minutes later, Max came in. He wasn't alone.

"Levi, this is Jack Murdock. Jack, Levi Komakov. Jack works the paramilitary side, like I used to." Max gave Tess a hug and a kiss then took the two men into the library. "I have good news and bad news, Levi. The bad news is that the Seventh Floor won't authorize the operation. They think the political climate's too volatile over there right now." When Levi opened his mouth to protest, Max held up his hand. "The good news is that we're going anyway. Jack has agreed to throw his career on the line, right along with mine, and he's coming with us."

"Max, I can't let you do that. I have my own plane. I can go by myself."

"You need us. You need our knowledge of these guys. As good as you are, you'd be a babe in the woods over there. Besides, while you may speak Farsi, you don't speak Arabic."

"And you do?"

"No, but I do," Jack said with a grin. "And if you think you're keeping me out of this, you're nuts. I'd like to nuke the whole lot of them, but since I can't arrange that, taking out a clan leader or two will have to do."

Levi looked over at Jack. He was about the same age as Levi and Max—though maybe three or four years younger—lean and just as well built. He had laugh lines around his eyes that showed a strong sense of humor and dark brown hair with a reddish hue that had Irish heritage written all over it. But it was the look in his lime-green eyes that tipped Levi off the most, as did the contained grace when he moved. "Special Forces?" he asked.

"Navy SEALS," Jack replied with a smile. "I've been in the Middle East many times in service to my country. Now I'm going for fun."

Max took a stack of papers from his briefcase and spread them out on the coffee table. "Maps and satellite photos of the area around Ahasama's palace. Do we know for sure which clan leader has her, Levi? Is it Ahasama?"

"I won't know until she stops moving and the transmitter can get a read on the coordinates," Levi said with a grimace. "Ahasama's the only one we've heard about."

"Well, we need to find out for sure. I don't want to

get her back from one and then have another one grab her later," Max told him.

"Bloody hell!"

"Calm down, guys," Jack said. "I think we can take care of that. All we have to do is blow the palace when we're done and send photos around to the other clan leaders as evidence of what happens when they mess with this woman. It wouldn't work for Ahasama, but it will for the others if we take *him* out." He paused for a moment then grinned. "And if we find out that a different clan leader has her, we take Ahasama out anyway. The guy deserves it, and I'm not opposed to a little collateral damage."

"You really think that's a good idea, Jack?" Max sounded a bit leery. "I think taking out one clan leader is enough for this trip, don't you? I don't want to start a war."

"Do you have any idea how many American women that bastard has kidnapped? Besides, if we take him out carefully, we can make it look like a clan war."

"He's got a point, Max," Levi said. "If there's any chance he'll come after Andi again, I'm all for taking him out."

"Well, let's see who has her, before we decide," Max hedged. "What time did they take her, Levi?"

"About four this morning—California time."

"The flight will probably last eleven to fourteen hours, depending on the speed of the plane, the prevailing winds, and how many times they had to stop and refuel." Max looked at his watch. "It's after ten p.m. Eastern Time now and they would've had a tail wind for most of the way. Check the receiver again and see if she's stopped moving."

Levi pulled it out of his pocket. "Yes." He showed the coordinates to Max and Jack.

"That's Ahasama's place, all right," Jack said. "In fact, those are the coordinates of the harem quarters." He just shrugged at their shocked expressions. "Trust me, guys. I know those coordinates. I've wanted to take that bastard out for years."

Max sighed with relief. "We got a break, Levi."

Levi just stared at him, trying to figure out how anything about this could be considered a break. He'd opened his mouth to voice that opinion when Max continued.

"Ahasama's tied up in New York for the next three weeks at a conference. He won't be home until the sixth of June. That means Andi's safe. For now. He'll most likely have given orders that she's not to be touched until he gets there. He'll want to be the first."

"So, as long as we get her out by then, she won't be hurt?" Levi could scarcely believe it.

"She'll probably be scared and disoriented, but no, they won't hurt her," Jack assured him. "She won't be molested by anyone until he gets home."

Levi felt weak with relief. "Thank heavens."

"Then let's plan this operation," Max said, spreading the photos out on the desk as Tess brought in coffee and sandwiches.

Levi didn't particularly like the way Jack looked at Tess, but she didn't seem to notice and Max didn't seem worried. Levi grabbed a sandwich and a cup of coffee and turned his attention to the mission.

Saturday, May 18th, 10:03 a.m., the palace of Mohammed Amal Ahasama in Sydaria:

Andi stared around her in dismay. Time seemed abstract and disjointed. How could it still be mid-morning? It was dawn when the men had broken down the door of the cabin and many hours had elapsed since then. Then her brain caught up, and she realized there was probably a time difference of about ten to twelve hours. Which meant it was night where Levi was.

She knew he would have gone to Virginia to see Max, and they would be planning a rescue mission. She hoped they came soon, but she knew it could take them a week or more to organize such an intricate operation. *I'll just have to be patient,* she told herself, *and make the best of the situation.*

The men had taken her from the plane to the palace in a limo, about an hour's drive, then to a small bedroom, which apparently would be hers—if she had pieced together their broken English correctly. After she'd seen the bedroom, they brought her to what they called "the common room" and left. The harem's common room was the most bizarre place she could imagine. Nothing Levi told her had prepared her for this. Oriental rugs covered the tile floors. Beautiful tapestries and sheets of colored chiffon hung from the walls. Above her head was a domed ceiling with three large skylights. The room looked like a Moroccan brothel, or at least what she *imagined* one would look like.

The fifteen other girls in the room, sitting on the floor or on cushions that looked like bean bag chairs, just stared at her. The girls were all dressed in exotic costumes that looked like they were made for belly dancers. Andi sighed. She had to get out of this place. Maybe she should just leave tonight. Then she looked more closely at the other girls. Only one of them looked Middle Eastern. The rest were Caucasian, probably American or English—light complexioned with blonde, light brown, or red hair—and were her age or younger. They were all lovely.

Most wore a look of fear, while a few of them had the vacant look of numbness and defeat. Andi's heart went out to them and she sighed again.

These girls needed her help. As much as she hated to even think about it, she'd have to stay put until Levi came for her or until she could take the girls and escape. She knew Levi would help them get home. He wouldn't leave any girl in this situation. That just wasn't Levi. But if they were going to pull off such a huge rescue mission, she would have to do what she could from the inside and teach the other girls what he'd taught her.

Scanning the common room, she wondered if any of the girls here were spies for the guards. Levi had warned her that could happen and told her she'd have to be careful. Picking a redhead with the most open-looking face, she went over and introduced herself. "Hi, I'm Andi. What's your name? Have you been here very long?"

"Cindy." She shook Andi's hand. "I've been here a year." Her hand dropped back into her lap and her face crumbled, tears filling her lovely blue eyes. "And it's terrible."

Andi put her arms around Cindy's shoulders and whispered, "It's okay. Everything will be all right. Can all the girls here be trusted?"

Cindy sniffed and nodded. "I think so. We all hate it here. But what difference does it make?"

Andi wondered how much to tell her. "I'm planning on taking off the first chance I get," she whispered conspiratorially. "You could come with me."

Though she was speaking softly, some of the girls apparently heard as they began whispering to the others. When Andi looked up, every girl in the harem was standing in front of her, their eyes filled with hope.

"I'll take anyone with me who wants to go," she said, still whispering. For all she knew the place was bugged. Levi had warned her about that, too. "But I need to scope out the palace and the grounds first so I can work up a plan. And I can teach you to defend yourselves, if you're willing."

"But what can we do against men with guns?" This girl's accent sounded like Levi's.

Andi felt a rush of homesickness. She missed him so much. "You're English?"

"Yes, I'm Katrina. But you didn't answer my question."

"My boyfriend was in the British SAS and he taught me how to deal with armed men. I can teach you. Ahasama isn't going to be here for three more weeks. At least that's what he said. So we have time to prepare and plan. That's if you want to go. So, who's in?" Andi counted the hands. All fifteen girls in the room were in. "Do you know if this room is bugged? Are there microphones or video cameras?"

Katrina shook her head. "Ahasama doesn't think we can escape, especially since he built the wall. The desert goes on for miles around this place. There's no way you could get across it in one night. No one can survive in the desert."

"I can," Andi declared. "I spent the last month learning how to survive in a desert. And I can show all of you. It won't be easy, but we can do it. It's time you fought back."

"Some of us have tried to escape before," Cindy said. "Only the guards came after us and dragged us back. Then they put up the wall. Now, we can't even try."

"Sure we can," Andi assured them. "I'll make a bomb and blow a hole in the wall."

"Are you for *real*?" one of the girls challenged. She sounded American and like she was feeling betrayed. "Can we trust you? Or is this all an act?"

Andi could relate. She'd been the same way before she found Levi. "What's your name?"

"I'm Mara."

She knew she had to reach these girls and get them to trust her. *What Levi would say to them?* she wondered. "No, Mara, it's not an act. We were warned that I would be kidnapped, and Levi tried to prevent it. But just in case it happened anyway, he taught me everything he could so I could escape and hide in the desert until he came to find me." She studied the girl for a moment. Her expression was probably the same one that had been on Andi's face when Levi first threw her over his shoulder and took off through the woods. "Trust me if you want to," she said, shrugging. "Don't, if you don't want to. I can relate. I was betrayed by my father, too." The girl gasped. "Did your father sell you, too?" Andi asked her. The girl nodded, tears welling up in her eyes. "Sucks, doesn't it?" Andi said to the group at large. "All I can tell you is that we can fight back. I'm going to fight and I'll teach anyone who wants me to. As for whether or not you can trust me—" She smiled as she remembered what Levi had told her. "Sometimes you just have to go with your instincts."

"But how will he find you?" the Middle Eastern girl demanded.

"What's your name?"

"Afya. But the desert all looks the same. We'll get lost there and they won't even find our bodies."

Andi opened her mouth to tell them about her transmitter then remembered what Pierre had said. She couldn't take the chance that one of these girls was a spy or that the room was really bugged. "Levi trained me," she said instead, "so he knows how to track me even when no one else does. He also knows who took me, so he knows where to start looking. Trust me, he'll find us."

Monday, May 20th, 5:35 p.m., the home of Max and Tess Maxwell:

"Doesn't the way Jack looks at you bother you, Tess?" Levi asked as he helped her cook a spaghetti dinner. "He looks at you like you're some kind of yummy treat and he wants to gobble you down whole."

Max and Jack were due any minute, but Levi had held his tongue about this all weekend and it was starting to get on his nerves. Tess was his best friend and he had loved her for as long as he'd known her. He didn't want Jack to offend her or make her feel uncomfortable in her own home.

But Tess only laughed. "That's just Jack," she said. "He looks at all women that way. He doesn't mean anything by it. He's a farm boy. Grew up on a horse ranch where he didn't meet many young women, so now I guess he's making up for lost time. I used to tease him about it, but he doesn't even know he's doing it."

"Right, luv. Tell me another. I really bought that one."

"Jack's harmless, Levi. Honest. As a matter of fact, he has the same ethical code as you do. Under all that macho crap you guys sling around, he's a really nice guy. And he's got a great sense of humor." She glanced up at him and smiled. "You worry about me too much."

"It's an old habit. Rescuing you used to seem like my full time occupation."

"I know and you did it so well, too. But you can't protect all the women in the world, Levi. Besides, what could Jack possibly want with a fat, pregnant woman, anyway?"

"That hardly describes you, luv. You're not fat and you don't look pregnant yet. You look more beautiful than I've ever seen you—and you look sexy."

It was true. She did. And looking at her, happy and fulfilled, warmed Levi's heart.

She put her arms around his neck and hugged him. "You always say the nicest things. But I really don't think you have to worry about Jack." She released him and gave him a wicked grin. "Besides, Max would kick his ass into the middle of next week if he ever made a pass at me."

"Only if Max got to him before I did."

Tess giggled and kissed his cheek just as Max and Jack came through the front door.

After dinner, they retired to the library to continue planning. So far it had been a frustrating experience. Over the weekend, they'd been studying maps and photos, tossing out ideas, and getting nowhere. Not knowing if Andi would still be at the palace when they got there, or if she'd have managed to escape, made planning difficult. Each option meant a different mission plan. There was also the fact that Ahasama's palace had over thirty guards and the rescue team only had the three of them.

And then there was the equipment.

"The problem is getting the specialized equipment we need," Max complained. "I can't just turn in a requisition form for it. And we'll need some very unusual gear."

"Anything we need, Jonas can get for us," Levi assured him. "Even if we have to get it from Pierre. He's already offered."

"Who's Jonas?" Jack asked.

Levi and Max exchanged glances.

"You probably don't want to know," Max said. "Let's just say that Levi's Connected and leave it at that."

"Connected?" Jack looked from one to the other. Then apparently the light dawned. "Oh, you mean *Connected* as in 'mob connections.'" He shrugged. "I don't have a problem with that if it'll help with the mission.

Besides, if the guy's willing to help, he can't be all bad."

Max smiled. "Yeah, he's actually a sweet old man. Okay, let's take a look at what we need. To start with, we need a plane. Can we use yours, Levi?"

"We can, but there's a problem. I'm not sure I can trust the flight crew. The spy who told Ahasama where to find us in the California desert got the information about where the plane dropped us off either from the crew or from the flight plan they filed. I don't want him to know the plane is coming here and figure out what we're doing. He'll warn Ahasama."

"Just because the plane comes to Virginia, it doesn't mean you plan to rescue the girl, does it?" Jack asked. "Besides, didn't you fly here commercially? He could track that, too, can't he?"

"No, Levi's right," Max told him before Levi could answer. "It's no secret in the Family that Levi's got connections to the CIA. In fact, I married Tess at Jonas's mansion in Boston and half the black ops community from six different countries attended. And when Levi married my secretary Leanne there, the same thing happened again." He paused and looked at Levi. "And if I know you, you anticipated that he might track you, so you used an old CIA identity no one knows about, didn't you?"

Levi's only response was a grin. He was surprised that hearing Leanne's name didn't cause him the pain it used to. He had *finally* moved on. Just as she would have wanted him to. He would always love and remember her in his heart, but the hole her death had left in his soul had been filled by Andi. Now all he had to do was to get Andi back. The thought that she might be lost to him forever was almost enough to incapacitate him, so he refused to think it. "If the plane comes to either Washington, DC, or Virginia," he confirmed, "it'll be clear to anyone in the

Family that I'm planning an operation to go get her and that you guys are involved."

"I think we can get around that," Max said. "I can get a new flight crew to pick up the plane and bring it here." He grinned. "And this one won't talk. I guarantee it. As for the problem with the flight plan, we can file one for someplace else then just fly the plane here."

"So we file a plan for Montana and then we just show up somewhere else?"

"No, Levi. We just don't show up anywhere at all."

"How's that work?" asked Jack.

"Levi, this happened after your time and, Jack, you haven't had a need to know about this yet. So what I'm about to tell you is strictly confidential." When both men nodded, Max continued. "The CIA has a secret airbase near The Farm that very few people know about. We can have Mike file a flight plan to Missoula to make it look like he's going to your cabin. Then Mike turns off the transponder and brings the plane to our airbase here instead. Mike is black ops. The base doesn't record any black ops planes that come in. So no one will know it's here."

"So the plane just basically disappears," Levi mused. "The spy won't know where I am. He may even think the plane crashed and I'm dead." He grinned. "I like it."

"That's my kind of plan," Jack agreed. "Sneaky."

Since they were all in agreement, Levi called his pilot, George, and told him that he was loaning the plane to a friend who wanted to go up to his cabin in Montana. He told George the friend's name was Joe Black and that George should release the plane to him without questions when Joe got to Boston. Reluctant though he seemed, George had no choice but to agree.

"Good," Max said when Levi hung up. "I'll call Mike and tell him. Mike's a renegade. He loves operations like this and he'll be glad to help. But why give his name as Joe Black?"

Levi handed him the Joseph Black ID and credit card Jonas had given him. "Have him use this for the fuel. Another gift from Jonas."

"You have a flight crew? Why don't you fly your own plane?" Jack asked.

"I can, but I don't have time to get the required hours to keep my credentials current. I'll fly it in a pinch, but it makes more sense right now to pay a flight crew."

Max called Mike and explained the operation they were planning. Mike was indeed a renegade. Intrigued by the mission concept, he pledged his whole crew to help from start to finish. They made arrangements for Mike to stop by The Farm tomorrow and pick up the ID and credit card.

When he hung up, Max said, "The personnel at the airbase won't question Mike when he brings the plane in. They're used to him keeping secrets. And he won't have to file a flight plan when we leave for Sydaria either."

"Perfect," Jack said with a grin. "I always knew you were clever, Max. So now that we have the plane, what else do we need?"

Levi walked over to Max's desk and studied the satellite photos of Ahasama's palace. "We'll need a double load of plastique and all the accessories, GPS locators, rifles, handguns, ammo, and encrypted tactical radios—I want the small ones that fit into your ear and can pick up a spider farting a half mile away. I also want the IVIS-equipped night-vision googles with thermal and infrared that can pick out heat signatures even through thick adobe walls. We'll need desert ghillie suits and also Sydarian attire of a clan and status that will let us go anywhere without question. And we'll need the same for Andi after we get her out." He took a quick breath. "We'll need food packs that are small and easy to carry. And water. As much water as the three of us can carry. If she manages to escape to the desert before we get there, I don't know what condition she'll be in when we find her. And we can use the food and water to barter with the locals if necessary. I also want the plastique to be the kind disguised to look like chewing gum or Hersey's candy bars in case we get searched for any reason." He looked up to see Max and Jack staring at him in shock. "What?"

"I see you've given this some thought," Max said. "If you already have the mission planned out, as well as the equipment, what did we waste the weekend for?"

Before Levi could respond, Jack voiced his concerns. "Some of that stuff even the CIA doesn't have. Where do you plan to get all this gear?"

"Anything you guys can't come up with, I'll get from Pierre," Levi said. "You don't know him, Jack, but Max does. He's a specialist in Miami and this high-tech stuff is all he does. And to answer *your* question, Max. Yes, I've thought about nothing else since I found out her kidnapping was inevitable. I've got several ideas for mission plans, and we'll have to have at least two—though some elements of both will be the same—because we don't know where she'll be."

"What's IVIS night vision?" Max wanted to know. While he'd done numerous black ops missions for the CIA during his career, he'd never been in the military.

"IVIS is a system that allows what one person sees to be immediately known to everyone in the team," Jack explained. "There'd be a small...ah...video screen, I guess you could call it, and usually a camera device, in the googles. So if Levi sees something through his googles, that image will show up on our screens as well. It allows everyone on the team to know what *any* member of the team knows. It's new and very cool, but I wasn't aware they had it available in googles. Usually, it just comes in tactical vehicles. Or at least that's how it was when I was in the military."

"I don't know what the military has now," Levi said, "but I called Pierre right after I called you, Max. And he's got everything we need. If you don't have Seventh Floor authorization for this, we may need to do it this way. That way, we aren't breaking any laws by using the Company's equipment. I don't want you and Jack to be collateral damage on this thing."

Max nodded. "I think you might be right," he said. "Call Jonas and make sure he agrees and then we'll call Pierre with our shopping list."

Jonas was in total agreement with the plan. He had gotten himself appointed as the executor of Merritt's estate, somehow, and was selling Merritt's property, so money wouldn't be a problem. And since this whole mess was Merritt's fault in the first place, neither Levi nor Jonas had any qualms about using his money to pay for it. As Merritt's only living relative, Andi would inherit everything that was left, anyway. And this was a good use for the money.

"I'm surprised that Merritt didn't leave a will," Levi told Jonas. "Andi was sure he wouldn't leave his property to her willingly."

Jonas coughed and cleared his throat. "Yes, well, I seem to recall finding a will that left his entire estate to his mistress. But I accidentally tripped as I was reading it, and it fell out of my hand into the fireplace and burned up. So we get to handle the estate as if there'd been no will. Luckily for Andi. After all, she's the real victim in all this. I'll see that the mistress gets a share, but most will go to Andi."

Levi burst out laughing. "I've got to hand it to you, old man, you're brilliant."

Jonas chuckled. "Thank you, son. As the head of a crime family, it's actually rather fun to be the good guy for a change. So just have Pierre bill everything to me and I'll take care of it."

"Thanks again, Jonas."

When Levi disconnected, he called Pierre and told him what was needed. Pierre promised to ship everything to Max's address within a week, so they should have it all in plenty of time.

"Well, that's taken care of," Levi told Max and Jack when he disconnected from Pierre. "Now all we have to do is come up with a plan." He looked at the other two men. "And we're agreed, that no matter what happens, we take out Ahasama?"

Max and Jack nodded.

Now that they had secured their equipment and the plane, all they needed was a plan—one that worked.

CHAPTER 16

*Friday, May 24th, 1:43 p.m., the palace of Mohammed
Amal Ahasama*:

No, no. Not that way," Andi told Katrina. "Straighten your wrist so that it's level with your arm and there's a straight line from your elbow to the end of your fist. Yes, that's right. Now lock your fist with your thumb underneath it, turn your wrist to the side so your thumb's toward your body, and draw your arm back as far as you can. That's good. Now hit it. Hard."

Katrina punched the bean bag chair as hard as she could.

Andi applauded. "Perfect!" she said. "If that'd been a guard, he would've really felt that. Now show me where my solar plexus is. Very good."

She looked around the common room at the other girls, each one practicing techniques. They had come a long way in just the week or so she'd been teaching them.

Andi thought back to all the lessons Levi had given her and her soul filled with longing. She missed him so much that sometimes it was hard to breathe. Every night in her dreams he held her, calling her "luv" in his sexy accent. But when she woke up in the morning and he wasn't with her, the longing made her chest ache so bad it felt like someone was cutting out her heart.

He'd come. He *had* to. Otherwise, none of them would survive. And the others had already been through so much. As she'd trained the girls, she'd listened to their stories. The horror of what they'd been subjected to made her shudder. Not only had their bodies been used against their will, but their self-esteem and self-respect had plummeted, breaking their spirits. Some of their stories of betrayal were even worse than hers. They told of incest, of beatings and other physical abuse, of verbal and mental abuse even *before* they were sold into slavery. Andi didn't know how they'd survived. She vowed to herself that if she could get them out of this, she'd find a way to help them all get their lives back. She didn't know how she'd do it, but she was determined that she would. That is, if *she* could survive long enough herself.

A movement she caught out of the corner of her eye interrupted her thoughts, and she turned to see Afya sneak into the room through the door that opened out onto the grounds. There was a guilty, furtive look on her face as she met Andi's gaze.

Levi had taught Andi to observe body language and facial expressions, and something about Afya made Andi's instincts twitch. She didn't trust the Middle-Eastern girl. And, if Afya's suspicious behavior wasn't enough, Andi had caught her talking to the guards late at night on more than one occasion. As they had spoken in their native tongue, Andi didn't understand what they were saying, but their interaction had been too relaxed and comfortable for Andi to believe Afya's sob-story of abduction and abuse any longer.

If Afya was a spy, Andi didn't want the guards to know everything she could do. This meant she had to be careful when teaching the other girls how to kill and how to cover their tracks so that Afya didn't figure out what they were doing. It also meant that Andi would have a harder time procuring the supplies she needed for their escape.

The day she'd arrived, Andi had gone on a tour of the palace grounds. She'd discovered a gigantic greenhouse where a lot of the palace's fresh produce was grown. They had bags and bags of ammonia-based fertilizer. Andi hadn't thought too much of it until she'd also discovered the diesel pumping station for fuel for the generators. So, using the skills Levi taught her, she'd been sneaking out to the greenhouse any night she could to make bombs. There were six bucket-sized bombs hidden in the greenhouse now. That should be enough. She hoped.

Deciding that it would help throw off suspicion, she'd started playing the submissive slave, along with wearing the clothes provided by the palace staff, to convince the guards she was fitting in well. Her closet was filled with skimpy outfits. Every top came to just below her breasts. All the pants were cut to hang below her navel and were slit up the sides all the way to her hips. Everything was made of translucent pastel materials, except for a beautiful full-length, hooded cloak made of lush deep purple velvet. It was the only thing in the wardrobe she liked.

She figured Levi would love her new clothes, but she hated wearing them when he wasn't here to see her and other men were. The outfits made her feel cheap. But it was necessary. For her feet, the closet provided only flimsy sandals—not much good for walking in the desert-like conditions outside the palace walls. She missed her sneakers. None of the other girls had anything but sandals, however, so they'd all be in the same boat.

As part of her plan to seduce the guards into thinking she was harmless, despite what Afya might tell them, she also took to wandering around the grounds at all hours so that if they saw her when she was doing something she wasn't supposed to be, they'd think she was on just another stroll and they wouldn't be suspicious. Levi had told her that anything she could do to lull her enemy into overconfidence would give her an advantage. And she'd need every advantage she could get!

Her plan was slowly coming together. From the kitchen staff, who were all women and very sympathetic to the girls in the harem, Andi had secured six boxes of "strike anywhere" matches. These held a critical element for the detonators she would begin to make in her room tonight. Every time Andi went to the kitchen she obtained something else she needed and took it back to her room. She now had an ice pick, which she could use as a weapon if she needed to, and several large cans of ground pepper. She wanted a can for each girl so if they needed to disguise their scent from dogs, they could.

The palace provided bottled water for the girls in the harem, since most of them were from places like England and America. The kitchen staff was careful with the water, writing a girl's name down on a list whenever she took a bottle. Andi was sure their paranoia had nothing to do with a water shortage and everything to do with making sure the girls didn't hoard the stuff to use in an escape attempt. Each girl was allowed only four bottles per day—the equivalent of eight glasses and the guards checked the list regularly to make sure no girl was taking too much. But they hadn't figured on Andi. She was hoarding it right under their noses. She took her four bottles a day like everyone else, but she was only drinking three. She was also sneaking into the kitchen every night and stealing an additional bottle. Although she wasn't getting much sleep, by the time they left she'd have thirty-two bottles of water hidden in her room—two for each girl who was going. If the kitchen staff noticed her thievery, they kept it to themselves.

Andi didn't tell the other girls what she was up to. They'd find out the night they left, when it was too late for Afya to stop them. Andi planned to leave on the night of June fourth, two days before Ahasama was scheduled to return. They should be far enough away by the time he got home that he couldn't find them. She hadn't told any of the girls when they were leaving. They needed the advantage of surprise more than anything else since the odds were so stacked against them. Levi had told her surprise was an advantage that could overcome a lot of obstacles.

Andi taught the girls self-defense with the same single-mindedness Levi had shown when teaching her. Not only was her life now on the line, she was responsible for fifteen other lives as well. She wondered if this was how he had felt teaching her. *What's he doing now? What's he planning? Is he even coming?* Every time her fear and loneliness got the better of her, a small voice in the back of her mind raised its ugly head, and she'd find herself wondering if he really loved her, if he really missed her, and if he would really come for her.

He did, didn't he?

He would, wouldn't he?

But the longer she was here, the stronger the voice got.

Monday, May 27th, 7:16 p.m., the home of Max and Tess Maxwell:

"No, Max, I don't think that will work," Levi said,

pointing to a spot on the satellite photo. "There's absolutely no cover if we go that way. But we could come down this draw here if we stay to the shadows. We'd be nearly invisible then."

"I think he's right, Max," Jack agreed. "The draw would also bring us in at a different angle to this ridge and that could be a real advantage. We'd be able to see a lot farther from this point than from the one we originally planned to use."

"I understand all that," Max argued. "And I agree. I just don't think that we'll be able to get Andi up that draw. She looks so darn fragile and, on the way back, we'll have to scale the same cliffs we repel down on the way there. Now, we could go down the draw on the way in and come back the way I suggested." He hesitated. "But there would still be no cover on the way out."

Levi snorted. "We shouldn't need cover on the way out, but I don't think you need to worry about Andi being fragile. The girl's got spunk. And she's a lot less fragile now than she was the last time you saw her, Max. I worked her pretty hard out in the desert."

"What all did you teach the girl?" Jack wanted to know.

"Everything I thought she needed to know to defend herself and survive in a harsh environment," Levi told him, his voice grim. "It was the only way I could protect her."

Max looked up at him. "We'll get her back, Levi. You know we will."

"Yeah, I know, Max."

"So getting back to this," Jack said, tapping the photo. "We go down and back through the draw. Now, who's going from this point to the palace to get Andi? There's not a lot of cover here either. I can probably do it if you want me to—if you think she would come with a stranger."

"I think we should let Levi do that," Max said with a grin. "He's known around the trade as the Ghost. I've watched him work. Even when you know he's there, you can't see him."

"This I've got to see," Jack quipped. "But even if—when—we get Andi, *she* won't be invisible and there's still no cover." He looked at Levi. "Unless you taught her that, too."

"Of course he did," Max confirmed.

Levi grinned. "She's not as good as we are, but she's good. We'll need to take a ghillie suit for her, though, but if we're careful, I'm sure we can keep from being spotted. Especially if we go at night. I also taught her bird call signals, so if I get close enough for her to hear me, she'll come running."

"That's good, because there may be other women in the harem," Jack pointed out. "And we might have to sneak her out without letting the others know what's happening."

Others? Levi looked at Max in horror to see Max looking at him the same way. Levi had been so focused on Andi's rescue that he hadn't even considered what to do with the other women in the harem. They couldn't just take Andi and leave the others there to suffer. And it was obvious from the expression on Max's face that he was thinking the very same thing.

"What do we do, Max?" he asked. "We can't just leave the others there and take Andi. That's not right."

Max sighed. "I know, Levi. But as Tess says to me, and probably to you on occasion, we can't protect every woman in the world." He ran a hand down his face. "If we take out Ahasama and can neutralize the guards, we can ask the women if any want help. I don't know what his harem consists of, but if it contains any women from Sydaria, they may not want help, especially from an American. To the Sydarians, the harem and the palace may seem like quite a step up in lifestyle from where they grew up." He sighed again. "I'm sure he has other Americans in his harem, but what percentage, I don't know. There could be three to rescue or even as many as ten." He turned to Jack. "Do you know?"

"I know he's been kidnapping American women. And we can probably assume that he's kidnapping them from other countries as well. But whether he sells most of them or keeps them, I don't know. From what I do know of the guy, I'd say he keeps more than he sells. So yeah, there will probably be other women in the harem from the US as well as England and Canada. The question is, what do we do about it?"

"And it may depend on Andi, too," Levi pointed out. "I told her to try to escape if she could. The coordinates on the receiver indicate that she's still at the palace, but by the time we get there, she may be gone. If she's in the desert, then we'll catch up with her there and never go near the harem. In that case, the best way to take out Ahasama would be a bomb at the side of the road." He paused for a moment, thinking. "That'd be the best case scenario, but it feels wrong. I say we take enough water and food for ten women and if we can rescue any others, we do it."

"That will be a lot of supplies to haul around and it will mean a riskier operation," Max grumbled. "But I agree that we can't leave any of them there if they want out. If we're that close and we're taking Ahasama out anyway, not helping the rest of the women feels criminal." He grinned at Levi. "And Andi will probably be pissed if we don't at least try."

"That she will, Max. That she will." Levi went back

to studying the satellite photo. "But we can't expect that any of the other women will be able to scale those cliffs, even with help. And that means, we have to find another way out, because the draw won't work." He threw up his hands in frustration. "Does it seem like we're getting nowhere? Every plan we come up with won't work."

Jack chuckled. "Not true. We're making progress. At least we know how we're getting in. That's farther along than we were yesterday."

Levi scowled at him. "Bloody hell, Jack. Didn't the SEALS teach you *anything*?"

Before Jack could retort, Max intervened. "What Levi's trying to say in his less-than-diplomatic way, Jack, is that while getting *in* is important, it doesn't mean squat unless we can also get back *out*."

Friday, May 31st, 10:21 a.m., the palace of Mohammed Amal Ahasama:

Andi was proud of her students. She'd complained to some of them that she needed to teach them to move quietly and the best place to do it was outside. But she was afraid the guards would get suspicious. So the girls had come up with the idea of making it look like a game. They giggled, talked, and laughed as she taught them how to place their feet so they could move silently through any terrain. Andi just hoped they'd remember not to giggle, talk, and laugh when they were doing this for real.

All the girls had gotten good at the self-defense techniques she'd taught them. When it came time to leave, she felt certain they could handle the guards. *One more week*, she told herself. *Just one more week.*

She'd seen a black and white photo of some cliffs in the harem quarters' hallway and asked one of the cooks, who spoke a little English, where the picture had been taken. The woman explained that the cliffs were local, about twenty miles due north. As this was the only geological feature in the surrounding area that could provide any shelter, Andi planned to head in that direction. Levi had taught her to navigate by the stars, and she was sure she could find the cliffs. They could hide out there until Levi reached her. As her plan came together, her confidence soared, and it was almost easy to believe—most of the time—that Levi loved her and really would come after her. All she had to do was survive. Just like he'd said.

She sighed. *Piece of cake, right?*

She'd collected sixteen large cans of ground black pepper. She hadn't seen any dogs during her walks around the grounds, but she wasn't taking any chances. If attention to detail was the key to success, she was going to consider every detail she could think of.

Running through scenario after scenario in her mind, she tried to think of anything more she could do to protect the girls. Two bottles of water apiece wouldn't keep them alive very long, but it should probably be enough to get them to the cliffs—if they were careful with it. And they really couldn't carry any more. From the photo of the cliffs, she knew that plants grew along the base. If vegetation was able to grow there in such an arid climate, there had to be *some* source of water. She could dig for it if she had to. And there was always the cacti.

She shuddered as she remembered the taste. But as Levi had said, "You'd be surprised what you can do when you have to, luv."

Even cacti might taste pretty good if it was the only source of water.

Afya was still a concern. Andi didn't trust her, but

she was afraid the other girls would object to leaving her behind. If she *was* a spy, she'd alert the guards and Andi would lose the element of surprise. So she decided not to tell them when they were leaving until right before they left. When they'd asked her for a specific date, she'd told them they'd be leaving the night of the fifth. That was still one day before Ahasama came home so they accepted it without question.

The only thing Andi had left to do was make the timing switches for the bombs. It had taken her until that morning to get all the parts she needed. The wire and analog clocks were easy, but the batteries had been almost impossible to find. She'd finally stolen some out of a flashlight one of the guards had left in the kitchen then hidden the rest of the flashlight so he wouldn't know. When it was time to go, everything should be ready.

As she lay in her bed that night, with the timing switches done and nothing to distract her from her thoughts, Andi tried to keep her spirits up, but it wasn't easy. She'd been here two weeks, and the small voice in her head kept reminding her that Levi hadn't come to get her yet. At every loud noise she heard in the darkness, she tensed, sure it was him. But night after night when he didn't come, she had to convince herself over and over that he would come. He *would*. She just had to be patient.

She knew she was being silly and insecure. That was the old Andi. But Levi was the only man she'd ever met who hadn't courted her because he wanted something from her father. Even Donald had turned out to be using her. Could she really trust Levi? Her instincts said yes, but they'd also told her she could trust Donald…well, at least that he was one of the good guys, which she supposed he was. After all, he had given her the opal neck-lace that had allowed Levi to find her the first time. Still…

The questions in her mind were driving her crazy. She couldn't lose faith in Levi. Whether he loved her or not, she loved him so much that if she lost him, she didn't think she could survive. Telling her little voice to shut up, she concentrated on what he'd said when he'd told her he had to kill her father. "I love you and I always will. If you never trust me on anything else, please trust me on this."

But what about *your father?* the little voice demand-ed.

Her father. Levi said he loved her in spite of her fa-ther. Yet how could he, knowing where she came from? When she was with him, he made it so easy to believe him. But he wasn't here now.

Then she remembered the faith Tess had in Levi, that he would come for her no matter what. Tess was his best friend and knew him better than anyone. But could Andi trust Tess?

She had to. If she didn't, she was lost. She just had to hold on. Somehow, she had to find the strength to believe that Levi *would* come.

7:58 p.m., the home of Max and Tess Maxwell:

Levi studied the outline of the plan they'd come up with. It was rough, but it was coming together. "I think we need to go with this, Max," he said. "Andi's been there over two weeks. She's going to think I'm not com-ing after her." He took a sip of his coffee, but he'd been concentrating on the plan so long, it was cold.

"Doesn't she trust you?" Jack asked him.

"Andi has issues with trust," Levi answered. "Because of her father, Darren Merritt—the Springfield wiseguy who died recently—Andi's been betrayed a number of times. Hell, it was her own father who sold her to Ahasama. And the last man she loved turned out to be an undercover FBI agent trying to use her to get information on her father's organization. Makes it bloody hard to trust *anyone* after things like that."

"We can't go before the fourth, Levi," Max reminded him. "This mission has two parts. We have to take out Ahasama and rescue Andi. If we don't complete the first part of the mission, she's not going to be any safer than she was before he took her. And Ahasama won't be home until the sixth."

"I know, Max." Levi sighed and raked his hands through his hair. "I'm just getting antsy. My gut's telling me something's wrong. There's something we're missing. I just don't know what it is."

"Part of that may be guilt," Max suggested. "And part of it may be just missing her. Andi's strong. You've made her that way. She'll get through this and she'll be waiting for us."

Remembering the time Andi had shot the two men in Montana, how she said that she'd always need him because he made her strong, Levi smiled. But it wasn't true. She was strong in herself. She had terrific courage and strength. She'd just had to get kidnapped to realize it. But Max was right that Levi felt guilty. He'd failed to protect her. And yes, he missed her. Bloody hell, he missed her so much he ached inside! He worried every minute about what she was going through and if she was okay. He'd been through a lot in his life, but he'd never felt a pain as punishing as the constant nagging terror he felt for Andi. He wanted her back—in his life, in his arms, in his bed. Just *back*!

He felt that if he couldn't hold her soon, reassure himself that she was whole and safe, he'd go mad. What he'd do if she decided to go off on her own rather than stay with him, he couldn't even imagine. Probably go crazy. He didn't think she would, but how could you ever really tell what someone else was thinking? Andi constantly surprised him. Would she surprise him in this, too, and leave him? Whether she did or not, he had to get her back. She didn't deserve to have to live like a slave. No woman did.

"It's only a few more days, Levi." When Levi didn't respond, Max touched his shoulder. "You okay?"

Levi looked over to see Max watching him. Knowing his emotions were playing across his face for all to see, Levi grimaced. "I know, Max, but I can't help but worry. Things like this aren't supposed to happen to normal people."

"Unfortunately, Andi's not normal," Jack interjected. "Not if she's anything like the picture you showed me. That kind of beauty's rare. The only way to make sure she's safe is to ensure that the rest of the clan leaders are too frightened to come after her. And that means we need to make an example out of Ahasama."

"We could blow the whole bloody palace to hell," Levi quipped sarcastically. "But that might be kind of hard on the rest of the family and staff."

Jack picked up one of the satellite photos and waved it. "We don't have to blow the whole palace. Look here." He pointed to a section of the back wing. "We know that Ahasama's quarters are here, and that no family or staff is allowed quarters in this section or the one next to it as he's too paranoid. So all we have to do to make a statement is to blow this section right here. Kind of like saying, 'we know where you sleep, so don't screw with us.'"

As much as Levi hated to admit it, Jack had a good

idea. "That just might work, Jack. I like it."

"Do we have enough plastique?" Max asked. "We have to prepare a bomb for the roadside attack as well."

"Levi ordered plenty," Jack told him. "We have more than enough."

"I always order plenty and I always set double charges. I like to be thorough."

Max laughed. "No, you just like to make a mess."

"Well, at least when I'm done, there's not enough DNA left to identify any bodies."

Tess brought in another pot of coffee. Levi poured a fresh cup and picked up the satellite photo that had the best view of the wall. "I can scale the wall with the rope ladder I used to get into the Merritt estate. I've got it in my luggage. But I'll have to blow a hole in it to get the women out. If I place the charge right here, where the wall is closest to the harem common room, they won't have far to run. And if they can see a way out, I'm hoping they'll be less likely to panic."

"They'll probably panic anyway. Who wouldn't when a Limey blows a hole in the wall right outside their back door?" Jack asked with a chuckle. "You might want to let them know what's going down before you destroy the wall and rush into the room in a ghillie suit and camo paint."

"I taught Andi a bird call signal for 'Duck and Cover,'" Levi explained. "If she's still in the harem when I get there and I give her that signal, I'm sure she'll tell the other girls to back away and get down. But I don't want to run in before the wall's down, because if there's a spy in the harem, the guards might find out I'm there before I'm ready."

"That's a good point," Max agreed. "What are we going to do if she's already escaped? Do you think she might try to take the other women with her?"

"I don't know what she'll do. She's so bloody unpredictable it's impossible to tell. That's just one of the many things I love about her." Levi thought for a moment. "You know, that may be the reason she hasn't left the palace. Because of the other women."

"But didn't you tell her to escape as soon as possible?"

"Of course I did, Jack. But Andi knows her own mind. If she thinks it's right to stay and help the other women, that's what she'll do. It never surprises me anymore when she doesn't do what I ask her to." Levi grinned at the memories suddenly flooding his mind. "I tell her I'm there to rescue her, she says I'm not me and screams bloody murder. I tell her not to lock the bathroom door, she locks the door and climbs out the bloody window. I tell her not to wait up, she does anyway. The woman's not big on cooperation."

"That doesn't seem to bother you."

"Nope. Just another thing to love about her."

Jack rolled his eyes. "The guy's got it bad."

Max nodded. "He does and I can't blame him. She's really special." He turned to Levi. "But you didn't answer my question. What do we do if she has escaped by the time we get there?"

Levi picked up the map. "That will depend on where her signal's coming from." He pointed to an airstrip on the map. "We have to land the plane here. It's the only abandoned airstrip anywhere close to where we need to be. And we can't land at the airport. That would be announcing our mission to the world. So in that way we're stuck. Agreed?" When Jack and Max both nodded, Levi continued. "So it depends on whether she's closer to us than to the palace or if she's on the other side of it. If she leaves the palace and goes north, then we'll have to go past the palace to get to her. In that case, we might as well stop and do what we have to do there. But if she goes another direction, we might run into her before we get to the palace and then we can just ask her the situation."

"You know," Max said, "there could be another reason she's waited as well. Did you tell her that it would take some time to put an operation together?"

"Yes, I told her it could be anywhere from one to three weeks. Why?"

"Andi's smart. That's one of the things that impressed me when you brought her over to meet us. If she knows the operation will take time to get moving, she may figure she has a better chance of survival by staying in the palace where she has food and water until just before Ahasama gets home. I'm sure the palace staff would know when he plans to come home. Wouldn't they, Jack?"

"They should. They're expected to prepare for his arrival. So it would be in his best interests to let them know. And if they know, you can bet the harem will know. You can't hide information in an environment like that. Servants like to talk."

"That makes bloody good sense," Levi agreed. "*If* that's why she's doing it. So I guess we should see the coordinates start changing on the fourth or fifth. Surely, she wouldn't wait until the sixth. That'd be suicide."

"No, I think if she's going, she'll go between now and the fifth. All we can do is wait and see what happens."

"But do you think she'll take any of the other women with her?" Jack asked. "It takes ten times the water to keep ten women alive as it does one."

"Again, you're asking me to predict the unpredictable. Guessing what Andi will do is like trying to carry water in your bare hands: you might get a little bit a little ways, but you won't get much very far."

"It'll depend on the other women, too," Max said. "You taught Andi to survive in the desert, but we don't know if they'll believe her and go with her when she asks. After all, Andi doesn't *look* someone with the skills of a black ops specialist."

Levi shrugged. "It's like I told Andi. You pay your dime and take your choice. So depending on where she is when we get there, we may be able to ask her. If not and we get to the palace before we get to her, one of us is going to have to go in and ask the other women if they want out." Levi looked the other two men in the eyes. "My conscience won't give me a choice and I don't think yours will either."

Both Jack and Max shook their heads.

Levi sighed. "There are so many unknowns on this mission. And that's without even taking Murphy's Law into consideration. What I wouldn't give for some real intel—a contact inside. Don't you have *anybody* in country you can trust, Max?"

"For an *unauthorized* mission? Not likely. If I'd gotten Seventh Floor approval, we'd have assets on the ground watching the palace. But Jack was the only one I knew I could trust to do this on the quiet." Max looked over at Jack. "What about you?"

"I was just thinking. I do have a snitch over there that we can trust. Well, I *think* we can trust him—at least enough to check out the palace for us and pass on what he knows honestly. For a fee. But we'd have to disguise it as a routine request. I couldn't mention the rescue mission. He can't keep a secret." He looked at his watch. "It's ten at night here, so that makes it nine in the morning there. I can call him right now if you like."

When Levi nodded, Jack went to the phone and dialed. He spoke in a foreign language for several minutes, and, although Levi couldn't understand what he was saying, he could tell from Jack's expression the news wasn't good.

"What is it?" Max and Levi asked simultaneously when Jack hung up.

"My friend said that there's a rumor going around that Ahasama's harem is planning an escape on the fifth, led by the new American woman. That has to be Andi. Another clan leader by the name of Ikalla has heard the rumor and plans to intercept the women as soon as they're far enough away from Ahasama's." Jack sighed. "It looks like you were right, Levi. She stayed to help the others. But there's a spy in the harem. So she'll be escaping one clan leader only to be caught by another. I'm sorry, man."

Before Levi could respond, his cell phone rang. "Yeah, Jonas, what is it?"

"Wilson just called me. I know it's late but he said he just heard and since he was leaving for Washington, DC, in the morning, he wanted to give me the news now."

"What news?"

"He told me your plane disappeared and you were presumed dead." Jonas chuckled. "I didn't believe that of course. I know you too well. I won't believe you're dead until I see the body."

"And what's the bad news?"

"How did you know there was bad news?

"Come on, old man, you wouldn't call me this late at night just to tell me I'm not dead."

"No, you're right, I wouldn't. The bad news is two-fold. First, the description we got of the man that accessed the flight plans filed in Boston could be anybody. No one at the airport recognized Jeff or Garry's pictures, but the description fits both of them—except for the full beard the man was wearing—as well as thousands of other guys. Second, Wilson can't find a penny out of place in either of their finances. If one of them is helping these guys, he's doing it for free."

"He could've worn a beard to disguise his face. But doing it for free doesn't sound like either Garry or Jeff."

"No, it doesn't. Garry has a half-brother in Washington, DC. The guy's some kind of big wig with a foreign government. Wilson says he has a lot more money than he should, based on his legitimate income. But they're thinking drugs, not kidnapping. They're taking a look at him, but that doesn't relate to our probl—"

"That's *it*, Jonas!" Levi exclaimed, suddenly remembering something. "That's the connection. The first time I rescued Andi, the kidnappers were talking about their boss being delayed by weather Back East. Garry and his half-brother must be in this together."

"With one doing the spying and the other doing the grunt work and collecting the money, which they stick in an off-shore account and both share. Yes, that makes sense," Jonas agreed. "I couldn't find any connection between Garry and the Indian reservation, but I bet we do when we check the brother." He paused. When he spoke again, his voice was cold. "Well, you concentrate on Andi, and I'll take care of Garry and his VIP half-brother."

"Whatever you're planning, Jonas, be careful and don't get caught."

"I never have," Jonas said with a laugh. "How are you coming on rescuing Andi?"

"We leave in a few more days. I'm hoping to have her back soon." There was no point in burdening Jonas with the all problems that kept cropping up.

"Well, good luck, son."

Levi hung up and turned to Jack. "So you're saying

that even if she escapes one place, she'll just end up in another?" When Jack nodded, Levi asked, "Where is Ikalla's palace?"

"About thirty miles from Ahasama's. We'll need to reevaluate our approaches, once we get there and find out where she is." Jack picked up the map and studied it a moment. Then he picked up another satellite photo. "Our early approaches will be good, regardless of where she is, but if she's at Ikalla's, we'll need to split off and head over to this ridge here." He tapped a spot on the photo. "Actually, there's a lot more cover around Ikalla's, so it will be easier to get in and out unseen."

Max took the map and photo from Jack. "Then let's go over the plan and see if we can't refine it. I want to load all the rest of the gear on the plane by Monday morning. Just in case something comes up and we're pressed for time. I can leave a little early and run out to the airbase before work." He exchanged a long look with Levi. "There's probably something we're missing, but we have to go with what we've got. Agreed?"

Levi and Jack both nodded.

"Don't forget we have to meet Mike and the crew at the plane at seven in the morning on Tuesday," Jack reminded them. "With the length of the flight and the eleven hour time difference, we should land in Sydaria late in the evening on Wednesday. That should give us enough time to get into position before Ahasama gets home on Thursday and to decide which way we need to go to find Andi."

As they went over their plan, Levi couldn't concentrate. All he could think was, *Don't give up on me, luv. I'm coming. Just hang in there for a few more days.*

Monday, June 3rd, 8:26 a.m.:

Levi had just taken his coffee into the library when Max came bursting through the front door, after leaving early to run the rest of the gear to the plane. Levi heard Tess ask what Max had forgotten but couldn't hear his reply. Then Max came running into the library.

"What is it?" Levi asked, shocked at the look on his friend's face. "What's wrong?"

"Grab your bags," Max ordered, grabbing the pile of maps and satellite photos. "We're leaving now. Jack's already on his way to the airbase with Mike and the crew," he said, rushing out the door and up the stairs before Levi could ask any of the questions scrambling his brain.

Levi headed for his room to collect his bags. When he returned to the library, Max was back with his own luggage. "Why are we going now?" Levi demanded. "What's happened?"

"Apparently Ahasama's meetings ended early. He's already left New York. If we leave now, we still might make it on time, but it's going to be close."

Max headed out the door with Levi right behind him. Tess kissed Max and hugged him goodbye then hugged Levi. She had tears in her eyes. He knew she was worried about Max. So was he. He was worried about everyone, especially Andi.

On the way to the airbase, he asked, "Do we know what changed his plans, Max?"

"No, and I only found out he left early by accident. I'd just gotten to the office when I overheard a call on speakerphone from one of the guys the Company has shadowing the people at the conference. He said Ahasama just packed his bags, checked out of the hotel, and told his limo driver to take him to the airport." Max sighed. "I can only assume it's because he's heard the rumors about the impending escape. But it doesn't really matter why he's going home early. We just have to be in place before he gets there."

"I've been expecting Andi to go at any time, but according to the receiver, she's still there," Levi said. "Maybe she can't get out."

"Or maybe she's biding her time and waiting for something. We'll just have to ask her when we get her back."

Tuesday, June 4th, 10:21 a.m., the palace of Mohammed Amal Ahasama:

Andi was ready. Having kept track of when dusk fell in this awful place, she knew it should be fully dark by ten tonight. All she had to do was wait until then to put her plan into action. She'd decided to leave a message for Ahasama. Four of her six bombs she'd rig to destroy his quarters. The other two would blow a hole in the wall, allowing their escape. When Ahasama got home on the sixth to find his harem gone and his half his palace reduced to rubble, maybe he'd understand that he couldn't kidnap American women without suffering some blowback.

She didn't plan to tell the girls they were leaving until after the bombs were in place, which wouldn't give Afya much time to stop them. She wished there were some way to leave the Middle-Eastern girl here, but she was worried the other girls wouldn't believe her if she accused Afya of being a spy. After all, Andi had no proof.

Reminding herself not to forget to steal a broom

from the kitchen before she left so they could sweep out their tracks in the sand, she wandered around the common room and watched the girls drill. The training had given them something to focus on and they practiced the techniques religiously. Thinking they were escaping tomorrow had fostered their hope and courage. Andi didn't think they'd complain about leaving early.

As the day wore on the responsibility of what she was attempting became more and more difficult to bear. What if she failed and some of these girls died? They were counting on her! What if she'd missed something— some detail that could prove detrimental? What obstacle hadn't she anticipated?

Her chest felt tight, constricted, and her stomach was so upset she couldn't eat. She never should've told the girls she could get them out of this. If she took them into the desert and they died, she'd be as guilty as if she'd murdered them. Maybe she should've just waited for Levi. But he hadn't *come*! Ahasama would be home in two days and Levi *still* wasn't here. Did he even think about her anymore? Tears blurred her vision as the doubts filled her mind. But the girls were counting on her, and she couldn't let them down. She had to go through with this.

Suddenly, Katrina came running into the common room from the kitchen. From the look on her face, Andi knew something was wrong. Katrina quickly made her way through the other girls to Andi's side.

"What is it, Katrina?" Andi whispered.

"I just went to get a bottle of water from the kitchen, and the cook told me that Ahasama's coming home today. He'll be here by tonight."

Andi stared at her. It couldn't be true. It couldn't be! Her plan had failed even before it started, and now she was out of time.

"What are we going to do?" Katrina whispered.

Andi could hear the terror in the girl's voice and knew she couldn't let herself go to pieces. She was the only hope these girls had. Somehow she had to get through this. "I don't know yet," she whispered. "But don't worry. I'll think of something."

CHAPTER 17

9:21 p.m.:

Andi gave a soft groan of resignation as two guards came into the common room, looked around, then headed straight for her. Glancing over at Afya, she saw a triumphant smile plastered on the Middle-Eastern girl's face. So it was true. Afya was a spy. That was why Ahasama had come home early.

But Andi was ready for this meeting. She'd spent the time, between when Katrina had told her the news and now, steeling her mind and coming to a decision. If Ahasama tried to harm her, she'd have to kill him. She really had no choice. Not only for herself, but for the women he had abused, and would continue to abuse, unless he was stopped. How many more would be kidnapped and sold into a life more terrible than Andi's sheltered existence could ever have prepared her for?

As invincible as these monsters might seem, Andi knew that every tyrant feared the day one of his victims would rise up and strike back. Or if he didn't, he should. If Ahasama hadn't realized it would happen eventually, that wasn't her problem. He should have considered the consequences of his actions.

The same was true for Afya. Her payback was coming. Andi would see to that.

The guards grabbed Andi's arms. She didn't resist. It would only put the other girls at risk. They watched her with terror in their eyes. She knew what they were thinking. It was starting for her, just like it had for them. Giving them all a reassuring smile, she let the guards drag her out of the room. Levi had prepared her for this. She wouldn't fail him—or the girls.

They pulled her through the palace to a pair of double doors, then through them, and down a long hallway to another door. Jerking her to an abrupt stop, one of the guards knocked, the sound like the toll of doom to Andi.

Ahasama answered the door. His disturbing smile chilled her blood and made the hairs on the back of her neck stand up. "Oh yes, my dear," he said. "Please come in. We have much to discuss." Taking her arm, he drew her into the room and closed the door in the guards' faces. "You made me leave my meeting early. But looking at you now, I have to say it was worth it."

They were in an opulent bedroom, so spacious it could have been a gymnasium. A gigantic four-post bed, with sheer curtains hanging from the canopy, stood in a far corner. Red leather couches and chairs were stationed in several small groupings on the Persian rugs that covered the dark wood floor. A stone fireplace ran the length of another wall, but it looked like it had never been used. An oak desk, larger than any she had ever seen, stood against another wall. What looked like original Rembrandt and Leonardo da Vinci paintings hung under their own lights on panels set into the beige silk wallpaper that covered the walls. Incense burned in a holder on the corner of the desk, its sickly sweet and spicy smell nauseating her.

She decided to start out defiant. It would make her

surrender more believable. When Ahasama ran his fingers down her arm, she lifted her chin and hissed, "What do you want with me?"

"Only your cooperation."

Ignoring the pain that word invoked, she refused to lower her gaze. "And just what does that consist of?"

Ahasama's fingers left her arm to stroke her cheek. She forced herself not to shudder. Then he walked around her, appraising her like a Thoroughbred at a horse auction. It made her feel cheap and degraded. But his eyes were wary. No doubt Afya had informed him about what she'd been up to the last three weeks. Taking a deep breath, she waited.

Suddenly, with no change of expression, he backhanded her. The force of the blow had her stumbling back a full two steps. She tasted blood and raised a hand to her throbbing face. *Not yet*, she told herself, struggling to control her temper. *Remember your training and wait for the right moment. You'll only get one shot at him.*

"That, my dear," he said calmly, "is for teaching the other girls to fight. It was foolish. As is your plan to escape. You can't hide anything from me. I have spies in the harem."

"I see Afya told you everything," Andi growled, watching his eyes.

They flickered and darkened. "Well, your father said you were intelligent, so I am not really surprised that you figured it out." He walked around her again, his smile evil. "Yes, Afya is my eyes and ears in the harem. I pay her very well and I do not allow her to be used as the others are used. As you will be used, if you choose to stay."

He reached out to stroke her cheek again and she flinched. His smile widened.

Andi clenched her fists at her sides. "What do you mean, if I *choose* to stay? I didn't think I had a choice."

"Of course you have a choice. You can cooperate, sign the papers of marriage, and surrender to your fate— or I will kill you." He chuckled. "And if you are waiting for your *boyfriend* to come and save you, you are going to be waiting a long time. It seems that his plane disappeared on the way to Montana, and all on board were lost."

Andi felt as if he'd punched her in the heart. Levi was *dead*? It couldn't be. Was this why he hadn't come? *No! I can't give into this now. I have to stay focused.* The girls were depending on her. She forced the pain and heartache to the back of her mind and faced her tormentor. "How do I know you're telling the truth?"

"You do not believe me? Well, my dear, you should face the facts. You have been here three weeks, and he has not come for you, even though I have been away and it would have been the perfect time to do it." He shrugged. "So either he is dead and he cannot come, or he has decided that you are just another woman and not that important after all."

He was voicing her worst fears, but she refused to surrender to them. She had to be strong. Still, Ahasama would expect her to break down, now that her hope was gone.

If she played along, she could use it against him. Hanging her head in defeat, she let tears fill her eyes. When she looked up at Ahasama, he was wearing a gloating, triumphant smile.

"So what exactly does cooperation involve?" she asked again.

"You will sign the papers of marriage so that I have the legal right to keep you. Then you will pleasure any man I present you to, without complaint and without question, starting with me tonight."

Andi cringed, hating the thought of him, or any man

but Levi, touching her. "I'm an American citizen, you know. I do have rights."

"You have rights in your own country. But in this country, women have no rights. The only way to survive is to do as you are told."

Hanging her head again, she thought of Levi. If Ahasama wanted cooperation, he was in for a surprise. She didn't even cooperate with Levi all the time, and she *loved* him. He *couldn't* be dead. *Please, God, don't let him be dead! But whether he is or not, I can't give into this!*

She shook her head and opened her mouth to defy him again, but he held up a hand. "We have many ways to kill in this country, none of them pleasant," he said. "It will not be a quick or painless death you are choosing. So be very sure that you are willing to subject yourself to severe humiliation and pain before you refuse my offer."

Andi thought of the stories she'd heard, about how women were treated in Middle Eastern countries, and shuddered. "May I see these marriage papers?" she asked meekly.

"Of course, my dear."

He handed the papers to her and she looked through them without really seeing them.

"You'd really kill me if I don't sign?"

"Yes. I would. As exquisite as you are, it would be a shame. But if that is the price I have to pay to keep my harem in line, I will pay it."

"Then I really don't have a choice at all, do I?"

Another gloating, triumphant smile. "No, you do not."

Andi sighed, trying to sound defeated. "Do you have a pen?"

He pointed. "On the desk."

Andi walked over to the desk and signed "Jane Doe"

in an illegible scrawl. Then she stayed where she was and held the papers out a few inches.

As expected, Ahasama walked right up to her, eager to collect them. He reached for them, but she let them slip from her fingers to the floor. When he glared at her and pulled back his arm to strike her again, she hurled the side of her hand into the front of his throat with all the rage-fueled force she could muster.

His hands flew to his neck. She'd practiced on enough dummies to know she'd crushed his larynx. Struggling for air he would never get, he collapsed at her feet and glared up at her in horror.

"I'm sorry," she said. "But you should have realized that not every woman is going to stand there and take your abuse. Sometimes we fight back."

She watched him until his eyes glazed over then felt for a pulse in his neck. Certain he was dead, she locked the bedroom door. Then she grabbed him by his robes and dragged him over to the bed, where she hoisted him onto it and pulled the covers over him, silently thanking Levi for all the pushups and weight lifting he'd made her do. The clock on the desk told her it was just after ten.

Like the girls' common room, Ahasama's bedroom had a small door leading out to the grounds. After closing all the drapes in the room, she slipped outside. It was dark enough now that no one could see her if she was careful and stayed out of the lights. No one would expect her back in the harem until morning, so she had plenty of time.

Creeping as quickly as possible without making noise, she snuck into the greenhouse and retrieved her bombs.

She put two bombs behind some bushes at the spot along the wall where she wanted to break through. Then she took the other four and placed them around Ahasama's bedroom, hiding them as well as she could in the shrubbery.

It was late enough that the kitchen staff would have gone to their quarters for the day, so she went through the kitchen to her bedroom, grabbing a broom on the way. In her bedroom, she put the broom with the rest of the gear they would take with them across the desert then gathered up the detonators, wire, and timing switches. Back outside, she hooked up the detonators and wired the bombs together like Levi had shown her. Then she wired up two timing switches and set the clocks for forty-five minutes. That should give her enough time to take care of Afya and get the girls ready.

If all went well, when hands of the clocks came around to the right time, the wires connected to the minute hands would touch the wires connected to the batteries and the circuits would be complete, detonating the bombs. Hopefully. If not, she'd have to punt!

Finished, she hurried to the back door of the common room. It was time to deal with Afya. As she slipped inside, she noticed the girls sprawled around the room, looking as if their last hope had died.

"Why all the long faces?" she asked as she closed the door.

The girls all jumped and then stared at her as if unable to speak.

Finally, Katrina said, "What happened? Did he hurt you? We all thought—"

"No, he didn't hurt me," she assured them. "And as for what happened, why don't we ask Afya?"

"Me?" The squeak in Afya's voice betrayed her.

"Ahasama and I had a little talk," Andi told her. Then she turned to the others. "Afya's his spy. That's why none of your earlier escapes succeeded. He pays her and doesn't use her the way he uses all of you." She glanced back at Afya. "Isn't that right? And that's why he came back early—because you told the guards we were leaving tomorrow, didn't you?"

Everyone turned to stare at Afya. The look on her face was all the evidence they needed.

Mara jumped up and rushed at Afya, taking the Middle-Eastern girl completely by surprise. "You bitch!" Mara screamed, punching her in the solar plexus.

Pulling Afya's hair, Mara drew her head down and rammed the heel of her palm into Afya's nose. It made a very satisfying crunch. Afya screamed in pain as the rest of the girls joined in. Without much trouble they had her pinned down on the floor and were punching and kicking every inch of her. Cindy slapped her hand over Afya's mouth to muffle her screams.

Andi pulled the hangings from the walls and tore them into strips. "Here," she said, intervening before the girls could kill Afya. "Tie her up. The bombs are going to explode in about thirty minutes and we have to be ready to leave."

"But what about Ahasama?" Cindy asked, anxiety replacing the anger in her eyes.

"He's dead. I killed him." The girls stared at her in shock and disbelief. "Hurry now," she ordered. "I'll tell you all about it later."

Watching as they bound Afya's wrists and ankles and tied a gag around her mouth, Andi winced, remembering her own kidnapping, but this time she didn't intervene. The girls weren't gentle. They probably blamed Afya for some of the terror they'd experienced. Well, they were right.

When they were done, Andi looked each girl in the eyes. "I have water for all of you in my room and everything else I could get to make this a success. But success or failure, I'm getting out of here tonight. Anyone who wants to come with me can. I'll do my best to keep you alive until we can find help." She paused and took a deep breath. "But I can't make any promises. All I can do is try."

The girls were stunned for a moment then they all started talking at once.

"You killed Ahasama?"

"What happened to your face?"

"We're leaving *now*?"

"I want to come!"

"What do we do now?"

"Should we kill Afya, too?"

"One at a time," Andi said. When they quieted, she continued, "Remember there are guards around, so we have to be quiet. We don't need to kill Afya. She's no longer a threat. I only killed Ahasama because he left me no choice. But we don't have much time for questions. Now who's coming with me?" Every girl there raised her hand. "Good, then here's what we need to do. First, all of you run to your rooms and grab a cloak. I have one, so you probably do, too."

They all nodded and ran off, leaving her alone with Afya. Andi stared down at the bound woman. Blood ran down her face, soaking into the gag and crusting in her hair. "I'm sorry about your nose, Afya," she said, not bothering to sound it. "But when you betray people, you have to expect they might get even someday."

Afya yelled through her gag—no doubt cursing at her—but Andi walked away, glad she couldn't understand the words.

The girls were back with their cloaks in record time. Andi told them to pick up Afya and follow her. She took them to her bedroom where they dumped Afya on the bed. Then Andi handed each girl two bottles of water and a can of ground pepper. When they started asking questions again, she shushed them and said she would answer all their questions later. A couple of girls stuck their bottles in the waistband of their belly-dancer pants, which were cut loose to drop low around their hips. Andi thought it looked like a good idea, so she did the same. She also took the two that had been planned for Afya. The pepper can fit nicely as well. Then she grabbed her cloak and the broom, and led them all back to the common room.

"We've got about ten or fifteen minutes before the bombs go off," she explained. "But we need to get the three guards stationed on the grounds near here out of the way first. Any suggestions on how we get them to come in here so we can take them out and tie them up?"

"I can scream," Katrina offered. "That should get them to come running. And I remember you telling us that if we acted like we wanted to have sex with them, it would make it easier to take them out."

Andi smiled at how much these girls had grown in the short time she'd been there. Then, taking cover out of sight in the hallway, where the guards wouldn't see her and get suspicious, she peeked around the corner and whispered, "Okay, go for it."

Katrina, Mara, and Cindy put their cloaks, water, and pepper cans in the corner. Katrina let out a blood curdling scream. Then another. The three guards patrolling grounds outside the harem came charging into the room.

"What's going on in here?" one of them shouted.

The three girls sauntered toward them, exaggerating the swing of their hips.

"I was lonely," Katrina purred. "You wouldn't mind keeping me company, would you?" She slid a hand enticingly over her bare stomach for good measure.

Confusion and shock warred across the guards' faces, and Andi could barely suppress her laughter.

When Katrina reached her target, she glanced around discreetly to ensure that her teammates had as well. Then she slid her hands up his chest, put her arms around his neck, pulled his head down, and slammed hers into his nose. She released him and he staggered back, screaming in pain. Before he could bring up his gun, her knee met his groin. When he collapsed, others girls ran to help tie him up.

Andi looked over and saw that the other two guards were down and being tied up as well. Once the men were immobilized, the girls gagged them then took turns kicking and punching them. After what the girls had been through, Andi couldn't blame them, but she knew they were running out of time.

"Drag them over here away from the door," she ordered. "And all of you, back away from the windows. I don't know how big the explosion will be."

The girls crowded around her. A few minutes later a huge blast rocked the room. The skylights in the domed ceiling crashed to the floor. The girls all screamed and huddled against the wall.

Just as the dust was settling, another gigantic explosion rocked the back half of the palace. Any guards still standing would now be running to Ahasama's room, not the harem.

"Checkmate," Andi said, hearing the same satisfaction in her voice she'd heard in Levi's when he'd blown up the cabin in Washington. He couldn't be dead. He *couldn't* be.

Don't think about it, she commanded herself. *There's no time now.*

"That's our cue, girls," she said when the aftershocks stopped. "Put on your cloaks, everyone." Andi threw her own cloak over her shoulders, picked up her broom, and retrieved one of the guard's guns. "Everyone got your water?" The girls all nodded. "Good. Grab the other guns and follow me."

She headed for the door, the fourteen other girls right behind her.

Outside, the air was filled with dust. As it slowly dissipated, Andi stared at the wall. She'd expected the bombs to create a hole big enough for them to crawl through one at a time. Instead, she saw a six foot gap where there was simply no wall at all.

Might have used a bit too much, she mused. *Oh well…*

She climbed over the pile of broken masonry and debris, wishing she had actual shoes instead of the flimsy palace sandals. Once outside the wall, she stopped to help the others across. When all were assembled, she looked up at the sky. *North. There, that way.*

Following the stars, she led them across the desert into an unknown future.

11:43 p.m. somewhere in the Sydarian desert:

"Dammit!" Levi growled into his headset. "Max, Andi's heading north from the palace. That's the last direction I wanted her to go."

The receiver coordinates were heading steadily away from the rescue team.

"Just be glad she's out of there," Max countered. "At least, we know she got out before Ahasama got home."

"If she did, she cut it awfully close," Jack said. "He should have been home two or three hours already but her signal didn't start moving until about an hour ago. Unless he got delayed by an accident or something."

They were still several miles from the palace. Because of patrols in the area that they hadn't counted on, they'd had to skirt around to the south and come in from a different direction. Now they wouldn't reach the palace until dawn. Andi's signal was moving slowly and steadily, which meant she was walking. So she hadn't been captured. At least that was something.

"If she didn't leave before Ahasama got there, how do you suppose she got out?" Max asked. "It's not like Ahasama would just let her go."

"I don't know, but I'll bloody well bet it was creative. That girl constantly surprises me. Heaven only knows what she did," Levi grunted quietly as he climbed over a boulder. "I just wish she'd come toward *us*." Then he dropped to the ground. "Freeze!" he whispered into the radio.

Instantly, Max and Jack hit the ground and froze. Two men in clan attire, armed with rifles and carrying lanterns, rounded the point of a draw and headed toward them. One of the men stopped to relieve himself three yards from where Levi was silently impersonating desert vegetation. When he'd finished urinating and straightened his clothing, the man turned and talked to his friend for several moments before they finally moved on. Once they were out of sight, Max and Jack crept up to where Levi was holding point position. As their best shadow, Levi always took point. Max and Jack were good, but Levi had been trained by the best—an ex-Russian *Spetsnaz* officer.

Jack knelt down and touched Levi's arm. "They said there was an attack at the palace," he whispered. "They don't know what happened, but they don't think it was an accident."

"An attack?" Levi repeated. "Did they say what kind?"

"No, but that could be the reason Andi was able to

get out after Ahasama got home. If something happened to distract him, she probably saw her chance and took it."

"And that's probably why we've run into all these bloody patrols," Levi grumbled. "Why couldn't she have just come south? If one of these patrols finds her, she'll be in even more trouble. Over this terrain, we may not catch up with her for days."

"Yes, Levi, but we *will* catch up with her," Max assured him. "That's the important thing."

Wednesday, June 5th, 4:21 a.m., on a ridge overlooking the palace of Mohammed Amal Ahasama:

Levi, Max, and Jack had trudged over the arid landscape for hours. By the time they arrived at their destination, the eastern sky had started to get light. Crawling on their bellies to the top of the ridge above Ahasama's palace, they stared through their high-powered scopes in shock. The back wing where Ahasama lived had disintegrated and taken a large part of the next wing with it. A six-foot section of the wall had also disintegrated. Three guards and one harem girl were wandering around with bandages on their noses. The other guards were patrolling the grounds, armed with machine guns and angry expressions. Law enforcement officers and men in clan attire were standing around, trying to look important, while firemen fought the fires still smoldering in the back wing.

"Somebody sure FUBARed this place," Jack whispered. "What the hell happened?"

"Well, if I had to guess," Levi deduced with a chuckle, "I'd say Andi used a little too much explosive for the job she was trying to do."

"*Andi* did this?" Jack shook his head. "No way! What the hell did you teach her?"

"I taught her to bloody well defend herself, and it looks like she did a bang-up job." Levi pointed to the small body bag on the ground near the back wing. Firemen were still adding pieces of something to it. "See that body bag. There were no children in this part of the palace. Right, Jack?" When Jack nodded, Levi continued, "So what do you want to bet that Ahasama's in that bag—in pieces? Andi must have killed him before she blew up his bedroom."

"His bedroom and half the house." Max patted Levi on the shoulder. "Good job, teach. And she uses about as much explosive as you do, too."

"She's done our job for us," Jack grumbled. "There's nothing left for us to do. If Ahasama's dead, all we have to do is find her. Unless you think there are more women here. I see one down there, but that's it."

"I would say that's probably a spy." Levi grinned in delight. "See her nose and the noses of those three guards with her? That looks like Andi's handiwork. My guess is she killed Ahasama, took out the spy and those three guards, blew the back wing and the wall, collected the rest of the women, and split. Isn't that what you would have done?"

"Yes, but I've had a lot more training than Andi." Jack sighed. "Max, I think you need to hire this guy to come teach at The Farm."

Max chuckled. "Not a chance. I don't want my guys speaking like a Brit."

Levi ignored them. Damn, he was proud of Andi. Now all they had to do was find her. He looked at his receiver. From his current position, he was about twenty miles from catching her. She'd walked only about nine miles from the palace so far, but he'd have to backtrack to a point where he could get past the patrols without being spotted. So he wouldn't catch up with her for several hours. But he was hot on her trail and closing in.

"Let's go, guys," he said. "She's getting farther away by the minute. And we'll have to go around for miles before we can even start after her."

They started crawling backward from the ridge. So Andi had taken out Ahasama. Levi hoped she was okay with it. He wanted to be there to hold her and ask her how she felt about it. She seemed to understand that killing in self-defense was sometimes necessary, but he knew deep down it hurt her to take a life. Although she'd told him she was fine, he knew she'd been having nightmares after she shot the two men in Montana and again after killing her father. He'd never said anything, waiting for her to bring it up, but she hadn't. He was a light sleeper, however, and had awakened each time to listen to her mumbling and moaning in her sleep. Fearing these last three weeks had been so hard on her they might have changed her, he wasn't sure what he'd see when he looked into her eyes again.

Hours later, in the early evening, as they continued to track Andi's signal, a sandstorm blew up. Knowing how deadly they could be, Levi, Max, and Jack covered their faces and hunkered down to wait it out. But Levi's gut twisted with fear that it would reach Andi, wherever she was, and, if it did, she might not survive it.

7:00 p.m. somewhere north of the palace of Mohammed Amal Ahasama:

Walking single file, Andi had led the girls through the night and into the early morning. As the stars faded out, she'd spotted a distant mountain on the horizon that looked to be due north and used it for daytime navigation.

The temperatures during the day had been brutal—well over one hundred degrees. Andi made the girls take shelter in the shade of a draw and sleep during the hottest part of the day to conserve their energy. With the heat came excruciating thirst, dragging them down further. She'd told them to be careful with their water and only take a sip or two when they couldn't stand it any longer. She already knew the water wouldn't last as long as she'd hoped, and she was worried.

When the heat faded to bearable, they'd started walking again. So far, no one had come looking for them. She hoped the mess she left back at the palace would keep everyone busy for a while. The girls had diligently swept out their tracks with the broom, taking turns, the last girl in line walking backward and sweeping as she went. It made the going slower, but Andi was sure it was worth it.

"What about the pepper?" a girl named Angela asked.

"If you think you'll be tracked by dogs and you can put enough pepper on your trail, the dogs will breathe it in," Andi said, recounting what Levi had told her. "It hurts their noses and sometimes they'll refuse to follow the trail. It doesn't always work, but it's better than nothing. I don't think we'll have to worry about it on this trip, though, but Levi taught me to be prepared for everything I could."

The wind had picked up, making the going just that much more difficult.

They'd been walking about an hour since their last rest when the desert suddenly turned against them. A sandstorm blew up. Andi could see it on the horizon, rapidly moving toward them—a dark wall of windblown sand several stories high.

"Hurry," she called to the other girls. "Cover yourselves with your cloaks and hunker down on the ground.

Make an air pocket so you can breathe. Quickly now, we don't have much time."

She got all the girls down and showed them how to make an air pocket. By the time she got them all situated, the storm was upon them. There was barely time for her to get herself ready.

The sand was ferocious, slipping under her cloak and stinging every inch of bare skin it could reach. Wind howled around her, screeching in her ears. Above the roar of the storm, she could hear some of the girls screaming. Andi couldn't blame them. At least Levi had given her some idea of what to expect in a sandstorm. The other girls were completely unprepared.

Levi.

He couldn't really be dead, could he? It might explain why he hadn't come for her, but why would he go to Montana in the first place? Max lived in Virginia. But if his plane had disappeared—the pain she'd suppressed since Ahasama gave her the news finally broke through and she sobbed into her cloak as the raging sand tore at her body. She wasn't sure what to do if Levi wasn't coming. Maybe she could find a village with a phone. She could call Max. He would come if he could. Had Levi managed to tell him what happened? But Max didn't have a receiver for her transmitter. Jonas would help. Maybe she should call him. There was a receiver in the blue box in her room at his estate. And he would know what had really happened to Levi. If Jonas confirmed what Ahasama had told her, Andi didn't much care what happened to her, but the other girls still needed help.

Loneliness, stronger than any she'd ever known before, pulsed through her chest, mixing with the longing she felt for his arms, his grin, his warmth—his love. It ached so much, it stole her breath.

Life had no meaning without him. Any man she met

from now on would only be a dim echo of him.

The storm and her pain seem to rage on for hours. By the time the storm was finally over, Andi had run out of tears. It was stupid to cry and she knew it. Tears only depleted her of precious moisture, dehydrating her faster. She forced herself to get up and brush the sand off her cloak. Then she helped the other girls to their feet and inspected their skin. They all had abrasions, but nothing that time wouldn't heal.

"Well, at least that'll cover our tracks," she told them all with a cheerfulness she didn't feel, "and help us out if Ahasama's men are looking for us."

"Will your boyfriend still be able to find you?" one of the girls asked.

"Yes, don't worry. He'll find me." *If he's alive and looking, anyway.* Then she took a deep breath. "Come on. Let's see how far we can get after our restful little nap."

The girls laughed as she'd intended, and she led them on toward the mountain, her hope and faith dwindling with every step she took.

11:00 p.m. somewhere in the Sydarian desert:

Levi stretched his neck muscles from side to side as he settled into his next point position and scoped out the terrain. After the heat of the day, the cool night breezes felt good. The sand roiled into little dust devils around him, dancing in the zephyrs. He breathed deeply. The air smelled fresh, as if the sandstorm had scoured it clean. A half-moon hung in the sky above him, giving his night-vision goggles plenty of light to work with. The landscape around him glowed almost as bright as day.

Andi's signal was moving again. She'd survived the storm and was continuing north. Still several hours behind her, he gritted his teeth with frustration. Every time the receiver showed she was stationary, the rescue team pressed on, trying to shorten the distance between them. It was working—but not fast enough.

He hadn't seen any patrols since they'd left the area around Ahasama's palace. So he was confident she hadn't been captured. The land was probably too inhospitable for the Sydarians to patrol. Which didn't bode well for Andi.

Dammit, he wanted her back, needed to hold and comfort her—whether *she* needed it or not. She'd been gone so long now, he almost couldn't remember the smell of her hair. But he could recall her laugh and the surprising things she'd said. He ran over and over them in his mind, remembering how loving and giving she was. Damn, he missed her!

"Hey, did you go to sleep up there?" Max's whisper rasped in his earpiece. "Care to give us a sit rep?"

Levi suppressed a chuckle and focused on the task at hand. "The situation is that I was thinking about Andi and got distracted. It's clear. Come ahead."

"Next time I go on one of these field trips," Jack growled over the radio, "remind me not to take a lovesick point man."

"Yeah?" Levi growled back. "I can't wait to see what you're like when you fall in love."

"*I* already pity the poor girl," Max added with a grin as he came up beside Levi.

"None of that now," Jack ordered as he joined them. "I'm good to my women."

"Of course you are," Max agreed. "You just have a small problem with commitment. I wish I had a dollar for every time one of your women has cried on Tess's shoulder because your relationship was going nowhere. I could retire."

"It's not a problem with commitment," Jack insisted. "I just haven't found the right one."

"Yeah, I know the feeling," Levi told him. "And now that I've found mine, I want her back. So if we're through discussing our love lives, why don't we move out?" Just as he started to rise, he heard a familiar noise. Rotors. "Freeze!" He dropped to the ground and watched as a small black helicopter dipped low over the horizon to the south. "Searching for Andi?" he whispered.

"Probably," Max whispered back. "You know, I don't know how Andi knew to go north, but it looks like she was dead right in her choice. They're concentrating most of their searches in the south."

"She may have been dead right," Levi said grimly, "but if we don't reach her soon, it won't matter. She's going to be just dead. She's been out here for over twenty-four hours without water. She can't go much longer in these conditions and survive."

"You're not giving yourself or her enough credit, Levi," Max pointed out. "I know you taught her how to survive in an environment like this. So she must have had a plan for water before she set out. Either she took it with her, or she knows where to get it." He patted Levi's shoulder. "We'll get there in time, I promise you."

"I hope to bloody hell you're right, Max." As the sound of the rotors faded into the distance, Levi stood up. "The chopper's gone, so let's move out."

Thursday, June 6th, 9:40 p.m.:

Andi could see the cliffs ahead of her. *Finally.*

It had taken her two days to get them here. Their water had been gone for several hours, though she'd insisted the girls keep the empty bottles as well as the cans of pepper. "Let's not leave bread crumbs like Hansel and Gretel," she told them. "We don't know who might be looking for us."

She didn't want to be found by anyone but Levi. But if he wasn't coming, she didn't know what to do now that she'd reached her goal. *One thing at a time. For now, just get to the cliffs.*

They hadn't needed the pepper as there had been no sign of any dogs, but they could still use it to blind their pursuers if need be. From the profusion of plants growing along the bottom of the cliffs, it seemed likely there would be a source of water. Runoff from the cliffs? Possibly, but runoff meant rain, and it obviously didn't rain here very often.

She could hear what sounded like a helicopter in the distance, but the darkening sky overhead was vast and empty. Still, she hurried the girls forward. When a small black shape appeared suddenly over the edge of the horizon, she yelled, "Drop! Everybody hit the ground. And keep perfectly still." With the encroaching darkness and the dark color of their cloaks, she hoped they would be unrecognizable as people. "Don't move till it's gone," she whispered.

The chopper circled slowly, no doubt searching the area, before finally moving off. When it was out of sight and she could no longer hear it, she gathered everyone up and headed for the cliffs at a run. By the time they hit the base of the cliffs, they were all out of breath and dying of thirst. As she'd hoped, there was a small stream running along the edge of the wall of rock.

"Water!" the girls cried, dipping in their bottles and drinking without reservation.

Andi was about to tell them it might not be safe to drink then realized it didn't matter. Without water, they'd die anyway. If they got sick, they got sick. She stuck her own bottle in the stream until it was full and then drank deeply. It was cool and tasted like heaven. When she'd drunk her fill, she dipped her feet into the water and cooled them.

On the other side of the stream was a cave, carved into the base of the cliffs. She'd expected to have to climb the rocks to find shelter. In the morning when it was light, she'd explore it and, if it was safe, they could hide there from the heat of the sun tomorrow. Then she could decide what to do next. Maybe there was a village nearby. With such an easily accessible source of water here, there would probably be people close by. The other girls might know. Or she could climb the cliffs tomorrow and take a look around.

She gathered the girls into the cover of the plants and bushes that grew along the stream. They all collapsed around her and immediately fell asleep. Andi pulled her cloak tighter around herself against the chilly night breeze and drifted off to sleep, wondering if she should post a guard. Probably, but if she was so exhausted, she couldn't stay awake, the other girls were most likely even more so. For now, she'd have to trust in luck.

Friday, June 7th, 4:05 a.m.:

The sky was just beginning to lighten in the east when Katrina shook Andi awake. "The helicopter came back," she whispered. "It woke me up. Then the noise stopped and now I hear men's voices."

Andi listened then nodded. Yes, she heard men's voices, too. They weren't speaking English, either. *This cannot be happening! It just can't. To come all this way just to get caught.* She didn't want to have to kill anyone else just to survive. But she refused to let these girls go back to another harem and would do whatever was necessary to protect them.

She and Katrina woke the others. Then, motioning to them, she took them across the stream to the cave. She hated to ask them to go inside when she wasn't sure it was safe. But it looked like their only option.

"We'll have to hide in here," she breathed. "It may not work, but it's our only chance. If they're from that helicopter, they may already know we're here." Tears filled her eyes. "I'm sorry to ask you to go in there, because it may be dangerous."

"We'll fight," Katrina whispered, determination etched on her face. "There are fifteen of us and it doesn't sound like there are very many of them."

"That helicopter couldn't hold too many men," Mara said.

"That's probably true," Andi agreed as quietly as she could and still be heard. "But they probably have guns. We have three, but do any of you know how to use one?"

The girls all shook their heads. Andi sighed. "I do, but that's leaves one against however many men they do have."

"What's to know?" Katrina demanded. "I've seen enough movies to know you just have to make sure the safety's off and the muzzle's pointed in the right direction before you pull the trigger. And if they get close enough, which they'll have to if they want to capture us, how can we miss?"

"She's right," Mara agreed. "And even if we don't hit anything, we'll scare the hell out of them. Maybe they'll go away and leave us alone."

Andi shook her head. "I don't think so. We're merchandise to them. Valuable merchandise. As well as witnesses to their debauchery. They don't want to kill us. But if we get away, we'll let the world know what's going on here. And they can't afford that. If they can't recapture us and take us into custody, they'll kill us all rather than risk us getting away. So if we want to escape, we'll have to kill them." She hesitated and looked them all in the eyes. "Are you guys all okay with that?"

Fourteen heads nodded. Tammy, one of the more quiet girls, clenched her hands into fists. "I'll die before I'll go to another harem. I can't go back. I just can't!" she exclaimed, clearly on the verge of tears.

"Then we fight," Andi agreed. "Katrina, Mara, and I will position ourselves on the cliffs and act as snipers. You girls feign surrender until you're close enough to kill them. Leave your cloaks here." She gestured at the mouth of the cave. "They could hinder your movements. Besides, it won't hurt to show a little skin," she explained. "Stand on the other side of the stream, and when the men approach you, just do like I taught you. Julie, you're the strongest of the group, so you take the leader. When you hear me whistle, drop to the ground."

Julie grinned. "Got it.

When they'd all nodded agreement, Andi lined them up in a row. "Wait for my signal then drop to the ground. I'll take out the leader and as many others as I can, but you need to be ready to act as soon as I do, because you won't have much time, and I don't think I can shoot them all before they return fire. Katrina and Mara, climb up in those rocks as high as you can and find a place where you can look down on the area. But don't shoot if you don't have to. If you do, aim high. You don't want to hit one of the other girls by mistake."

"Should we hide?"

"No, let them see that we're armed and on higher ground. It'll give them something to think about."

Clamping down on her fear and letting her rage flow through her, Andi climbed up into the rocks, searching for a good shooting position, and prepared to meet her doom.

Again.

CHAPTER 18

Levi breathed a deep sigh of relief as he came out the mouth of the long draw they'd been following. They'd done it. Andi was only minutes away now. Wherever she was, she'd stayed put long enough for him to catch up with her. Unless she'd gotten hurt and couldn't move.

Her signal was still transmitting normally, which meant she was alive. If she died, the signal changed and went out as a beacon any police force could track. Pierre had done that as a way of preparing the one holding the receiver for what they would find at the end of their search. As long as Andi was alive, Levi didn't care. Injuries would heal. He'd deal with anything, as long as he had her back.

He dropped to the ground and scoped out the terrain ahead.

"Levi, seven o'clock!" Max whispered urgently.

Levi turned his scope to the southwest. "Bloody hell," he whispered. "It's that damn chopper again. What's it doing on the ground?"

"What do you want to bet they got to Andi before us?" Jack said. "I'm afraid we don't have time for stealth anymore, guys. We just need to go."

"I agree," Max replied. "But let's go with caution all the same."

"Bugger caution," Levi snapped. "I just caught up with her. I'm not letting someone take off with her in a chopper." He got to his feet and headed at a quiet run around the point of the draw with Max and Jack right behind him. They ran into a small valley and stopped dead.

To the left, a line of cliffs rose toward the sky with a small stream at the base. Just in front of the stream stood twelve young women. But Andi was nowhere to be seen. Scanning the AO in desperation, he noticed movement in the rocks above. There she was, taking a position on the cliffs with a rifle. Levi had never seen her look more beautiful. She was dressed in a pair of flowing pants made of a translucent soft pink material that glimmered in the diminishing darkness. The pants were slit up the sides, exposing her shapely legs. Her top was made of the same material and only came down to just below her breasts, leaving her midriff bare. The sleeves of the top were split down the outside seams from her shoulder to her wrists, showing off her arms. Her long hair was mussed and tousled around her face and shoulders like an auburn cloud. But it was the rifle snugged into her shoulder and the fire in her eyes that made him smile.

Levi heard Jack's soft whistle in his earpiece as he came up beside him. "She's breathtaking! And she not only got them to the only shelter for miles around, she got them here *armed*. She's freaking amazing."

"That she is," Levi whispered back. "But take your eyes off her for one damn minute and focus on what she's aiming at?"

Four men were walking toward the women: three dressed as guards and carrying rifles, one in the attire of a clan leader and carrying a pistol.

"That's Ikalla," Jack informed him. "I guess the rumors were true. He waited for her to escape and then searched for her until he found her."

"What do you want to do, Levi?" Max asked. "Do you want to take them out? I know *you*, at least, can hit them from here."

"I don't know what to do," he confessed. "Should I rush in and rescue her, or wait to see if she needs help first? I hate to interfere if she can handle it. She's fought hard to get here and deserves some payback. It seems a shame to take over now."

He looked around at the terrain. "Let's get out of sight and creep closer. The only reason no one's seen us is because the two groups are totally focused on each other. I'd like to let her handle it if she can. But I want to be in a position to help if she needs it."

"Head for those bushes near the stream to the right," Jack suggested. "There's more cover over there and we'll be close enough to prevent anything bad from happening."

Levi looked to his right. Jack's idea was a good one. He led off and crept silently through the lessening darkness to a clump of bushes at the edge of the stream, arriving at his destination just as the four men reached the women.

Andi fired a warning shot from her position on the cliffs. The ground near Ikalla's feet exploded. The man stopped dead and held up his hands.

"Who are you and what do you want?" she demanded.

Levi had to stifle a moan. It was so good to hear her voice.

"You must be Miss Merritt," Ikalla said in heavily accented English. "I am very impressed with how you handled Ahasama. I have been searching everywhere for you, my dear."

"I'm not *your dear*. Now that you've found us, what do you want?"

"Why, to add you to my harem, of course."

"Of course," Andi sneered. "Now, why didn't I think of that?"

Levi heard Jack snicker over his radio. He could relate. Andi was magnificent. He couldn't wait to see what she'd do next.

"I don't think you quite understand your position, young ladies," Ikalla informed them. "There isn't a village or settlement within miles of here. Without food you'll die very quickly. I admire your bravery, but is your freedom really worth dying for?"

"You're damn right it is!"

"Really? You would rather die than be treated like queens? And you, Miss Merritt, will have a special place of honor in my home."

Levi couldn't read the look on Andi's face, as her expression was hidden by the shadows that played across her cheek, but Jack obviously wasn't convinced. "Right," he scoffed in a whisper. "Pull the lady's other leg, why don't you?"

Ikalla motioned to his guards and they spread out beside him. Something was about to happen. Levi could sense it.

"I don't like this," Max whispered.

"We can't just go barging in on them," Levi insisted. "One of the girls might get killed. Give Andi some time. He hasn't beaten her yet."

Andi pointed the rifle at Ikalla. "Bullshit!" she yelled. "A harem's a harem, and we want no part of it. If you want to live, turn around and go back to where you came from. Forget you ever found us."

"I am afraid I cannot do that." Ikalla gestured to his guards again. They stepped back and spread out a little farther. "I'll give you a choice, Miss Merritt," he said. "You can come quietly, or my guards will kill you right now." He pointed back over his shoulder. "I have a helicopter waiting to take you all to safety."

From their fanned position, the guards raised their rifles. In the bushes, Levi, Max, and Jack did the same. Levi sighted in on Ikalla's head. Then one of the women surprised them by walking toward Ikalla. Three other women followed, approaching the guards.

"I'm Julie," the first woman whimpered. "Please don't shoot. I'll come quietly," she told him meekly, clutching at his robes. "But first, I need to kiss you."

The other girls mimicked Julie's actions.

Levi heard Jack's sharp intake of breath. "What the hell are they doing?"

"What they're supposed to do," Levi whispered back. "They have to get close enough to take them out. Apparently, Andi passed on what I taught her. Now shut up and watch."

"Are you sure, Levi?" Max asked. "He's a lot bigger than she is."

"If Andi's a good teacher, there'll be a lot of power in that little package," Levi insisted. "Believe me, I know."

Ikalla, however, seemed more inclined to agree with Jack. "Why would you want to kiss me?" he asked incredulously.

"If we're going to have a place of honor in your harem," she cooed, "we have to know that you can satisfy us. Why do you think we took out Ahasama?"

Ikalla gasped.

Levi grinned.

Andi whistled.

And all hell broke loose.

Julie dropped to the ground, a gunshot rang out, and

Ikalla's chest exploded. The three other women, who were wrapped around the guards, brought their knees up hard, slamming them into the men's groins. Another shot rang out and one man's groans suddenly stopped.

One of the women brought the side of her hand down forcibly on the front of a fallen guard's neck. He grabbed at his throat, gurgling, his eyes wide with horror.

The last remaining guard struggled to his feet, brought up his gun, and slammed it into a woman's head. She crumpled. He twisted, cursing, and fired wildly. One of the women on the rocks cried out and dropped her rifle. More bullets splattered the cliffs. Andi screamed.

Oh, shit! Levi squeezed his trigger, the silenced rifle emitting only a soft puff of sound. The guard dropped like a stone. But it was too late.

Andi had crumpled, blood spreading over her chest.

"She's been hit!" he cried.

Bolting to his feet, he raced for the cliffs with Max and Jack on his heels. A gunshot rang out, the bullet slamming into the ground to their left. Levi skidded to a halt.

"Hold it right there," the only women left standing on the cliffs told him. "Who the hell are you and what are you doing here?"

"We're Americans and we've come to take you home," Levi told her, struggling to restrain his temper. "But you've got wounded, so drop your weapon and let me help her." Turning to Max, he growled, "Deal with this," and sprinted toward Andi's still form on the rocks.

The other woman who'd been shot had staggered over to check on Andi, though one of her arms was bleeding badly. "I can't find a pulse," she whimpered.

"*No!*" Levi shouted. "She can't be dead. I won't let her be!"

He picked Andi up in his arms and carried her down

the cliffs. One of the women spread a cloak out on the ground. Levi gently laid Andi down on it and felt for a pulse in her neck. Despair filled his mind when he didn't find one.

"Damn you, Andi. Don't do this to me! Jack," he called over his shoulder. "See if there's a first-aid kit and AED in that chopper. Max, take care of the other wounded women, will you?"

"Already on it," Max said as he poured water over a woman's arm.

Levi started CPR on Andi. "Come on, baby," he pleaded. "Come on back now."

"Got it," Jack told him, dropping to his knees beside Andi. "First-aid kit with an AED."

"Thank heavens." Levi tore open Andi's blood-soaked top. "Break the AED open and set it up." He pulled a clean handkerchief out of his pocket and wiped the blood from her chest. "Looks like the bullet missed her heart."

"Then why isn't she breathing," Max demanded.

"Shock," Jack said. "I imagine the shock and adrenalin worked together to send her into ventricular fibrillation. Here," he said, shoving the leads at Levi. "Attach these to her chest, upper right and lower left."

Keeping his emotions locked down under an iron clamp, Levi dried small areas of skin with his handkerchief and attached the adhesive pads to Andi's chest. A high-pitched tone sounded.

"Clear," Jack called.

Andi's body jerked. When it stopped, Levi checked for a pulse. Nothing. "Again," he demanded.

"Levi—" Jack began.

"Again, dammit! She's bloody well *not* going to die. I refuse to let her. Come on, baby," he chanted. "Come on, Andi. Come back to me now, luv."

Another high-pitched tone sounded. Andi's body jerked again.

Levi felt for a pulse. Nothing. "No!" A wave of grief and agony slammed into him, shattering his control. "You are bloody well *not* going to die, luv. Do you hear me?"

He shoved Jack roughly out of the way and reset the AED. He refused to let her go. He couldn't fail her again, not this way. At the sound of the tone, he pushed the button. Andi's body jerked. Then he heard a soft inhale as her lungs filled. She moaned and coughed weakly. Levi nearly burst into tears.

"Out of my way," Jack ordered. "Let me stop the bleeding or we'll lose her again."

Levi backed away and let the man work. Jack had been a US Navy SEAL and they had some of the best medical training in the military. And Levi was too shaken up to be any good to her now, anyway. *What the hell was I thinking?* he asked himself. *I should have taken Ikalla and his guards out as soon as we got here.*

"You wanted to let her handle it if she could, remember?" Max said, coming up beside him.

Levi stared at him. "Did I say that out loud?"

"You didn't have to. I could read it on your face."

"It's my fault she's injured."

"No, it's Ikalla and his guards' fault. None of this would have happened except for them."

"Max—"

"Levi?" Andi called weakly.

He rushed back to her side. "I'm here, luv."

"Oh, Levi," she cried as his arm encircled her shoulders. "You came!"

"Of course, I came, luv," he whispered into her hair. "I told you I would." It felt so good to finally hold her again, he could hardly breathe. "Didn't you trust me?"

"Ahasama said you were d—dead. I—I thought I

would never see you again," she stammered as tears streamed down her cheeks.

"Don't cry, luv. It's all right now. I'm here." He cupped her face. "I see you did exactly what I told you and escaped into the desert as soon as you got here."

She smiled as he'd intended. "No, I had to play teacher first." She took a deep, stuttering breath before continuing. "I couldn't leave the girls there, and they needed to know how to fight so they could come with me."

"Why am I not surprised?"

Max cleared his throat. "We probably should get her out of here, Levi. Jack says there's a US Navy ship anchored out in the gulf. They'd have a doctor and facilities to treat her properly."

Andi shook her head. "I'm not leaving without the others," she insisted. "We can't leave them here."

Levi ran his hand over her hair. "We're not leaving anyone here," he promised. "My plane will be a little crowded on the way home, but we'll all fit."

The women cheered.

"Can you fly that chopper, Jack?" Max asked. "And will it hold all of us?"

Jack nodded. "I think we can all fit. It will be a heavy load, but doable. But let's move it. It's getting light and it's a ways to the gulf."

Levi picked Andi up and carried her gently to the chopper. He had her back and it was finally over. Now it was time to see if she wanted him to let her go. After what he'd done, he could hardly blame her if she did.

11:27 a.m., aboard the USS Maverick:

Andi opened her eyes and tried to see past all the

tubes and machines surrounding her. Apparently, she was going to live, at least if the amount of pain in her chest was any indication. Why did it still hurt so much? The bullet was out, the wound stitched closed. Shouldn't the pain be ebbing?

"Hey, luv. How're you feeling?"

She turned her head to see Levi standing by the bed. "Hurts."

"Yeah, I can imagine. Let me get the medic to give you a shot."

"No, don't go."

He took her hand, squeezed it. "I'll just be a moment." He stuck his head out of the door and called to someone, "She's awake and hurting."

A few seconds later, a man came in with a syringe. He gave her a shot, nodded to Levi, then left again.

"How is everyone?" she asked.

"So far, so good," Levi said. "The ship-to-shore phone lines have been busy. The CIA bosses have forgiven Max and Jack for our little field trip because the information the girls have on the clan leaders is so valuable. All the girls have been promised new identities when everything is wrapped up. And Wilson says a lot of the girls' fathers will soon be facing charges."

"That's good," Andi mumbled. She was glad. She'd been tossing around ideas to help them all, but she didn't even know her own future yet. "Levi—" She yawned.

He kissed her forehead. "Sleep, luv. We'll talk later."

11.35 a.m., the apartment of Garry Farahani, Boston, Massachusetts:

Garry rushed around his apartment like a madman,

throwing clothes, papers, and essential possessions into the two open suitcases on his bed. When he'd heard the news this morning, he'd panicked, come home "sick" from work, and started packing. He'd warned Jamar. Hadn't he *warned* him? "Don't let Ahasama's men kill Komakov," he'd told him. *So what did the morons do? They shot the* girl*!*

"Dammit!" Garry swiped a hand over his forehead, wiping away the beads of sweat that kept forming there. "If they thought we'd be in danger by killing Komakov, what the hell do they think is going to happen now?"

Even if the girl survived, Komakov would want payback. From what the man had told Special Agent McCarty, if the girl was hurt, none of their lives were worth crap. Well, Garry wasn't waiting around for Komakov to come after *him*. He was taking the money he'd hidden away in an off-shore bank and finding a nice, safe hole where the bastard would *never* find him. He'd change his identity, his personality—his face, if he had to—but he wasn't paying for someone else's stupidity.

"Hell, *I* didn't shoot the damn girl. Why should I have to die?"

"You didn't shoot her, but you helped others sell her into slavery," said an unfamiliar voice just as Garry felt a sting in his neck. "And you betrayed Jonas."

Garry spun around, or tried to. But his legs didn't seem to work. His muscles refused to hold him up, and he collapsed on the floor beside the bed. His vision was failing. The blurry image of a man leaned over him.

"Who're y—you?" Garry demanded, his word slurring. "H—How'd you get in h—here?"

"My name's not important. But my message is. Jonas sends his greetings."

"J—Jonas?" Garry stammered around a tongue that felt suddenly thick. "But Koma—"

"Sshh, sleep now," the man said.

Garry felt a searing pain in his neck and the world dissolved to nothingness.

4:42 p.m., the Sydarian Embassy:

"Answer the phone, dammit," Jamar growled.

But it just kept ringing and ringing. Where in the hell was Garry? Jamar knew his brother was worried, but he was surely overreacting. Since neither he nor Jamar had anything to do with the shooting of the Merritt girl, it made no sense to think that this Levi Komakov would be coming after them. But Jamar had been trying to call his brother for hours to no avail. *Where the hell is he?*

Maybe Garry had left a message with Bas. Jamar moved to the desk and pressed the intercom. "Bas, did my brother call and leave a message for me?"

Silence greeted his query. That was strange. Bas *never* left his post without telling him. Come to think of it, if Garry *had* left a message, Bas would surely have given it to him already.

"Bas? Are you there?"

"He's tied up at the moment," said a strange voice behind him. "But don't you worry, you won't be needing him any more today. In fact, you won't be needing anything anymore."

Jamar turned and saw a man dressed in a janitor's uniform standing next to a laundry cart. "Who are you and how did you get in here?"

"That's the same thing your scumbag brother asked, just before he died," the man said. "Such a family resemblance."

"Garry, dead?" Jamar swallowed hard. Then he took

a deep breath and straightened his shoulders. "I have diplomatic immunity—" he began.

The man chuckled and raised a funny-looking gun, cutting Jamar off. "Sorry, man, that don't count for shit with me," he said as he pulled the trigger and shot a dart into Jamar's neck.

Monday, June 10th, 4:11 p.m. aboard the USS Maverick:

Hearing muffled voices, Andi opened her eyes.

"...Garry disappeared, along with his half-brother, the Sydarian ambassador, in Washington, DC," Levi was saying softly. "No one knows what happened to them."

"So what *did* happen to them?" Jack asked just as softly.

Max chuckled. "Are you sure you want to know?"

"Yeah, I do."

"I doubt we'll ever know for certain," Levi said. "But I think it's safe to say that Jonas sent one of his guys to take care of them?"

"And this guy just made them *disappear*?"

"Jonas takes a dim view of men who hurt women. Garry knew the rules when he came to work for him—hurt innocent people and you die. I'd say that selling young women into sexual slavery qualifies big time. If Garry forgot to mention the risks to his half-brother...well, that's not really Jonas's problem."

Jack stared at him. "And you're *okay* with this?"

"I'm not going to lose any sleep over it, if that's what you're asking. Kidnappers, terrorists, human traffickers—scum like that—have no right to breathe the same air as decent humans. If they don't like the blowback from their actions, they should think of that before they make their career choices."

"I agree with Levi," Andi said, her voice little more than a croak. "Those poor girls with me went through hell, mentally as well as physically, so some man could make a profit. People like that forfeit their right to live."

"Well said, luv," Levi told her, hurrying to her bedside. "How're you feeling?"

"Throat's dry," she croaked, grateful when Levi held a cup of water to her lips. She drank deeply, sighed, and laid her head back down on the pillow. "Thanks."

"We'll leave you two alone," Max said. "Come on, Jack." He gave Andi a kiss on the forehead. "Glad you're still with us, kiddo."

"Thanks, Max. Bye. Bye, Jack." She looked at Levi. "Why'd they leave?"

"Because I need to talk to you."

"Oh." The seriousness of his tone had her tensing. *Is he going to tell me he's through with me? Does he think I'm damaged goods now?* "What about?"

He stroked a finger over the healing bruise on her face where Ahasama had struck here. "Can you ever forgive me?"

She frowned. "For what?"

"For letting you get shot. I should have killed the buggers the minute we arrived and saw the situation, but—"

"Bullshit," she snapped, rising up on her elbows. Pain shot through her. Crying out, she flopped back down on the bed. "No, no, I'm okay. It just hurt for a second," she said when Levi started for the door. When he returned to her side, she glared at him. "You were letting me handle it, remember? And I needed to. So did those girls. Don't you dare feel guilty, you hear me?"

He saluted. "Yes, ma'am."

She sighed wearily. The outburst had sapped her

strength. "It's finally over," she said after a moment. "Isn't it?"

"Well, there are still a few loose ends to tie up for the other women," he said. "But, yes, for you, it's over. None of the other clan leaders will be coming after you. Jack told his friend in Sydaria that you've had black ops training and took out both Ahasama and Ikalla single-handedly. That rumor is now spreading like wildfire. They're all terrified of you, so I think you'll be safe."

She turned her head, afraid to meet his eyes. "So, what do I do now?"

"What do you want to do, luv?"

"I've decided I want the money Jonas set aside for me, after all." She felt him tense beside her and her heart soared. Was he worried *she* would leave *him*? She could only hope. "I want to use it to set up a trust fund for the girls who came back with me from Sydaria, so they can go to college, or use it to start a new life, or whatever." She heard him gasp softly and figured she'd surprised him. "They can't go home, not if their families were responsible for their kidnappings in the first place, and they don't have a lot of other options," she said. "This would give them a chance."

His fingers tightened around her hand. "That's sounds like a good use for the money," he said, his voice rough. "Have I told you how proud I am of the way you handled yourself over there?"

"Only a few hundred times."

"Not nearly enough, luv." He hooked his fingers around her chin and tugged until her eyes met his. "But what about you, Andi? What do *you* want?"

She couldn't read his expression and didn't know if she should tell him. "That depends on you," she hedged. "What do you want?"

"What *you* want depends on what *I* want?" His grin

made her breath catch. "How's that work?"

"Tell me," she demanded stubbornly. "What do you want, Levi?"

"I want to get you a new identity."

Andi blinked in surprise. Of all the responses she'd imagined, this one threw her for a loop. "But—" She swallowed. "A new identity? Why?" With her father dead and the Sydarian clan leaders scared shitless, there was no reason to change her identity. Was there?

"I think it might be easier and safer for you if your name wasn't Andi Merritt." Levi watched her face. "Do you *want* to keep your father's name?"

"Not particularly. I like Andi, but I could do without the Merritt, I suppose. What do you suggest? Andi Smith?"

"I think we can come up with something more original than Smith."

"Such as?"

"What do you think of Andi *Komakov*?"

"Andi Koma—" She gasped as she realized what he was saying. At least she hoped he was. She met his eyes. They were wary—afraid she might refuse him? "Levi Komakov, are you asking me to marry you?"

"And if I am, luv?"

Andi couldn't stop the joy that broke out on her face. She knew he could see it. It was reflected in his grin. But she wasn't giving in so easily. "I think you'd probably get more *cooperation* if you asked me properly."

Levi laughed, hugged her tight, then gave her a searing kiss. When he raised his head, everything she'd ever wanted was shining in his eyes. "Anderson Merritt," he said softly and formally, "I love you more than anything or anyone in the world. Will you marry me?"

"Yes, Levi Komakov, I will," she replied in the same tone. "It just so happens, I love you, too."

He kissed her again. "I love you, Andi, more than you will ever know," he murmured, his voice laden with feeling.

Andi knew she'd finally found a man she could love, who would love her in return. "Not as much as I love you."

"You can tell yourself that, luv, if you want to," he said with a chuckle, "as much as you like—for all the good it will do you. You'll never win this argument, but I'm happy to let you try."

EPILOGUE

Saturday, July 27th, 4:10 p.m., the estate of Jonas Demopulus:

Jonas sat in his study, his head in his hands. "I'm getting too old for this shit," he told himself.

Being the head of an organized crime family had seemed like such a great adventure in his early forties when he'd taken over after the sudden death of his father. He'd had so many grand and lofty ideas then. But, in reality, it turned out be little more than dealing with a myriad of minor problems, refereeing petty squabbles between rival underbosses, and maintaining a constant vigilance to ensure that his people played by the rules. *His* rules. Which included sticking with what the law called "victimless" crimes. He didn't tolerate selling drugs and hurting innocent people or cops—least of all, human trafficking!

It was a lot harder than he'd thought it would be when he was young and idealistic—as the Darren Merritt case had just proven.

And now this.

Jonas sighed and picked up the letter that had been delivered by courier that afternoon. Horses. Personally,

Jonas knew nothing about them, except that they ate tons of hay and grain and produced twice as much manure. But if the letter from his grandniece, Jordan Nash, was any indication, Jonas needed to act and act quickly.

"This is more Levi's forte than mine," he mused.

But Levi was off on his honeymoon and wasn't expected back for three more weeks. No, Jonas would have to figure this problem out on his own. Or *would* he?

Levi had left strict instructions for Jonas to call his cell phone—anytime, day or night—if *anything* came up that he couldn't handle. Jonas had assured him that the Family could survive for a month without him, but Jordan's letter had changed that.

"Not that Levi needs to cut his honeymoon short, but I could sure use his advice." Jonas reached for his phone. "I'll just have to make sure he understands that."

Levi answered on the first ring. "Hey, Jonas, what's up?"

"You sound like you were expecting me," Jonas replied with a chuckle.

Levi snorted. "Well, it's been a week, and actually, I was expecting to hear from you a lot sooner than this. Things must be quiet there."

"They were. Until this afternoon."

"What happened?" Levi demanded, all trace of humor gone from his voice.

"I got a letter from my grandniece, Jordan. You remember her, don't you?"

"How could I forget? She's the little beauty from down under. A stunning piece of eye candy, if I recall."

Jonas heard a slap in the background and Levi laughed.

"Ouch. Careful what you're banging on there, luv," he told his new bride. "You might break something important."

Andi mumbled something that Jonas couldn't make out and Levi laughed again.

"Anyway, Jonas, what's the problem? Is Jordan in trouble?"

"I'm not sure. She says that our prized race horses are dying from mysterious causes and she thinks it's deliberate. I need to send someone to our ranch near Lynchburg, Virginia, to check it out, but I need to do it covertly."

"You want me to go?" Levi asked.

"No, no, son. I won't have you coming back sooner than you planned on my account, but I was hoping that you could suggest someone with similar skills who might be willing to take this on, preferably someone that no one in the Family knows."

"He should probably be somewhat familiar with horses, too, I imagine," Levi said. "I don't know of anyone off hand, but let me—wait, on second thought, I know just the guy."

"Who?"

"Jack Murdock. You met him at my wedding, remember? He went with Max and me when we rescued Andi and the other women in Sydaria. He's covert ops, so he'd be perfect."

"He's CIA. Is he going to want to take on a private job for us?"

"Probably not. But give Max a call. He owes us and he can convince Jack." Levi chuckled. "Yeah, the more I think about it, the more it seems perfect. Jack could use being taken down a peg or two, and Jordan's just the spitfire to do it."

"He wouldn't hurt her, would he?" Jonas asked, concerned. "After what she's already been through, the last thing I want is to foist someone off on her who might hurt her—in *any* way."

"Oh, *hell* no. Jack's a good guy—just a bit too cocky. Call Max. Let him know the particulars and he'll fill Jack in." Levi paused and chuckled again. "I promise you, Jonas, Jack won't hurt Jordan. However, I can't promise you that *she* won't inflict a little well-deserved pain on *him*."

END OF BOOK 2

ACKNOWLEDGEMENTS

Before I became a published author, I had no clue the amount of work that went into a book, or the number of people it took. I have so many people to thank and to acknowledge for their help in making this book a reality:

A big, big thanks to my editors, Mike, Cora, and Faith, for their marvelous insights and keen eyes.

Also, thanks to my critique group for their patience, understanding, and helpful ideas: Fe, Stacie, Dee, Robyn, Linda, Cara, and Julie. Thanks, guys, for your help with plot, characters, and general support. I wouldn't be this far without you. You made a big difference.

Lastly, thanks to Levi, Max, Jack, and Jonas (well, their real-life counterparts, anyway) for vetting my story and making sure it rang true. You guys are the best!

About the Author

Award-winning author, Pepper O'Neal is a researcher, a writer, and an adrenalin junkie. She has a doctorate in education and spent several years in Mexico and the Caribbean working as researcher for an educational resource firm based out of Mexico City. During that time, she met and befriended many adventurers like herself, including former CIA officers and members of organized crime. Her fiction is heavily influenced by the stories they shared with her, as well her own experiences abroad.

O'Neal attributes both her love of adventure and her compulsion to write fiction to her Irish and Cherokee ancestors. When she's not at her computer, O'Neal spends her time taking long walks in the forests near her home or playing with her three cats. And of course, planning the next adventure.

http://www.pepperoneal.com